As She Was Discovering Tigony

AFRICAN HUMANITIES AND THE ARTS

SERIES EDITOR
Kenneth Harrow

The African Humanities and the Arts series mirrors the agenda of the African Studies Center at Michigan State University and its commitment to the study of Africa. The series examines all aspects of cultural research—including art, literature, film, and religion.

As She Was Discovering Tigony

Olympe Bhêly-Quenum

TRANSLATED BY Tomi Adeaga

MICHIGAN STATE UNIVERSITY PRESS
East Lansing

♾ The paper used in this publication meets the minimum requirements
of ANSI/NISO Z39.48-1992 (R 1997) (Permanence of Paper).

Michigan State University Press
East Lansing, Michigan 48823-5245

Printed and bound in the United States of America.

26 25 24 23 22 21 20 19 18 17 1 2 3 4 5 6 7 8 9 10

LIBRARY OF CONGRESS CATALOGING-IN-PUBLICATION DATA
Names: Bhêly-Quenum, Olympe, author. | Adeaga, Tomi, 1968– translator.
Title: As she was discovering Tigony / Olympe Bhêly-Quenum;
translated by Tomi Adeaga. Other titles: C'etait a Tigony. English
Description: East Lansing : Michigan State University Press, [2016]
| Series: African humanities and the arts
Identifiers: LCCN 2015041933| ISBN 9781611862096 (pbk. : alk. paper)
| ISBN 9781609174958 (pdf) | ISBN 9781628952681 (epub)
| ISBN 9781628962680 (kindle)
Subjects: LCSH: African literature (French).
Classification: LCC PQ3989.2.B5 C4813 2016 | DDC 843/.914—dc23 LC record
available at http://lccn.loc.gov/2015041933

Book design by Charlie Sharp, Sharp Des!gns, East Lansing, Michigan
Cover design by Shaun Allshouse, www.shaunallshouse.com

Michigan State University Press is a member of the Green Press Initiative and is committed to developing and encouraging ecologically responsible publishing practices. For more information about the Green Press Initiative and the use of recycled paper in book publishing, please visit *www.greenpressinitiative.org.*

Visit Michigan State University Press at *www.msupress.org*

FOREWORD

Kenneth Harrow

Olympe Bhêly-Quenum (b. 1928) belongs to the first generation of francophone African authors of fiction. Coming after the Negritude poets of the 1930s, African authors of the 1950s embraced a two-sided strategy of combating colonialism. Those like Mongo Beti or Ferdinand Oyono exposed the ills of the colonial system, while others like Camara Laye, or the Anglophones like Chinua Achebe, sought to validate their own indigenous cultures, "writing back" to the derogatory images of colonial literature. Bhêly-Quenum's extraordinary career began with his first novel, *Un piège sans fin*, published in 1960, the same year that Dahomey, his home country (now called Benin) became independent. In most of his fiction he has followed both tracks of those early postcolonial authors by remaining close to his original culture, indeed his family culture, and by exposing the biases of a Eurocentric view of Africa that he had come to know firsthand.

At an early age he set out to travel to Ghana and to his grandmother's homeland of Nigeria, where he was able to learn English. In 1945, in Dahomey, he passed a competitive exam and was hired by John Walkden, a Unilever Company, as an assistant warehouseman "able to understand and read English" (www.obhelyquenum.com). After three years he was able to leave for France where he pursued his secondary education in Avranches, Normandy, and received a

Baccalaureate majoring in classic letters (French, Latin, Greek, and English), minoring in philosophy. He taught classical languages and literature from 1955 to 1960 when he succeeded in publishing his first novel, *Un piège sans fin*, with Stock in Paris. The novel was translated into English as *Snares without End* (1966).

In 1960, Dahomey (later renamed the Republic of Benin) became independent, and in 1961, Bhêly-Quenum again changed direction in his career. He was then a well-known author. He undertook a course of diplomatic studies in 1961–63, training at the Institut des hautes études d'Outre-Mer (IHEOM) in Paris, at Quai d'Orsay (the French Foreign Office), at the Diplomatic Academy in The Hague, and in the French consulates-general in Genoa, Milan, and Florence, and in the French Embassy in Rome. He obtained his diploma and was certified in diplomacy by the IHEOM.

However, diplomacy didn't appeal to him and he turned to journalism and became editor in chief and then director of an African magazine, *La Vie Africaine*, which he directed until 1964 when the publication folded. He then founded, with his wife, the French-English bilingual magazine *L'Afrique actuelle* that he directed until 1968 before he joined UNESCO headquarters in Paris where he was employed as an African issues specialist in the Office of Public Information.

While working at UNESCO he resumed his study of sociology at the Sorbonne, where he completed his socio-anthropological essay *Trance and Possession in the Voodoo Alladahouin*, deepening his fascination with African religion, an inheritance from his mother and his maternal grandmother that remained despite his Catholic upbringing. Eventually those personal and academic interests in *vodun* (the African religion most closely associated with Dahomey and, eventually, its New World incarnation in Haiti termed "voodoo") bore fruit in much of his best-known fiction.

Over the years since then he has increasingly published works that evoke his maternal traditional association with Beninois *vodun* as his mother was a priestess. His prose is that of classical French as he was educated in French and lived in France for more than half a century. But his background in Beninois religion, and in Fon and Yoruba language and culture, marked his personality and his writing where he typically sought to achieve a synthesis of his African traditions, his classical training in France, and his love for the classics and Western culture, especially Greek.

He summarizes the synthesis of influences that have marked his life from the times that preceded the end of colonialism down to the present: "Fon de naissance mais d'ascendance yorouba par sa grand mère maternelle, immergé dès l'enfance dans le culte, vodou, franc maçon, chrétien fervent, passionné de lettres classiques, tour à tour ou en même temps professeur, diplomate, fonctionnaire international, mais surtout et toujours écrivain, nègre noir jusqu'à la moelle mais marié à une Normande, aujourd'hui enfin, retraité suractif, basé plus que vivant dans un minuscule village du Gard" (Fon by birth but Yoruba originally through his maternal grandmother, immersed since childhood in *vodun* through his priestess mother, Free Mason, fervent Christian believer, passionately attached to classical letters—at once teacher, diplomat, international bureaucrat, but above all writer, Black African down to the marrow, but married to a Norman Frenchwoman, today retired and based in a small village in the Gard region) (www.facebook.com/QuenumBhelyOlympe).

He has published regularly since 1960, his most famous work being *Le Chant du lac* (1965), for which he won a major literary award, Le Grand Prix littérature d'Afrique Noire, in 1966. His other major works, besides *Un Piège sans fin*, include *Un Enfant d'Afrique* (1970), *L'initié* (1979), *Les Appels du vodou* (1994), and collections of short stories, *Liaison d'un été* (with stories going back to 1949), *La Naissance de l'abikou* (1998), and *Promenade dans le forêt* (2006). In 2000 *C'était à Tigony* appeared.

Although Bhêly-Quenum is known primarily as an author of long fiction, Willfried F. Feuser has called him "One of the great masters of the African short story," and speaks of the force and troubling beauty of a short story entitled "La Reine au bras d'or" (Feuser 1981).

On his own website Bhêly-Quenum recounts an encounter he had in his youth that proved to be important for him, if not determinant for his career. He tells us the first story in *Liaison d'un été* was written after he met André Breton in 1949, at the age of twenty-one, and recounted to Breton a dream. Astonished, Breton declared, "C'est étrange, mais c'est du rêve à l'état brut. Je vois que vous n'avez pas encore lu Freud, mais vous devriez écrire ce rêve avant de devenir écrivain" (It's strange, but it's a dream in its pure state. I see that you haven't read Freud yet, but you should write down this dream before becoming a writer) (www.obhelyquenum.com).

On Breton's death Bhêly-Quenum wrote that "without the instigation of the poet, I would never have thought about writing down the dream"—and by extension, creating the works inspired in that manner. Like Césaire, Bhêly-Quenum's meeting with Breton proved consequential.

Later Bhêly-Quenum dedicated *Liaison d'un été* (1968) to Breton. Subsequently, in publishing his first novel, *Années du bac de Kouglo*, written shortly after his meeting with Breton in 1949, he states, "le rêve de 1949, plus précisément sa transcription en suivant le conseil d'André Breton, était fondateur: le fondement de nombre de mes écrits" (the dream of 1949, and more precisely its transcription following André Breton's advice, was fundamental: it provided the foundation for a number of my writings) (www.grioo.com/forum/viewtopic.php?t=2214&start=400).

Snares without End deals with the tragedy of a good man who experiences misfortunes throughout much of his life. After his father's cattle herd is destroyed by a disease his wife becomes suspicious of him, driving him to commit a senseless crime. He is imprisoned and wishes to die, but then escapes punishment when his friends die in a rockslide. The despair and misfortunes evoke the dark side of an existential condition, evocative of the forces of fate that hover over human attempts to exercise their free will and agency.

With *Le Chant du lac* his reputation was assured. He evokes the mysteries not of existence, but of African spirituality lodged beneath the cold waters of the lake, the site so often linked in West African imaginary with spirits, like Mammy Wata. The monstrous forces lying beneath the lake attempt to draw down to their depths a woman and her two children, along with her faithful boatman. Its central drama turns on the struggle between two worlds: that represented by the educated youth who return to their home village in Dahomey from France where they absorbed the ideological impress of "modernity," and the local fishermen and villages who respected their "traditional" water gods, paying annual homage to them in fear of their destructive powers. The struggle for what turns into the life of the gods of old entails a motif that runs through much of the arts of twentieth-century Africa, as seen in the phantasmagoric scenes of Souleymane Cissé's films where the departure of the gods is seen as leaving a demythologized new generation vulnerable to the abusive neocolonial or postcolonial state whose armed forces are no longer guided by scruples. The promise of the new day, youth empowered by education, respectful of tradition and elders, aware of heritage, and yet no longer the same as before the ambiguous colonial venture, these are tropes that mark much of Bhêly-Quenum's fiction. Bhêly-Quenum describes this image of a new world, a New Africa, as one where the dawn, splendid in its light, still weeps for the passing of its gods, its elders as a "symbole évident d'une Afrique qu'inquiètent et fascinent à la fois son passé et son avenir" (obvious symbol of an Africa unsettled and yet fascinated by its past and its future) (www.obhelyquenum.com/livres/le-chant-du-lac.html).

On his own website, Bhêly-Quenum adds to this description of his novel the autobiographical claim to be the son "d'une grande prêtresse" (of a high *vodun* priestess), which authorizes him to lead the reader "dans les arcanes d'un monde dont il connaît les norms" (through the labyrinth of a world whose norms he knows well). The end of *Le Chant du lac* evokes the shattering effect on the entire community who hear the drums announce the news of the death of the gods. This unfathomable announcement is echoed in the most potent novels of Achebe, *Things Fall Apart*, which deals not only with the arrival of colonialism but with the passage of the religious worldviews of the Igbo from traditionalist beliefs to missionary Christianity, and *Arrow of God*, where the fall of the high priest is accompanied by the conversion of his son to the Europeans' religion.

The tensions enlisted by the clashing epistemologies are famously described by Cheikh Hamidou Kane as "Une aventure ambiguë," that is, not just an ambiguous tension but a deadly contagion of thought that results in the death and suicide of Africa's "new" generation. *Vodun* as a generational life-and-death struggle against modernity returns again in *Les appels du vodou* (1994), which goes much further in providing full descriptions of *vodun* practices, incantations, and beliefs. It presents a portrait of the great priestess who is the protagonist's mother, her life in the aristocratic circle described by her family, the call of the divinity in service of his order, and the entire glorious nature of the vocation. One dimension of this novel, then, is purely testimonial, or even anthropological.

In part this feeling of distance is due to the narrative discourse. Bhêly-Quenum writes in a distinctively intellectual, at times scholarly tone. The protagonist of the novel, Agblo, is the son of a Christian father and a *vodun* priestess mother. The mores of his family, and of the society at Gléxwé, are decidedly mixed. His grandmother is Egba, and she maintains Yoruba practices. His family is noted for the eminence of its vodon priests. And yet Agblo, the reincarnation of an illustrious vodon ancestor, marries a French woman and resides in France. Like the city of Gléxwé itself, better known as Ouidah, the children of this society are baptized with Christian names and infused with vodon beliefs, accepting the two together. *Les appels du vodou* depicts a celebration of death in the grand old way as known to the world of vodon adherents, and thus can be taken as an important attestation to the impulse to seek self-validation through one's heritage.

C'était à Tigony is a novel that concerns itself with the central issues of the day in an age of neoliberal capitalism, with a frame provided by a giant multinational corporation investing in extractive industries, an autocratic state ruler cast in the modern vein as "democrat" of the people who dissimulates the corrupt relationship with European powers, and the vast struggle of the unemployed masses set against the backdrop of poverty and detritus on the one bank of the river and the familiar contours of wealthy denizens living on the other. In short, an updated version of the colonial divide now sustained in a postcolonial Africa. However, although the novel sets the action in play with a massive national strike, and with a chorus of voices of the people echoing the complaints of the "wretched of the earth," the drama of the narrative comes to turn on several key interpersonal relations. The central one involves Dorcas Keurléonan-Moricet, a white geophysicist posted to Africa, who falls in love with a young African, Ségué n'Di, and reveals to him the joys of physical love that her husband was incapable of providing her with. The enlightened couple represent an ideal of openness, sensuality, and authenticity in the sense of early existential thought. The binary division of the characters, echoing the strictures of neoliberal ideology, demands that the counterparts of corruption, bigotry, and hatred are located in the oppressive white figures who are emblematic of neoliberalism operating in Africa today, alongside a cast of ignorant and vicious Africans and Europeans. The good are assisted by the "old African Hand" journalist, a sensualist and intellectual bonvivant, and another range of idealized children, reassuring elders, and in particular, an Ethiopian Jewish woman of aristocratic bearing who recites the Song of Songs and the Haggadah in Hebrew.

If *Le Chant du lac* evoked the trials of a "young" Africa seeking to forge the path for its future between an idealized past and an unstoppable future, *C'était à Tigony* brings us into that future world, two generations later, and it is not only far from having liberated itself from the heritage of neocolonialism, it finds itself confronting not only the inadequacies of the postcolonial regime, but more ominously, the unstoppable forces of the multinational corporation—with no more spirits of the sky or the mountains or the sea to turn to. Here it is the neoliberal order working against a new generation of Africans and Europeans armed with the best weapons of High Culture, at home in any corner of Africa or of Europe—the Afropolitans and their lover-allies among the Euro-cosmopolitans.

C'était à Tigony caps the career of one of Africa's major authors whose life spans the entire breadth of contemporary African fictions, and whose earlier works have been celebrated and well known to readers and scholars of African literature.

REFERENCES

Bhêly-Quenum, Olympe. *Promenade dans la forêt* (Précédemment paru sous le titre *Liaison d'un été*). Http://forum.potomitan.info/viewtopic.php?f=7&t=828.

Bhêly-Quenum, Olympe. 1981. *Snares without End*. Harlow, UK: Longman.

Feuser, Willfried F. 1981. "Introduction." In *Jazz and Palm Wine*, by Olympe Bhêly-Quenum. Harlow, UK: Longman.

Harrow, Kenneth. "Les appels du vodou by Olympe Bhêly-Quenum." *World Literature Today* 69, no. 4 (1995): 867–68.

"UNESCO: Livres de l'Afrique." Espace de Discussion. Www.grioo.com/forum/viewtopic.php?t=2214&start=400.

Wauthier, Claude. "Un auteur à découvrir: Olympe Bhely-Quenum entre l'Europe et l'Afrique." RFI Service Pro. Www1.rfi.fr/fichiers/MFI/CultureSociete/987.asp.

Www.facebook.com/QuenumBhelyOlympe.

Www.obhelyquenum.com.

As She Was Discovering Tigony

If, then, there is some end of the things we do, which we desire for its own sake (everything else being desired for the sake of this), and if we do not choose everything for the sake of something else . . . clearly this must be the good and the chief good. Will not the knowledge of it, then, have a great influence on life? Shall we not, like archers who have a mark to aim at, be more likely to hit upon what is right?

—Aristotle, *Nicomachean Ethics* (translated by W. D. Ross)

Our misfortunes, the stranger replied, are not of recent date; we drank the bitter draught of that time, a draught all the more dreadful because, along with so many other wretches, our fondest hopes were dashed. For, who could deny that at the first ray of the sun rising over the horizon, when we heard tell of rights common to all men, of invigorating liberty and longed-for equality, who could deny that he felt his heart leap and throb against his freer chest with more vibrant movements? Everyone then hoped to enjoy his existence; the chains which bound so many countries, clasped by the hand of idleness and self-interest, seemed to loosen. Did every oppressed nation not turn its gaze towards the capital of the world, the glorious title that this city has so long rightly borne, and which it never more deserved than at that time? Were the names of men who first proclaimed liberty not equal to the most famous names borne up to the stars?

Everyone felt courage, soul, and speech reborn within him. No tongues were silent; old men, mature men, and adolescents spoke aloud, full of sublime thoughts and feelings. But soon, the heavens darkened: a race of perverse men, unworthy of being the instrument of good, disputed the fruits of dominance; they massacred each other, oppressed their neighboring peoples, their new brothers, and sent among them swarms of rapacious men. The leaders plundered on a vast scale, their subalterns, down to the least among them, robbed us, and piled up their spoils; they seemed to have no other fear than that of letting something escape their plunder for the morrow.

—Gœthe, *Hermann and Dorothea*

CHAPTER 1

It was at Tigony, a town in the middle of a huge valley surrounded by mountains with steep slopes and scattered villages. The Kiniéroko traverses the whole of the country called Wanakawa. At Tigony, the capital, the Kirinikimoja Bridge and the bridge on the Kiniéroko span a part of the river. Rectangular huts on the bank with thatched roofs, perched on the platform on the side of Mount Kiniyinka, give the impression that you climb in a circle, when coming from the center of the town at five kilometers; you enter the village from the northern side.

At each breath of wind, beautiful eucalyptus with voluminous trunks shake their branches with leaves like countless fans in the valley. The forest stretches at the foot of the Kiniyinka on about a hundred hectares and gets blurred along a broad sidewalk of dividers that separate a two-lane road from the river.

From the perspective of the strikers, in front of the Monomotapa cinema, the forest seems to have been rooted on the mountain and its curve before growing several kilometers on the river upon whose phlegmatic waves—except in thunderstorms—sun rays danced about during the daytime and the stars shimmered at night.

Mrs. Dorcas Keurléonan-Moricet, a geophysicist working for an applied geographic, geophysics, and geodesy consortium, was canvassing the region when she received a note from the multinational company, through which the head office wanted her to undertake "a summary investigation highlighting the general information that could not be disregarded."

She was not a sociologist and made this known through an unsubtle fax; in response, the head of the consortium handled her with kid gloves by answering that it was about a duty "that would not be in vain, if your investigations proved to be promising; in doing this, the consortium also falls back on your demographic and statistics skills."

As the situation eased, Mrs. Keurléonan-Moricet used her spare time to survey the roads, the quarters, and the suburbs of Tigony. She went to the province, discovered the country, taking notes, filling untidy pages without knowing what she would do with them. There were no indications from the head office that a report should be sent to them, but having grasped the realities as parts of the problems in the country, it opened her eyes, raising her as if to best understand herself. There came a day when she read her notes again, reflected on them, and sat in front of her computer and began revising the text with the aim of leaving no stone unturned.

After some time, the worms also grow as big as the flies, which lay their eggs on suitable grounds. The area permanently exhales a fetid odor that is not mitigated by the maritime wind, which blows in puffs. Constant like the hands of a clock, malnourished children, with stomachs filled with the same food poor in protein, relieve themselves facing the sea or by turning their backs to it. A beach that could have been beautiful, attractive to tourists and strollers, is thus transformed into a dump where household refuse accumulates, in which big rats rummage, black-skinned pigs and fierce emaciated dogs squabble over leftover food in wild fights. These are more visible than those darker ones, motivated by jealousy and hatred among the people in Wanakawa.

The picture is not better when you casually watch Tigony, stretched on the edge of the ochre fine sands and shores of the Kiniéroko. To prove this, considerable effort has been put in less than a quarter of a decade after independence: 68 percent of the huts with mud walls or bamboo were replaced with cinder-block buildings, even reinforced concrete; tarred avenues, new lined and marked roads; the city gets bigger, hundreds of luxury houses and buildings with more than ten floors are erected all over the place; the provinces become depopulated, unfortunately to Tigony's benefit, where refuse piles up on the street corners of some quarters.

A city without character or original style? In order to appreciate its beauty and charms, it should be discovered by surprising it at dawn or daybreak. It is the political as well as economic capital, but also a cosmopolitan city, with human dregs—scumbags, riffraff, crooks, and human garbage polluting the unfathomable political administration, and even justice. Arbitrarily restricted to residential quarters, middle-class and popular zones, it was not unusual to observe in the former what you would have thought specific to the latter: dumps, wavy lots, inconceivable to link to such areas, refuse, which piles up in easements from which, by nightfall, the least burdened crawl with heterogeneous fauna; the sexually unbalanced; swindlers, drug addicts, harmless fools, as other corners served as the toilets for the demoralized night-owls who would love to produce a picture of these men in a hurry to get rich at the people's expense, instead of providing the country with public toilets."

Suppressed people are rendered powerless and reduced to silence. Would there be a day or uprising like that of May '68? Nothing is certain; it is in fact unimaginable that it could occur with the same violence as in France: Tigony is a peaceful region with a mosaic of ethnic varieties. A route that starts from the bridge on the Kiniéroko at Konioroijé, passes through the European quarters of the colonial period, then spans the area of the railway network like that of the new districts to return to its starting point, touching the river, and circumscribing the Kiniéroko big market, would demarcate the district with unspeakable accuracy in the course of construction.

Not only the non-natives, called the "Westerners," but also the natives themselves know and enquire about it. Is the government aware of it? What solutions does it propose? The "Northern countries" companies, for which Wanakawa is transformed into economic manna, could they propose their intervention collectively, to avoid haste? It would not be in vain that at one point in time or the other, their accomplishments and contributions are obvious enough for the people to be aware of it.

From within the imaginary topographic demarcation, the stench, heavy with miasmas that hang over the city, rises day and night, which the government, supposedly, tries to cleanse; indeed, the project does not focus on Tigony, but its suburbs, to reclaim and transform cultivated lands into building areas, thanks to men who filled and drained immense marshy areas where new districts emerged with modern constructions. Nevertheless, one cannot help but hold one's nose when passing by the gutters in a number of the districts; water stagnates in the drains that smother thick watery grasses, whereas, they could be cleansed with little or no expense by making them push carpets of water hyacinth.

Young goats, pigs, fowls, cats, and dogs crushed by cars and thrown in refuse dumps decompose under the sun; such reports are not extremely rare in the city of Tigony, on the side of the big market. The urbanization of the suburb too, as well as the lack of civic spirit, present alarming problems that the press recently deplored: "When will we stop seeing women who urinate upright, legs wide apart, children between five and six years squatted on garbage dumps in broad daylight? The entire country lacks adequate health facilities."

Quasi-daily street scenes prove that freedom of speech is costly: a minister's air-conditioned Mercedes Benz stops without anyone knowing the reason behind it; tramps recognize the politician, look at him, and spit in disgust; three old women curse him in an obscene language; a group of students hurl insults with political implications. "Colonization's rhizome generates neocolonialism that is studded with the little available to the people reduced to poverty."

The minister does not react, listens, looks at the unemployed people passing by, indifferent, crunching maize or sorghum beignets, a piece of coconut, an ear of roasted corn. A brigand relieves a passerby of the proceeds of her business; the fruit of petty theft passes on to the hands of an accomplice and they escape. The Mercedes, about to carry on its way, does not start. The woman who was robbed wails, calls on the gods to come to her aid; the police are absent, and even if present—I've already seen it happen—would be impassive.

Witness among so many others, I approach the official car; I hardly had the time to open my mouth before the minister of Internal Affairs challenged me: "Dear Mrs. Keurléonan-Moricet, I know that you have carried out a survey for a few weeks; it is legal that a consortium that is interested in a country counts on the physical information provided by private sources. Born in this country, I am not unaware of the places that you cover. Before you came here, a gun was held to my throat near the gutters. I saw cadavers of cattle in decomposition, also horrors that escape your wisdom and to which a native of Wanakawa will never draw your attention: we are a proud folk who are reluctant to exploit our poverty and even our obvious problems. If you wish, dear madam, my colleagues from the Ministry of Health, Urbanism, Information, and Communication will provide you with the complementary data whenever you need it."

I thanked him; we went our separate ways and I had the feeling of having been cut into pieces.

"The horrors that escape my wisdom—" Where are they coming from? Deathly stinky odors with an overwhelming filth reach the Kiulari' University Hospital; I felt as if my body were soaked and reeking with them until I got into my car. At the Saïnifuki port, tons of coffee covered with tarpaulin awaited the cargo liners for

their transport to Inshakiu, which needs them. In Kilakila, the grapefruit province, hundreds of tons rotted in jute baskets or Hessian sacks, whereas there is scarcity in Tigony, where it is still expensive. The fish marketing industry such as the snapper, barracuda, grouper, and shrimp collapsed; no one forgets that hardly a year after independence, Wanakawa froze them and exported them to Europe.

Sprinkled with cynical foreign businessmen who "pump" their resources, sharks lying in wait for economic potential, to dispossess those who should first benefit from it, the country seems to be perched on a steep slope. The downtrodden, those who feel wretched, oppressed, emasculated, and bled white, groan, rendered powerless by the repressive state apparatus, locked by an autocratic dictator.

Plethoric and scrawny, the unemployed cohort, which accounts for 49 percent of the population, gathers on all street corners.

"What did we do to our gods to be where we are in our poverty?" "God himself must be against us, if he exists."

I heard this type of reflection more than a hundred times across the country. An unemployed man with a bony, hectic, scrawny face in a pair of trousers and a colorless, tattered shirt chanted a song that was translated for me:

The earth, the earth no longer turns
Although in my country
My country is
Where I die of hunger
Poverty assails me there
Others have jobs
Even if the job is insignificant
It provides something to eat
When will I get something of my own?
It's better to die
Than to live the way I live.

One of his friends stared at him, making faces. "He! He! Mwuki, you're inspired today."

"It is like this when he thinks of his ancestors," someone else said.

We should leave those who have gone in peace
They profit forever from the sun of death
They no longer need jobs in the country beyond

There is no unemployment in the land of the dead
And me, Mwuki, I say:
The earth, the earth, no longer turns well
It no longer turns well in our country
And ours is that which dies of hunger
Dies of hunger on the garbage dumps
Oye! Listen! Listen! We are dying of hunger, poverty, and death
Of hunger, mass poverty
Oye! Listen, Listen! Our night loincloth is vermin
Oye! Listen, Listen! Wanakawa
Country of riches for the Whites
African country, hostile to the Negro
Hostile to its rejected Negro children
Oye! Listen, Listen! And on the roads where we wander
Dogs without owners
Or slave owners
Foreigners
Oye! Listen, Listen!

"If the translation is correct, the chant is edifying, and there is the need to react: stay, but do not live closed-in and indifferent, or leave."

She left the ergonomic seat on which she liked to work on her knees, with her back straight, arms stretched in the air, and let herself be served a glass of milk. Returning to the computer, she saw herself full length in the living room mirror and eyed the image: big, squared shoulders; discretely luscious sculptured body; sumptuous, plaited chestnut hair, arranged below the nape of her neck and left free, which she arranged in a half-hitch knot or loose braid, or sometimes in a ponytail with an ivory, ebony, or silver ring, except when she gathered it in a chignon, cleverly brought below the nape of the neck like a diva.

Mrs. Keurléonan-Moricet read her notes again, and then adjusted the text that she had taken. The notes, photographs on the sharp realities, seemed to her to be harsher than the text. "Of what use is this? There's the rub," she said in a low voice, turning off the computer.

CHAPTER 2

THEY WERE SIX FROM THE SAME VILLAGE ON THE TRACK ROAD ON THE NORTHern side of Mount Kiniyinka. Since their youth, each time that they descended it, this road made them feel as if they were moving forward, crouching toward the river on the other side of the eucalyptus forest, and that it unraveled under their feet while they caught sight of water in the river below, packed in the valley where its crested wavelets of scattered scum scintillated under the sun, lapping with a sluggish rhythm against the banks.

"Old n'Ata no longer likes going into town and makes no secret of it," Nakiyinka said.

"We know it, but he does not seem to be fed up with life; he talks about it nonstop and as soon as he opens his mouth, the past returns to the present," Ségué n'Di said.

"After having listened to him, we now look foolish going into town and I wonder what we are going to do there," Foyiola said.

"Grandfather circumnavigated many problems; age counts when you know how to manage them well," retorted Ségué n'Di, turning toward her, a distant first cousin with whom things had not worked out well because she wanted to emigrate whereas he still loved her and a lot kept him close to his roots and his grandfather.

"Experience of age, please; is that enough for him who for years doesn't leave the village anymore, to analyze the present with such accuracy and relevance? That's disconcerting and demoralizing," Nakiyinka said.

"Not me . . . not always. You noticed that his face looked like a stunned and sad mask when I referred to unemployment and the unemployed people?" Ségué n'Di—big, muscular, long faced, and poised, with fine features—said.

"As for me—in fact our Old Man's thoughts that clung more to my brain—when he complained that 'too many young people get too much education; I am not sad that boys and girls attend the white man's school; but so much knowledge acquired from these people who have more than us, of what use is that? There are fertile lands, forests, mountains abounding in unused resources; rivers also sometimes offer gold nuggets; I see one on the neck of my little Foyiola. Who among you, young ones, is interested in all that? Even peasants have turned their backs on the land, under the pretext that they work for nothing or for too little; badly rewarded efforts, and this and that. Here, they rush toward the cities in search of employments that they did not learn! My grandchildren, this serious disease called unemployment, would it be less scandalous if people bought the fruit of the peasants' labor at cost price or moderately? Would those who learned from the white man be unemployed, if in addition they had thought of going into our local professions that they could practice? My grandchildren, your problems and emotions—'"

Foyiola interrupted. "You are upset because you want to leave the country—"

"I want to leave because I cannot find work there; I am upset because our n'Ata is right."

"Me too, I also listened to him; you rendered his words perfectly. I admit that they sometimes nauseated me. If he were not our grandfather, uncle, and my granduncle, yes my nakinakafu; I would have called him an old cynical man," Sélikiyi intervened.

"Hello! Was he not right?" Ségué n'Di was astonished.

"I don't know anymore. I felt like vomiting, probably because he was quite right."

The road seemed to accelerate their speed. More than one tripped and landed on his backside or knees, provoking a chortling laughter.

"Do you go downtown to admire the white man, bureaucrats, and the underworld?" Nakiyinka said ironically.

"The underworld proliferates; you do not need the city to be in it. Unemployment makes it look bigger, delinquency becomes widespread, and it is distressing. In Itayikani, a European woman, who I was not the only one to see in areas that you can hardly associate her with—with dirt everywhere, which is shameful—approached people, listened to them while taking notes. Was it necessary to talk a lot about our problems and offload everything about our country?"

"Of course not, Sélikiyi; notwithstanding, do you think that it would be in our interest, out of too much decency or dignity, to hide certain realities from the Westerners, I mean those that they will not see or will never understand without our cooperation?" Ségué n'Di questioned.

"Agreed, but these people often take sides with the government in power. Like prostitutes, they change sides when nothing works anymore where they operate. They're coming to 'collaborate' with the people? They are afraid of them," Foyiola said.

"Well done, little sister! Go and talk to the journalist with her hair tied in a ponytail on her neck. Make her understand that without an organization or resolute action of representatives of the Wanakawa people, we go overboard; that in a year or two, the twenty- to forty-year-olds will fall in the horde of the eternally unemployed. Freaked out at the thought of the fizzling of the interests of the international aid organizations, she alerts the appropriate authorities, and presto! Hound the miscreant citizens. I am very wary and pessimistic," Sélikiyi said.

"Yes, yes—of what use will this general strike that we are preparing be? Have you already heard the crises and cries of rage from protesters in Wanakawa? And here we are on the way to take part in a demonstration. OK, but I'm leaving after this act of solidarity," Foyiola said.

"You too, you doubt it? If it is that, go back to the village," Ségué n'Di said in a calm voice, though he could barely conceal his irritation.

He imagined tomorrow and heard the clamor of crowds from the districts of the city and the suburbs walking in the pale-blue coolness of a day with faint light. The solar disc came out on the horizon like an immense blossoming egg; the pure song of a bird rose up to Mount Nariékiyingy and it was that of the beginning . . .

"It is good, we are not alone," could be heard among those who joined the Kiniyinka group.

"Would it not be sad if we were the only ones going there?" Sélikiyi said.

"I wonder where to spend the night if this runs late," his neighbor said.

"At Tigony, it is rare that you do not meet a friend in whose house you can spend the night."

"Then, there is the forest. You can crash there without danger: in a group, you won't have to worry about thieves."

"If you find yourself among people of our village, go up together; if not, hit the hay in the hall of the *Daily Encounter* and *L'Afrique actuelle*," Ségué n'Di said.

"You are the one who sells the newspapers, not all of us; unless you're not with us," Foyiola said, putting an affectionate hand on his shoulder.

"Even without me, those of us from the village would have nothing to fear. Um'Kantalikani is the new night guard."

"What? Good heavens, how was he able to find that?" Nakiyinka exclaimed.

"They were looking for a hardworking man, not a coward, someone able to get rid of his attackers. Mr. Greenough, you know, the old Irish journalist, wanted me to find him someone that fits this curriculum vitae . . ."

"And you thought of someone from Mount Kiniyinka. Well done! One less unemployed," said Sélikiyi, who exclaimed on seeing groups coming from the other slopes: "Great! A lot of people will be there, our brave sisters will come to our rescue!"

"Without the women, what good can we achieve, we the men in this country? Nothing! Not even with muscle!" one of the newcomers said.

"You are right to insist that without the women, and not 'our sisters,' like the other person over there said. Whoa! It is not only your young girlfriends who are there! We are also there, we your mothers; in spite of our big butts, our breasts that don't stand upright anymore, we climb down the mountain; yes, and these people who create the mess in the country, they will know us," a woman energetically threatened.

"Come on! Let's move on! It is not the time to eye fifty-year-olds!" someone else said, talking to the two young newcomers.

Driven from their homes by a feeling of justice and solidarity, the townsfolk, and suburban dwellers, who did not want to pass for an insignificant number on the fringes of the Democratic and Social Movement demonstration for the Revival of Wanakawa (MDSPRW), poured forth into the streets of the capital. People on the mountains poured in without haste, taking care not to fall into the ravine, but the steepness of the way made the steps go faster, and the "natives from up there" maintained a balance on the winding roads. Those from another mountainside took their usual tracks; no one saw them, you could only hear their voices as well as the dull beat of their steps sweeping dust up the laterite ground moistened by fine rain that had fallen at early dawn. Roads exhaled an odor of earth cooled by a heavy shower, and you could feel this emanation like it was the breathing of the land.

"How would we react if our national police, those underdeveloped, potbellied, white mercenaries and other thugs of these politicians, received the order to go against the demonstration?"

"We shall see. The country is not yet democratic and could go after a crowd that demonstrates peacefully!"

"Peacefully, that is the MDSPRW's watchword; all the same, we must plan the tactics to be adopted if—"

"He is right, talking like that; these people, armed with guns, bludgeons, and—"

"You ask yourself if they will dare to attack people without stones or sticks and who do not expect a scuffle."

"That's right. Those people, you could say that they are paid to beat people, even to kill, and us, we have nothing, and we go down empty-handed."

"My children, we are happy to hear that you are not taking any weapons with you; it is better to be even without a penknife to peel an orange. When they beat my little Kiriniyo to death, they said that he had a shoka! A hatchet in the hands of an eleven-year-old kid! May the earth swallow them!" an octogenarian said, wiping her tears.

"Where would we have found a gun? What would we have bought it with? Without any money, we don't even have enough to fill a basket every day . . .

"Yes then! You have to be a fool or an idiot to be buried alive, to spend the little money you have on a pistol, machete, or shoka."

"What they use with so much anger and skill—whether the order comes 'from the government' as they say, or themselves alone—are the weapons of shame. Their fathers had never manufactured any, but the West provides them to kill off the under—no, those "in the process of development."

"He sells them to them, at what price, by all our gods?"

"Me, I prefer to say provide, since weapons are part of the 'aid package' for the development of our country, eh!"

"I got it!"

"Ho! Young ones, this hogwash does not dictate what you do if there is a blow—"

"We have already said it. The question: Would they use that against unarmed citizens?"

"My foot! You are really naive, really an asshole! You do not know those 'brothers' of ours when they leave the tribal hut for the government side, or when, as they say, they start finding their bearings."

"Do I know them? A bit, but . . .

"It has already happened elsewhere on the continent; why not here as well?"

"I think that if we are many—and I believe we will be, given the noise of the footsteps going on down—so, if we are like that, we can oppose them—the nonviolent force of the people of Wanakawa."

Laughter rose through the crowd, followed by a long silence broken by a sexagenarian in shabby patched-up black velvet trousers and a sleeveless undershirt, which smelled of sweat.

"Force or what? And so on and so forth, a collective massacre swallowed with resignation."

"I would rather say selflessly like martyrs."

"Who talks like that? What martyrs? I do not know what we would do if . . ."

"Me, I hit if I am hit; they already killed my eldest brother; thus, an eye for an eye . . ."

"As for me, nothing; we go down to express our dissatisfactions and to state our wishes."

"That is it, and we go there like calves that are brought to the slaughterhouse, I believe."

CHAPTER 3

THE MULTITUDE GREW INCREASINGLY DENSE AS IT REACHED THE FOOT OF THE mountain; parents, friends, and inhabitants of the same village mixed with other groups and lost sight of each other. They laughed, greeted each other, embraced each other, delighted to see faces they did not see any more in Wanakawa, hugged with amazement those whom they had thought dead. Like a huge wave when the sea spreads out, a quiet joy animated the multitude moving toward the right bank of Kiniéroko, as if it pushed them in the back; the lamps along the river were dimly lit and everyone wondered.

The impressive reinforced steel and concrete structure that spanned the river connecting the Northern Tigony riverbank to the Southern Tigony riverbank was also illuminated. The "classy city" was located on this side where businesses were scattered in the residential districts with posh residences equipped with swimming pools, courts reserved to the young workers of the foreign countries whose diplomatic mission was accredited to Wanakawa, as well as their senior official counterparts in the International Cooperation Mission (ICM). It was also the district of the Ministries of the Interior, Information and Communication, Defense, Economics, Finances, and Budget. The Northern Tigony riverbank accommodated important administrative departments on a site far away from the

Kinikifunkuyingy Palace. Wrapped as if in a pompous boubou of rare arboreal and floral essence, the immense palace was the pride of a thirty hectare estate fenced by a five-meter high granite wall, equipped with a criminal device: whoever came within two meters of the wall received an electric shock. Firing at the presidential residence would produce a boomerang effect. Mountains and valleys surrounded an elite class who had promoted those who were organized into a new middle-class of opportunists, upstarts oblivious of their roots and social environment. But Mrs. Myriam Haïlé-Haïkouni also had her private property in this area and despised these "nouveau riches"; there, you found discrete villas with charming paths ensconced within the woods, in the heart of the valleys that belonged to some sons and daughters of Wanakawa called "the successful."

The crowd pouring down the valleys, the suburbs, and the riverfronts moved toward Southern Tigony like magma, with a cold determination of mountain men whose fighting instinct appeared to have won. The link with those from the water regions and provincial towns bore out as soon as they arrived. The initial multitude increased as it absorbed them and beefed up. The quiet crowd laboriously kept the watchword of the workers' associations and trade unions hurt by the injustice of the government in place. But protests were heard here and there against "the degradation of the social network," "the deterioration of cultural authenticity in favor of those helping to import cultures with no local significance or of interest for Wanakawa." "The disintegration of the nation's active forces and the considerable profits that the governmental circle draws from it": they denounced the "unemployment in progress," while the government tricks the youth and unemployed multitude, incessantly promising a colossal fiction called "job creation."

The repressive police force tried to channel the crowd from their armored vans. A steady voice rose from the loudspeakers connected to several places throughout the country.

"We urgently ask the law and order officers to stop choking us, the minister of Internal Affairs to recall his men and women. Our legitimate and peaceful protest won't tolerate any provocative gestures."

Simultaneously translated in African national languages, English, and Spanish, the declaration triggered the crowd's mirth as they applauded. The presence of Westerners worried the riot police and the police. A motorcyclist without using sirens went from one van to another, accelerated, moved away, then turned back and questioned the chief coordinator of the demonstration. There was a brief talk between them; Maïlidi allowed him to broadcast his message and we heard the loudspeakers say: "The minister of Internal Affairs wants foreigners to leave this demonstration immediately! The minister for Internal Affairs refuses to take responsibility in case of any accident."

"What foreigners? Who is a foreigner in Wanakawa? Those who joined the natives are loyal! Men and women with good intentions who have acknowledged the legitimacy of our uncertain demands!" the spokesman for the demonstration retorted. Starting from the fourth ranks, the song of the Career Workers of Oum'Iniafori, like the swell in its wide progression, grew as if in tiers to the first rows, to rise immediately again before crashing on the shore. The crowd joined hands instinctively; the national anthem in Kirokoroni starting like plainsong, sounding almost guttural behind hardly open lips. It was ample, supple air, rising from deep within the body, seeming as if it rose from the ground, soaring up to those who sang or listened.

Despite their anxiety, the police forces honored the order not to do anything that looked like a provocation or a simple intimidation. The human magma angled toward the police headquarters from the bridge on Kiniéroko. On the pedestrian crossing, the pavements on the Béhanzin, Samory Touré, Chaka, and Soundjata Keita Avenues and the Naga, Dr. Agrey, Victor Hugo, Emile Zola, and Baudelaire Avenues that this multitude took were onlookers. Some were amused, others dumbfounded; the "societies of the marginalized" rushed up from the peripheral areas where Mrs. Keurléonan-Moricet had investigated before jotting in her notebook: "Scrofulous tramps in sticky, crazy rags, with naked flanks who don't stop scratching their butts; or mocking or astonished, show their erection to kids of eight to ten years who look in the heaps of refuse for something to alleviate their hunger."

"These 'citizens' from whom you solicited votes during elections, just as you had done with the dead, yelled 'cheers' at the demonstrators from time to time."

"You are right! We are right, we must go on!"

"Yes, we really must kill off the guy from the state government who doesn't have any dream for the country!"

"Likewise his minister friends, fuckers of our virgins!"

"And also without life plans!"

"Not even for our chicks that they take from us!"

"And one can't say boo! Bastards!"

"I say we have to do them in! Cut their throats like pigs!"

"Yes, they are all pigs!"

"Fattened! Big and heavy in unbelievably big luxurious cars!"

"Yes, like the gods!"

"The gods, they gave them chickens, libations when we were kids, right?"

"Not me, I'm a Christian, knucklehead!"

"You are wrong, it's the gospel! The gods, if they exist, they must equip the pricks of politicians!"

"Hahhahaha! So, no more fucking, dick at half-mast, and our women are unemployed!"

"Cheers! Cheers! Cheers!"

"Walk, walk, group of pigs, the land will never be otherwise!"

"Wanakawa's bottom is still on the ground! This is not an idle ballad that we need!"

"You're right. It's a public scandal; take up your arms, citizens!"

"Go to hell, riffraff politics!"

Without issuing threats, the riot police asked them to be less noisy, shut up, or clear out.

"Yeah, you're right, we will shut up," one of them answered, arms in the air, taking the heavens as witness.

Their cries of rage reached the others, making them feel as if they also had done the same thing, at the same time as the poundings of their feet on the roads betrayed the anger that the majority suppressed. Some of them worried themselves sick.

A young woman in a locally made wrapper, camisole, and a culvert headscarf detached herself from the crowd and gave a sealed envelope to a police officer, telling him to hand it over to the police commissioner himself. The march came to a standstill.

"At your service, madam," the police officer accepted it.

"We'll wait for you to return before we continue on our way."

The police officer returned shortly after, preceded by the senior civil servant, amazed as much at the size of the crowd as at its silence. The crowd shook as it saw him behind the iron gate. The same process took place at the Ministry of Internal Affairs, where a European who called himself "personal adviser to the minister" came to the iron gate after the petition was sent.

The crowd broke out. The song of "Granite Careers" rose once more, peaceful, throbbing, heavy with panting and hope. You could picture workers with sweat running down crushed by the effort; you could hear the groans of the wounded, the drop by drop of their blood, the cries of those who, no longer able, still had to continue, the gnashing of teeth of pains held in because they were convinced that tomorrow would be a new day and Utopia and hope would become a sole reality. But the people, too disappointed at the unfulfilled promises, saw through this voice of death hanging in the sunny azure sky and, as if plagued by a life force, the demonstration rushed to the surroundings of the Kinikifunkuyingy Palace, where it came to a standstill. Although a beautiful song, the national anthem was heard in a great murmur rising from the human tide in singsong pattern, which was unsettling.

The great palace's iron gates opened, and two men in civvies, ostensibly different from the official guard, came to the front of the crowd. A petition was also entrusted to them, and they quickly left. Unable to turn back without causing a traffic jam that could have paralyzed the traffic for hours, the crowd took to the Afrique Libérée Avenue still holding hands.

The marchers' organization and discipline deceived the repressive police force, aggravated the government, and made the president wary and suspicious. For two hours, the trampling of the crowd on the avenue circumvented the Tchen'Kêti Square, took the Kotoka Bridge that People's Republic of China had set up above the Humba, a branch of the Kiniéroko, then the crowd flowed northwest of Mount Kiniyinka where it split and spread out.

CHAPTER 4

One of the two people that held Ségué n'Di's hand was a European woman. Like many others, they hardly looked at each other, but they exchanged a friendly smile as soon as they held each other's hands. Mrs. Dorcas Keurléonan-Moricet would have liked that Gaëtan was one of those who held her hand in this crowd of strangers, predominantly Africans. She knew that the Official Secrets Act did not allow an official of the International Cooperation Mission (ICM) to take part in such a demonstration. The agency had its headquarters in Tigony, and Gaëtan Keurléonan was the deputy secretary general; his wife demonstrated, although he had declared it "indecent, even unhealthy, to involve herself in an issue that is above all African. I perfectly understand that you are interested in some African problems and your passion for the Black continent, but to get yourself entangled in a protest march with a crowd set to be plethoric, you, the wife of an international senior officer, isn't it excessive?"

She ignored such arguments whose vanity and contempt had angered her. Dressed in a short-sleeved denim dress, buttoned from the chest to above the knees, but slightly open on the calves that the slit bared when she walked, Mrs. Keurléonan-Moricet wore sunglasses and a locally made raffia hat beneath which hung her braided hair that oscillated when she walked. From time to time, a fine finger-pressure was exerted on Ségué n'Di's hand; he thought that it was a tic, but held this hand gently, and even ended up speaking to his neighbor.

"You are really good, madam, you and your countrymen. Since independence, this is the first time that Westerners publicly commiserate with us."

"I'm happy to hear you say that. Do not make speeches, but take matured decisions and act; those in power seldom resist the people's force when they take to the streets."

"This unimaginable multitude is extraordinary . . ."

"A good sign; the whole country would have had to be on the streets—"

"That will come. A number of demonstrators came on foot, from more than thirty kilometers."

"Really?" Dorcas was astonished.

"I affirm and assure you, madam, that in the city, many of the African houses as well as each village on the sides of Mount Kiniyinka will take in whoever knocks on the door, whether they know them or not."

"Perfect organization."

"The demonstration, not the accommodation, and so on: culture and tradition function for us in this way."

"I knew a bit of it and do not doubt it; it is nevertheless interesting to watch."

She had the feeling of having found a native who could help her to complete her research. She turned her face toward him and inquired about his activities in Wanakawa.

"Unemployed trade employee, I am a news vendor, canvassing the field, in search of a good job."

Next, they talked about different things, and when the crowd scattered, assuming that she lived in a nearby residential area, Ségué n'Di suggested that he accompany her to the other side of the Kirinikimoja Bridge, "if you do not meet Westerners with whom you could . . ."

"I would like to walk a bit of the way in your company, or—walk in the eucalyptus grove," she said in a tired voice, and they left the road for the forest.

Mrs. Keurléonan-Moricet did not let go the hand of the twenty-five-year-old African man. He was slim sized, slender, and muscular, with quiet steps; there was something reassuring as well in his manner of holding her hand as in the tone of his voice. She apologized for being undeniably indiscreet but asked him about his "way of life now that he no longer has a permanent job."

A native of Wanakawa does not respond to such a question, whatever the sympathy that prompted it. That he had not assuaged his hunger every day for fifteen months was his problem; also he answered that it was of no importance, that they could survive up there, in the Mount Kiniyinka villages.

Dorcas's hand tightened in his. The movements of her fingers transmitted more tenderness than affection.

"And yet?"

"You know madam; there are more unhappy people than me in Wanakawa. Not only the hobos and other misfits that you could notice during the demonstration, but also graduates without work, skilled workers fired after eight days with or without notice."

"I carried out a survey, oh! In short: my notes, which I must review, complete, and refine, will help me to understand some problems in this country. But tell me, please, what difficulties do you have? Your country is independent . . ."

"Independent, independent—you heard the minister of Internal Affairs? He estimated the number of the demonstrators to be two million five hundred thousand; the organizers cried out loud and strongly that there were some four million five hundred thousand, a quarter of the population registered. The presence of the Westerners was unique, anachronistic."

A crawling feeling had taken Dorcas's body by storm when her hand had touched the young man's in the moving crowd; the feeling remained in the forest, at once calm and sinuous, that made her ill at ease. Although conscious of playing with fire, a sign of this nature amused her, while also triggering an anguish that sometimes invaded her and that she bore with irony; she was feeling something slowly opening in her like a bud that completed its growth.

"Face to face with the irreversible," she heard her inner conscience say as the blossoming bud dispersed its perfume onto her, which she breathed in the eucalyptus woods. She raised their hands in each other and put her cheek on Ségué n'Di's backhand; the young man did not understand the significance of this movement and nearly withdrew his hand.

"My comment is not a derogatory criticism . . ."

"I have nothing to do with the pursuit of . . . the exploitation of Africa by the West with or without the Africans' knowledge. I am here as a geologist-geophysicist."

"That must be very interesting."

"Without doubt, corporations pay better in Africa than in France; I work hard; objectively, do I deserve these remunerations? I am not the one that fixed the scales and I do not have any reason to oppose it or to underestimate my skills."

"Why are you talking like this to a stranger?"

"Do I know?"

"The forest is fine at night; its scents are—how do you explain that? In any case, I love to walk there, sometimes till 2:00 or 3:00 a.m."

"Are you married?"

"I nearly did, and you?"

"My husband and I live in the European residence."

"He was not at the demonstration."

"It is a matter of choice."

"Excuse me, madam."

"Is it still far to your house?"

Ségué n'Di laughed gently. They were on the east side of Mount Kiniyinka when he changed route. Dorcas realized that they were going down.

"You do not live 'up there'?"

"I do; it would be exhausting for you to climb up there. I will take you back near your home."

"You do not want . . ."

"It is not that, madam. There is the fact that a hut in the night resembles another so much; if we happen to meet by chance again and we recognize each other . . ."

She had watched him out of the corner of her eyes many times under the city lights. In the darkness of the forest, his large black eyes, his fine face, thinner due to the lack of regular food was exposed to her imagination like in a mirror. She stopped. He was not much taller than her, and in the crowd she did not lift her head when she sometimes turned her head to talk to him. He could not help but throw furtive secretive glances at her; her beautifully proportioned face that revealed her wishes even before they were acted upon had struck him. She gave him her arm, as White couples did, but also of those Africans used to Western ways. Ségué n'Di saw them on the cinema screens when he could treat himself to such entertainment. He took pleasure in it. They walked on side by side; a feeling of well-being reigned in him without him knowing why.

"I certainly intrigue you."

"If tomorrow I told the story to those from my village with whom I went down into the city, or to my friends, that after the march, I walked in the forest with a European woman, they would claim that I had had a dream of an unemployed person and roar with laughter."

"Is that a response to my question?"

"I do not know; is it because she pities me? I do not like people pitying me. Would she want to prove that a White person can only see a domestic servant in a pathetic African, but is it not hypocritical to feel sorry for him? These are the ideas that have been running around in my head since we . . ."

"Please hold me by the waist, as if I were your ex-fiancée."

Her voice was full of fatigue. He hesitated, and she wrapped him in her arms, snuggled close to him, and kissed him at length on the lips. That also Ségué n'Di used to see in the cinema and did it as in a fiction when the eucalyptus leaves rustled under their panting bodies in a myrtle smell.

An hour later, holding hands while descending the mountainside, they stopped, and he made love to her again. Time shattered; the conjugal straitjacket came off; complete blooming, blossoming in the body. She had a staggering pleasure that he had thus wanted her, and she felt insane, hoisted on the back of Ségué n'Di carrying her; neither her nor him knowing where they were going or toward what. Twice the desire emerging from deep within him found her available, and she was conscious of being a woman and desirable.

CHAPTER 5

"I WILL TAKE YOU CLOSE TO YOUR HOME."

She took back his hand and squeezed it gently.

"Please, where do you live?"

"Up there in a village perched on the mountainside."

"I would like to visit your house, would you mind?" she said with a calm voice that seemed to filter the words of her desire or her wishes.

Ségué n'Di could not get over the fact that a Westerner married to an international civil servant had made love to him in a grove. Now uneasy that she wanted to visit his home, he thought briefly and an evasive smile was outlined on his lips.

"My house? I do not have a house, at best a hut with thatched roof in a tribal village."

"I have never been in a hut . . ."

"It is nothing extraordinary; four perforated walls with three windows or more; a door that closes badly that I leave ajar. I sleep on the floor on a mat or a straw mattress unrolled on a basic bed. Nothing appealing, but it is the tradition, our way of life that does not disgust us, even when we manage to provide ourselves with the basics that the West offers us."

"You do not want me to know where you live," she concluded, fitting her fingers between his. "Why not, after all that happened? We are so good together."

They walked at a leisurely pace, one after the other, fingers entwined. Now and again, she asked him questions that he answered, tersely precise.

"Thus, you have . . . almost no romantic life."

"Where do I find the means? If I were to believe the newspapers, AIDS kills love in your countries. In Wanakawa, it is unemployment and its consequences that burned off the impulse, even desire for love in me."

"It is awful . . . it is . . . terrible to listen to."

"I was hardly surprised that even people who did not know each other could speak freely to each other during the demonstration. But believe me, I cannot understand what followed; it is too fresh and like a dream of impossible things."

She pressed his hand gently. He knew that she was beside him, that neither she nor he was a character in a dream and that she was the one who had decided to have this adventure of desire and pleasure with a stranger. It was less because she was annoyed as she left the European residence than because, from the moment her hand had touched his, holding it with a gentle firmness, welding the demonstrators to each other, the burst of the unexpected grew in her like the birth of a new day.

"Why did we do that?" he asked in a low voice.

"Because there was desire; the reciprocity in a desire; we wanted each other. Am I mistaken?"

"Nevertheless, I would not have dared to do such a thing."

"I understand you, that is nature; I dared and went far, come what may. You could have not responded, you could . . ."

"I confess I was afraid. I do not understand what is happening between us, or what happened to me."

"Then?"

"Oh, old stifled desires awakened."

She laughed a soft whispery laughter. They took a break; she hugged him close, put her arms around him, head resting on his back, and said beside herself, "What freshness, there is such freshness in you!"

"I am simply sincere, honest to myself as I like to be with others."

"This sky is magnificent; it is as if it is near us," she said, eyes raised to the scintillating sky of myriad stars.

"The night, the sky above Mount Kiniyinka brings me a kind of appeasement.

Life seems to be bearable to me and worth living."

"I love this country where the heat of the days is bearable; the nights are of unimaginable mildness."

They reached the foot of the sleeping village, quiet, a night of tenderness, a mysterious moment. Dorcas relaxed, oddly felt the restless desire in her before this group of huts submerged in the night. Ségué n'Di pushed the latticework of the bamboo slat-ribbed entry and they entered a vast courtyard. Still holding her hand, he turned left, moved toward the first hut, and opened the door.

"There's no electricity. I am going to light the hurricane lamp," he said in a low voice.

In the shadows, Dorcas felt as if she was in a place that wasn't foreign to her, where her imagination skimmed through the things. A flame from a match, which looked like an incandescent needle, suddenly turned the place into a chiaroscuro as Ségué's hand raised the glass of the lamp, while the other lit the tiny flame. The igniferous wick filled the oblong sphere of soft reddish light that, radiant in the room, restored its half-light to the lot.

"I only have a chair, it is safe," and he asked her to sit down.

He put the lantern on a badly finished wooden eucalyptus table that he had made along with the chair. Dorcas watched him. He seemed more handsome to her than under the city lights. She left the chair for the edge of the bed made of nine forked columns inserted in the ground, which held crossbeams on which a large door mat was unrolled like two rush mats. He sat beside her. With an exhausted gesture, now feeling the tiredness after having arrived at this height of the city, tears filled her throat when she put her head back on his shoulder and murmured, "I'm thirsty."

"There is only water from the earthenware jar, over there. There are no drinking glasses; we serve ourselves in calabash bowls."

"That is of no importance . . ."

He took the bowl turned upside down on the wooden lid, which he removed from the earthenware jar, drew water, and swallowed three mouthfuls of it before offering the bowl to his guest who quenched her thirst and sighed as she returned the bowl.

"This is where I live; the hut belongs to me. The field spreads out over more than one hundred meters, over the side of the mountain. It is a legacy from my great-great-grandfather; my father lived in this hut when he was young."

"Where is he?"

Ségué n'Di made a sign like running water. She guessed and did not insist. Her hand shook a bit as she caressed his face, murmuring, "My poor friend."

"There are stories of the destitute worse than mine in this country."

"Alas! I observed Tigony, even the whole of Wanakawa during my travels."

"In fact, before the demonstration, my cousins and I talked about life and our parents. Someone said that he had met a European woman at Itayikani, perhaps a journalist, because she interviewed many people; his description of this woman's hair makes me think of yours."

"I was probably the one. I crisscrossed the country a bit for six months, asking questions. I could not say if my notes constitute an X-ray of your problems, but I was right about my thoughts on the minister of Internal Affairs."

"I understand your discretion and modesty. What you saw is nothing new; what is annoying is that the coming of joblessness worsens our problems. I say coming because I do not remember having known people without jobs when I was between fifteen and twenty years old; everyone had a job or profession that he lived on; you were also a peasant, farmer, day-to-day laborer in the companies belonging to Africans or Whites or a bureaucrat in the administration. So many possibilities have disappeared; the current generation, mine, drifts. What will become of us? Look at this demonstration that brought us side by side before bringing us to this hut; I did not take part in it for the sake of it. Alienated from society, I expect nothing from it. Only this had made me decide to go down to the road and join the crowd with sympathy for those who fight peacefully for their job and salary, and my solidarity with them, me who no longer fights for anything. The majority of my countrymen did not believe their eyes or their minds, on discovering Westerners in the crowd at the march. None has interacted with us; even when it was about our conviviality that they treat as 'vulgar folklore, always hilarious Negro antics.' I do not know why; I had said to my grandfather that if the situation degenerated, some Whites would go through fire for the frustrated people in this country, and he had retorted that it was up to us young ones to honestly get to know them. And today, they were many in this crowd, at the center of a just, collective revolt they could have let escalate. It was a magnificent experience . . ."

Elbows on knees, the lower part of her face in the hollow of her hands, Dorcas devoured him with her eyes, scrutinized his animated face, took a short break before she gazed at him anew. The room seemed to her to be brighter, also bigger, and she listened to him, holding onto each significant word, each group of thoughts as if she had included them in her notes.

"Oh, sorry, I got carried away and bored you; without doubt because I'm happy to have someone to confide my thoughts in and who listens."

"You cannot imagine how pleased I am to listen to you talk; in a short while, I have learned a lot more than from speeches by expatriates in a business meeting."

"What kind words! You are overindulgent with me."

She took his hand, clutched it hard, asking for his name; he told her.

"I am Dorcas."

"It is easier to pronounce," he said, laughing, then hugged her closely in a fraternal embrace, giving her affectionate slaps on the back the African way.

She broke down, landing beneath him in the sepia light and the sweetness of this rustic hut.

▪ ▪ ▪

The moon in the abundantly star-studded sky poured a soft gleam on Mount Kiniyinka when they left the hut and went down toward the misty myrtle covered forest. Hand in hand, he guided her on a footpath that he could follow with closed eyes. They entered into the pitch darkness of the woods. Suddenly, drunk with perfume that infiltrated and lit up in her, she said in a nearly high voice as if in a retort: "Oh, no! I'm not ashamed . . ."

"Why are you talking like this?"

"I do not know. I am going crazy, and it is nice!"

Ségué n'Di anticipated her desire; the quiet firmness as well as the sureness of his rhythm dazed her but made her deeply happy. Leaving the forest, they walked well away from each other on the Wanakawa Avenue. Cars and trucks passed by them at full speed. Homeless people begged or wandered on the pavements; on the other side of the two-way street, Africans, Europeans, or mixed couples walked along the riverbank, on which neon lights spread false daylight.

"We are there. Good night, Ségué n'Di," she said, giving him her hand that he squeezed, slightly inclining, then moved away.

CHAPTER 6

BEGGARS APPROACHED HIM LIKE SMALL GROUPS OF A FRATERNAL SOCIETY. HE knew this fauna that seemed to him to be more than normal. Hands outstretched, they came from here and there with madrepore movements.

"I have nothing," he said in a low pitiful voice.

"It's not tlue, lou've shomthin on lou!"

"I'm jobless; I have nothing on me."

"Liar!"

"Why do I have to lie? I have no job, no money."

"Sho me your pocket, liar who wants to give lothing!"

"Yes, he's even with a white woman!"

"Even hand in hand before."

"Once again, alone with your ear now . . ."

"She walked with our demonstrators, I had to see her home, didn't I? Right?"

"No need for more! You held her hand; you have a job, give here!"

"I say once more show us inside your pockets!"

"Show us your pockets!"

"Show us your pockets!" they cried in a chorus.

They were already a score; others approached, vociferating insults and swearwords: "Bbbastard! Complete asshole!"

"Well-heeled'son, yea!"

"Fucker of white women!"

"Yes, dey did that as wel!"

"And mangy despite!"

"And us, we've nothin' to eat!"

"Bbbastard, soiled at that!"

His lungs dried up with fear as he turned out his pocket. The hand of one of the beggars behind flattened on his shoulder. He started, gave a howl that made them burst into a noisy laughter; some held their sides, others were surprised. Ségué n'Di ran quickly, heart beating wildly, while the group laughed on the spot. On getting outside the bridge on Kiniéroko, he stopped and realized that he cried.

He often came across victims of the famine and emaciation without ever having seen as many as this night come together as clans of skeletal, loquacious men, ragged women with saggy tits and sticky long hairs; some carried their babies, who looked like they were at death's door with their swollen bellies, and who were relentlessly suckling breasts without milk.

"Ohhe man! Where're ya goin like that?" A man dressed in a coat that was too big for him, took him on, touching his felt hat by pulling it down on his face.

Amused, Ségué n'Di answered in a pleasant voice, "Well, to my home!"

"Oh boy, 'e iiiiis off home," the man retorted, speaking to an accomplice who remained in the shadows and who came to him at once. They moved forward in a rolling chorus gait.

Ségué n'Di took off as he suddenly noticed that one of them held a dagger. They began to chase him. He ran much faster and entered the forest. Believing he was now safe hardened him, but he did not stop, luring them more into an area where he was sure of being invincible, even if there were ten of them.

"Asshole! Bastard! Worthless man!"

"Bourgeois son-of-a-bitch! And coooward at that!"

"Come then, I am waiting for you."

"You're waiting for whom? You eve' dr'e to wait for us!"

"I am doing nothing other than that, old maid! Delinquents without balls!"

"Goddamn! Is he cursing us as well?"

He had found a big short stick, a club whose resistance he measured, made a weapon out of it, and went up to a fairly precipitous part of the mountain saddleback and stopped.

"What, are you already tired over there?

"Don't mess around, peazant!"

"Then, you are a real dipshiiiit!"

"You are delinquents! You don't smell good at all! Go and wash yourselves in the Kiniéroko!"

"Ah? Says who?"

"Shut your traps . . ."

"Whaat?"

"Your mouths, just measure them!"

"Oh no! Your mother's cunt! Peazant!" one of them counteracted, climbing the mountain.

"My mother, she is dead, attacked by rubbish like you. Perhaps you are the ones who killed her. I am waiting for you. Be brave, old ladies!"

"He is motherless, spit on the ground and leave!"

"Yes, for God's sake," said the other one who hesitated before following his friend.

"Your mothers and your grandmothers! Saggy balls! I don't give a damn about your pity! Dare come up here; you will be buried tomorrow."

They stopped, perplexed, grumbled inaudible swearwords, and turned on their heels. The image of his fleeing mother was profiled in front of him in a misty cone of light. He bent down, picked up a stone of the size of his fist, and, before realizing that it was no more in his hand, the forest resounded with a cry of terror that seemed to him like a call of despair.

▪ ▪ ▪

Softened by the limpid firmament strewn with stars, moonlight fell on Kiniyinka like a light rain. Old Nakinokofu was lying in his ironwood armchair made up of a seat and a backrest fitted in each other; he had inherited it after his grandfather's death, who had inherited it from his own father. The old man loved to stretch out on this armchair for siesta, but on nights like this one when, after having led him as if toward death, shortly after he had gone to bed, sleep evaded him until dawn. He then brought out two armchairs, stacked them together, lay down and gently drew his night-wrapper on his frail body.

Ségué n'Di loved this group of traditional houses where timeless practices, habits, and old customs were ingrained. If he found work, he would first of all build a house, far from the ancestral cocoon, a home different from his father's hut that for him sometimes exuded his parents' odor. It is impossible to reject such a home. Nevertheless, this night made him aware of other facts to which he had previously been indifferent: buildings of ten to twenty floors in a country where the vastness of open space could be dizzying; luxury hotels that the newspapers criticized for their "chronic underutilization"; magnificent buildings, bourgeois properties or offices of Western officials of the International Cooperation Mission, or rented to their fellow citizens, far-ranging traders who were afraid to invest in real estate in Africa. At a hundred meters from such buildings, you found bread, uneaten cooked meat, roasted chicken whose thighs and a part of the white flesh had been eaten, in the garbage cans. He was not shocked that there were residential districts, middle-class or working-class: Wanakawa could only be made up of posh or poor residences. But he could not help but like the sides of Mount Kiniyinka and this village where he saw his grandfather sitting in his antique armchair in the court. He walked up to him and lightly stroked the cloth lying close to his heart. He had such deep affection for his grandson who stayed in the village so as not to move too far from him, the tenderness in his gesture moved the good old man, who, with the same slowness as at the time when he had laid down, removed the part of the wrapper protecting his eyes, his snow-white head, and his emaciated face from the sun.

"You are late, my child."

"I came home after the demonstration."

"I heard you come back after the others, but you went out again—"

"It is a blissful night and I am not feeling sleepy," he said, hiding a small smile, in order not to recount his love affair to his grandfather from whom he couldn't hide anything in his life.

"A cry in the forest reached me as if in a dream."

"I heard it—"

"Don't stay out too late at night; don't cross the forest in the dead of the night. It has already been too awful for this village."

"You are right, n'Ata; I am more vigilant in the forest since Naa n'Ki left."

"Don't think about it again. Oh, it is not easy to not to think about it, when there are more unemployed people there as well as thugs. They attack during the day or at night; they even kill, don't they?"

"You should go to sleep, n'Ata."

"You too, child; he who sleeps well lives a long time."

"Since you said it, it must be true."

"If you sleep well, the gods and the spirits of the ancestors will certainly show you how to find a job in your sleep."

"Since you said it, it must be true."

"You say that, but you laugh inside."

"It is true n'Ata; that does not mean that I do not believe this word coming from deep within my grandfather."

"My poor little Ségué n'Di Nikaïniyingy, go to sleep; may the gods keep you safe."

"You said it, so shall it be, n'Ata. Sleep as well."

He left alleviated, relaxed. The inflections in the old man's voice had calmed him since his childhood, thus restoring his equilibrium without him knowing why it was like that! But this night of his meeting with Dorcas, as he arrived at his hut, the idea crossed his mind that after an uneasiness or quiet spell in his sleep the revered octogenarian could die. Panic-stricken, he wanted to return to sit close by him, to tell him about the demonstration, evoke "a whim of fate," without keeping the person who went hand in hand with him a secret; argue endlessly; keep n'Ata awake so that he did not die. "He will not pass away like this," he heard himself say. He glanced behind him and, before going into his thatched hut, an odd hallucination suddenly showed him the village breaking away from the mountain.

■ ■ ■

Old Nakinokofu was a craftsman sculptor who enjoyed working with hard wood, his preferred material, while using the rudimentary tools that he designed and that Ninkuinkali, the best blacksmith of the country, manufactured. As a child, Ségué n'Di, upright or on his knees, observed his n'Ata digging into a chunk of tree of more than one meter in diameter and admired it; he already loved him with this tenderness that now made him tremble. At that time, the transformation of a block into an armchair, a table, or a strange object filled him with wonder.

The feet of the tables were carved bases of designs such as monkey, eagle, soursop; of a peasant woman carrying her baby on her back or hoisted onto her hip as she nursed; a naked peasant with her agricultural tool fixed on her shoulder. An invented scene that had made him laugh a lot showed two naked women and also a naked man whose phallus was wrapped around all of them.

When Nakinokofu carved a statue or a ritual mask, he sat on a straw mat or a low tripod; the rough wood was on his knees or wedged between his legs. Focused, he wielded a twenty- to thirty-centimeters long hatchet; a knife or chisel cut into the rough shape, to sketch precise details, or to hollow out the angles. The image emerged in a vague way that he caught sight of as he sought the point of attack, which eluded his piercing glance that sparkled with skill and humor.

His oblong cranium with his thick crescent-shaped grizzly hair made him look younger than his age. Lips pressed together, he seemed to be meditating on creating objects with which he was seldom satisfied, always on the lookout for some problem to solve. How to overcome even his dissatisfaction with the work became his obsession. "To produce a work of art that is acknowledged today and after my death, a huge Utopia!" was his dream.

"How can you think like this, n'Ata?" Ségué n'Di asked him one day.

"You must not—you must never agree to live squatting. Stand up, be the best at your job because you've wished for and chosen what you do."

There was a long silence, then looking at him straight in the face, Ségué n'Di had said: "Gladly. And yet? I mean that to think that your creation must survive you and that you will still be talked of long after you have left this world!"

"My Ségué n'Di Nikaïniyingy, I do not really work to live from my profession that I love deeply. That is why I never complete an object, even an order, if while making it I do not have the feeling, the tactility, and the very certainty of giving birth to it like a woman giving birth. Listen carefully: even if the newborn baby would be a monster, it will have been conceived in an act of love and put in the world by a birth mother who will feel as if she is among the gods."

"You—let it rest, n'Ata."

"But no! Do what you enjoy doing; learn to produce something with your hands or with your head; be ambitious. I have lived like this for seventy-five years. A healthy ambition is not a disease, my child; the gods are not against those who have it."

"I repeat, n'Ata, at your age, you overwhelm me."

"You looked up to me, you wanted to follow my footsteps, 'to continue the tradition,' as you said, at the age of fifteen."

"You did not want me to do so."

"May the gods punish me if that was my thought: as your father was no longer alive, I wanted you to see the world differently, to aim high because you needed to help my daughter-in-law take care of your two brothers and sister;

it is the responsibility of the eldest child. I wanted you to be initiated into hard work by entering modern life. High hopes? Well, I wanted, I still want with all my heart, that you rise beyond your limits. Of course, this was for you, but also so that the village and the family community wouldn't remain stagnant, or go like a millipede behind the present world that I see and do not like."

Listening to him Ségué n'Di heard more than what the octogenarian said. He had the feeling that in his craftsman-sculptor heart and conscience there was no conflict between his desires, his choices that were so old and those, much higher, that he sought for his ninth grandson. Although he was attached to the ancestral house, he had attended the Westerners' school and absorbed their teaching, but had been unemployed for three years, getting along only by selling newspapers that he could not read.

"You are gifted, more intelligent than me . . ."

"It is not true, n'Ata! You are exaggerating and it is not right!" he had energetically protested.

"Don't be annoyed! Don't work yourself into such a state . . ."

"Because for once you are wrong! But . . ."

A low doubtful laughter that seemed to have come from far off gently shook the old man's body. After a brief silence, Ségué n'Di continued: "What I mean, because it's the truth, is that many of your positive words helped me. They made me overcome the negative feelings that often divert me from what I really can do."

"My child, I know; it is the reason why I want you to sit up: gear up and shoot for the distance. A man who has talents must make good use of them, with all his strength." Dazzled by an unlimited admiration, his "good old n'Ata," for the first time, had not looked like an eighty-five-year-old to him.

CHAPTER 7

"ARE YOU LEAVING, AGAIN CHILD?" HIS GRANDFATHER WHO WAS SITTING ON a high tripod on the veranda asked in his soft voice, on seeing him leave his hut.

"I will take newspapers to the residential area. These people are not happy as long as they do not read these papers."

"They live in luxury houses, red brick houses. The gods will provide one for you as well . . ."

"Since n'Ata has said it, so shall it be."

On his return from Naïnifuni where he had gone early with "Daddy Greenough," he had prepared the midday meal of pasta, cassava flour in red oil, seasoned barracuda fried on embers, tomatoes, onions, and ground pepper. As usual, lunch was marked with laconic remarks. Ségué n'Di liked this daily family-centered tête-à-tête; after siesta, he had no wish to go out of the village, but duty called him elsewhere. He came to his grandfather, bent forward, stroked his knees; the old man laid his hand on his head as if he blessed him. Then he stood up, lifted the double raffia sack containing the packages of newspapers onto his left shoulder, and left.

Nothing special attracted him to this district, and Dorcas had not seemed to him to be in the least embarrassed on discovering the hut in which he lived. He did not think of her when, after having distributed the newspapers, he arrived in front of the iron gate of the Kamsine hotel where he saw people around a large swimming pool. Men, women, and young people swam, dived, or chased each other. Their demonstration of joie de vivre as they fluttered around in the air made it seem as if they were rising toward the azure sky.

In Naïnifuni, the coastal security's ban of "all non-swimmers and swimmers, who are unaware of the dangers of the sea on this beach" did not prevent whoever felt like swimming from doing so. Waves excited him, but imagining what the old journalist who accompanied him would photograph or jot down in his notebook put him so much ill at ease that he dared not swim. Braving the tide by going far out where the sea opened up in the distance, he liked to do breaststrokes or swim on his back.

The ecological deterioration, like the filth to which the city council and the government closed their eyes, had made him ashamed. The fine sand beach stretched out over some kilometers covered with coconut trees; an avenue of pavements separated it from the sea. When, coming from Eastern Tigony, approaching Naïnifuni, you could catch sight of this area with couples and groups of friends picnicking—some seated, others lying down or half-lying on veined palm-tree leaves. Less than a hundred meters behind them, the old pier, a gangly iron structure, looked like an abandoned piece of art or a tough nut disgusted with life, one who commits suicide by plunging in the sea with stoic dignity.

At the wheel of his white Austin, Greenough threw a sad glance at the wharf; on his left were colonial-style buildings facing the ocean. The undertow of a broken wave, sometimes cleaning the seaweed floor, carried along unspeakable sediments that accumulated there. The car stopped, the journalist opened his notebook and took notes, when he wasn't pointing the lens of his Nikon at a passerby or a shocking or picturesque scene, before listening to Ségué n'Di express his feelings of revolt against events that the press did not cease drawing attention to, as the election was drawing near. The Austin started again and Greenough expressed his opinion: "I don't understand how the new inhabitants of the former European quarters can stand, without repugnance or protest, this degradation of places that delighted me thirty years ago. The revolution has produced a clique; it burdens this country, favors with its method the deterioration of public places where awful smells have taken the place of the former freshness."

The taste of spray was still on the tip of his lips. He had dropped a bundle of newspapers in foreign languages at the reception of the great hotel. Looking around the swimming pool, at women in bikinis, with sophisticated swimming suits, or as silly-looking prudes, his glance drifted from one swimmer to the other. A plump woman caressed the head of a portly handsome man, older than her and who seemed out of breath; his shaven cranium softened his bald head, which, standing up on tiptoes, she touched lightly with her lips and then looked fondly at him. He smiled, took her by the waist, crushed his lips on hers, and they dove in.

The sequence amused Ségué n'Di. When he recognized Dorcas, a feverish thrill covered him at once with goose pimples. Nicely proportioned body, the breasts in a seductive bra and the hips seemed to have been carved; water oozed out of her green jade swim cap. A man in a lifeguard's swimming suit put his arm around her shoulders, kissed her on the neck, and then, they jumped into the swimming pool.

Big, with an athletic stature, his portliness moderately spilling out of his shorts, he had a well-fed oval face, as if the head was cut out of granite. His curly fair hair had russet-red highlights. They swam on their backs; people laughingly splashed water on them. Ségué n'Di looked at them. The perfume and the softness of Dorcas's body that had pressed against him lingered within him.

Six days earlier, Gaëtan Yvan Keurléonan was on an assignment. As usual during the major dry season, when she liked to be on the construction site before the morning heat, his wife had left the villa at dawn. On the road to the construction site, the Range Rover had changed direction, gone round the forest, climbed the side of Mount Kiniéroko to stop on the verge at the beginning of the rise where Dorcas went on foot to the entrance of the sleeping village. She had pushed the lattice bamboo slats, crossed the courtyard, and crept sideways into the hut whose door remained ajar at night. He was had not been able to hide his astonishment, but had received her with the spontaneity of the end of a long wait; sharing sensual feelings and bliss, he had made love to her again, and then, she had murmured with a faraway voice: "Would you be so nice to awake me before the third crow of the cock?" She had slept, snoring gently. As if in a dream, Ségué n'Di had heard the rhythm of her respiration like the rustle of a river among mangroves and water grass.

"If I were your husband, madam representative, it is at the last crow of the cock that I would let you leave home," n'Kagoni had joked, looking round at the head overseers who did not like that she arrived as first on the construction site.

"It is the time that I got on the road," she had retorted in a casual voice.

"Hello! If that is the case, then not before 6:00 a.m.!" Aïn'ka had responded.

"Sleep early, wake up early; sometimes late, wake up early. This is the beginning of a good development program," she had smilingly retorted.

The inebriation of the sensual pleasure at daybreak followed her in her work; she quivered from time to time. She was taken out of where she spoke, put back on the road to Kiniéroko and its forest where the tangle of the branches gave to the sky the appearance of a worn fabric in shreds from which the stars watched over the heart of the forest.

▪ ▪ ▪

The head of the construction site waited for her directions to delineate the area to be dug. Last week, "a geological phenomenon" had more than troubled her: she had smelled "the odor of gold" exfiltrate from a peat bog and decided to undertake the work. Madjita did not like this "technocrat whim"; big, intelligent, with a little adolescent face despite his twenty-eight years of age, fine-featured, stubborn, sly, he had approached madam representative in a politely sullen manner.

"It would be digging for nothing: our ancestors knew the whole of the land; nothing is strange to us there. What does the Consortium for Applied Geography from Europe want the peat bog to contain?" he had objected.

"If beyond the peat, we meet more than just the peat, I will make myself be elected PRESIDENT!" "Old" Biirkany, fifty years, heavyset, eyes fizzy with malice, had stated.

"I was afraid that you would ask for my hand in marriage," Dorcas had said, and everyone had burst into laughter.

The general skepticism seemed to have been swept away, but today Madjita was no more convinced than some time ago.

"It would be a pity to have dug for nothing."

"I am a geophysicist, 'gefisitist' as some say. We sometimes have intuitions, inspirations as well."

"You are becoming a poet, madam," he said ironically.

"Mr. Madjita, you do not like poetry?"

"Poets? Sentimentalists!"

"Nothing but the realities of life we would let go of without a little bit of feeling, I would say even a bit of weakness!"

"You are really a poet, Mrs. Keurléonan-Moricet."

This beginning of endless argument annoyed her, but took her back to the time of her administrative move for the drilling in the varied species forest of the road that would equip Wanakawa with the infrastructure suitable for the consortium's project. After the research, the multinational company had wanted the government's approbation to take into account the reports from specialists and experts. She had negotiated without giving up an inch of ground; glad to have come out of a political-administrative imbroglio, she wanted to go much further and win.

"You have read my instructions, Mr. Madjita, please give your orders for the digging," she said, cutting him short.

Everything still kept her away from the work, but she also thought of her parents with their wish to instill an education in their children, which gave each of them a "practical basis," without neglecting their gifts, capacities, and skills; develop feeling, arouse the appropriateness of judgement, cultivate in themselves the respect for values and patrimony was the watchword. Paul-Emile Guy Moricet had explained, "Apprehend and define in a decisive way who you are, what you must do for yourself, for others, and achieve excellence."

"Yes, father, I was young. Everything is now different in independent Africa that you did not know: the realities are jeered at; the Africans that draw attention to them are called Utopians; an unimaginable lie overshadows the obvious facts. Foolish, emasculated people and me, your 'little Dorcas,' with my clever head, I am in love with a jobless man. Even without this chance, I do not want to be an accessory to the deceptions that lie at the base of claims about exaltations over human rights, liberty, equality, and fraternity so often proclaimed but hardly honored."

CHAPTER 8

"The forest has opened / the depth of its stomach for the birth of the beautiful road," sang skilled day laborers in an improvised tone. The road initially ran through the middle of the forest like a huge culvert running through the red earth; it was later filled up with rubble from a granite quarry, then covered with concrete asphalt three months later, after a stormy shower. Beginning fifteen kilometers from the city center, the artery crossed a vast region rich in vegetation without detracting from its life or its environment, to stop forty kilometers away from Mount Atakaïyiriko. Dense, deep, labyrinthine on both sides of the road, the forest imposed its vitality and seemed to offer the sky the summit of its bulky trees, or twisted as if writhing in torture, while the motorway with four tracks, a unique snake produced by Western technology, seemed to run under the vehicles attacking each other in a place where fear, from now on an old bad dream for the natives, had vanished.

At the foot of the trees where they stayed side by side like frightened children, lianas grew in feather-grasses climbing the full heights of the trunks. Looking at the work, Dorcas sensed the weather variations and looked at the sky, heavy with storm in spite of ephemeral sunny spells; its floodgates suddenly opened and a torrential thundershower quickly fell upon the landscape. The construction site workers ran to take refuge in the vehicles and started to palaver. The thunder loudly rumbled in the forest; the waters ran down the roadway and raced into ducts that diverted them into the river where the waterway finally ended up. One hour later, the floodgates closed again as quickly as they had opened; a subdued luminosity touched the road and the forest like the breathing of a sleeping baby.

On both sides of the disemboweled jungle, you could perceive the savannah and valley with lots on which houses seemed scattered or in groups, the roofs made of corrugated sheets or asbestos cement tiles, or peeping thatched huts that also seemed to shelter enemy clans.

Joining Tigony in the northeast of the forestry road, you came out of the forest below a slope of Mount Kiniyinka. The tops of the trees shook like flyswatters, spreading a myrtle scent in the air, while the thunderstorm that raged with anger still flowed in a very steep ravine. On the way back, under her astonished eyes and towering above the saddleback as well as the houses that she used to go by at night, Dorcas viewed the heights where the visible tops of the forest and the vastness of an infinite space could be seen.

▪ ▪ ▪

Day laborers had been hired; many hardly understood French or only spoke Kinokoroni, Koufini, or Kaïnifuku. People from border countries, hard-working laborers, had started digging as soon as the Wanakawanis, those recruited first, had finished clearing away the siliceous ground that covered the peat. The toil had lasted six months. Because Sunday is not a working day, those who wanted to work overtime met on the building site; Madjita supervised their work. Like Foyiola, Nouriki, Abdi, Ikili, Anka, and many others of his generation, he also thought of going into exile to Europe or elsewhere in Africa to seek a job worthy of his agronomist skills—skills that the political barriers of the one-party state diverted from the jobs that he had applied for. But what he saw coming from the subsoil broke through the walls of his skepticism and verified the reasoning of the consortium's representative, modifying his judgment on "the obstinacy of a technocrat" without convincing him to change his mind.

Four hundred and fifty steps cut into the silica led to the gold-bearing quartz galleries of more than two square kilometers. Dorcas had smelled the odor of metal before weighing up the distressed oscillations of her pendulum on the peat bog, during a solitary excursion far from Tigony. The consortium was informed without her dwelling too much on the reality, and the administrative process had followed. Discrete, convincing with quiet obstinacy, she had overcome the obstacles, sometimes scoffing at the African and Western experts who did not believe in it. Their studies had been without appeal: "no positive result has come out of the research carried out, and having given some hints, we do not see the need to continue them."

The accidental intrusion of such a breakthrough excluded all scientific analysis, but Dorcas did not bother to emphasize "the lack of perseverance, also insight by those who had buried this layer that the country concealed in its subsoil too quickly." Although devoid of emotion, regret replaced her joy in such a discovery, the idea that the transmission of her report would attract a horde of sharks who would rush to the manna. "The decolonized Wanakawa will be exploited again, with the complicity of African politicians."

▪ ▪ ▪

While taking a stroll, Ségué n'Di had visited the site on a bike; he had argued with the guards who threatened him with their bludgeons that as a citizen of the country and newspaper vendor, he wanted to see what the press had reported. Distrustful, wary, the men had looked him up and down, listening to him express himself sometimes in Kinokoroni or in another crude language, then they had left him to walk the broad length before going down in the main gallery. He had not been able to see anything there, but had left with the feeling of being locked up in an underground prison whose layout seemed to be like a reproduction in his imagination.

"Do you happen to know a metalworker?" Dorcas, to whom the protection of the entry of the main galleries was of concern, had asked him as she was about to leave.

He thought for one second, then went to the trunk where he stored his prized objects, and took out a sketch that he showed her in the light of the oil lamp. Slightly taken aback, she jumped with astonishment.

"It is the mines! Where did you get it from?"

"Guess."

"Hello! I did not know you had such a talent! When did you go over there? And they allowed a stranger to go inside?"

"The press—often ironical—sometimes writes a brief article on 'the gold bearing quartz mines of Wanakawa'; you cannot help but read them when you..."

"Find me a metalworker quickly, would you?"

"There are good workmen. In my opinion, none will be able to produce the kind of reinforced closure that you want. Why not order it in—?"

"It would be disastrous if I spoke to the ambassador or to the representative about it."

"You don't trust them?"

"With a few exceptions, nearly all the White people in Africa spy for their government: diplomats or youth workers, they are the governments' and lobbyists' ears and eyes."

"It is alarming . . ."

"Certainly, and I'm a European who works here as a technician, representative of a private international consortium."

"We don't discriminate between the overseas volunteers and those working for private companies."

"The private company is often independent, the sort that neither the governments nor the civil servants hardly like."

"You don't say! Why is it so?"

"In theory, an expert in a private company is better paid than a civil servant. On the other hand, the governments find it difficult to use us as intelligence agents."

"Damn! Our independent countries would be infiltrated, if not stuffed with agents that would stick their noses in our national problems. Perhaps even with tape recorders."

"My compatriots that are committed to these kinds of ignominies are not free; they oversee them and it is reciprocal."

Ségué n'Di stifled an uncontrollable laughter so as not to wake up his grandfather whose hut was about ten meters away from his, then he stated seriously: "The two of us, we had better be more discrete and careful."

"I will prepare a proposal for a metal gateway that I'll request from France or Germany. The installation could be carried out by local workers. What do you think of it? We cannot really bring people from Europe to Tigony for that!"

"I will find you special craftsmen from the traditional blacksmiths guild."

"Who are they? Would they be able to manufacture reinforced grill?"

"The members of an art guild are linked to each other by secrets inaccessible to uninitiated persons. They are unaware of iron door plating produced by Western technology, but they are able to cement the hinges, unhinge them. My grandfather is the oldest of the members of the Wanakawa art guild."

CHAPTER 9

ONE OF THE CONSEQUENCES OF THE DISCOVERY WAS THE INCREASE IN MANpower. Initially Mrs. Keurléonan-Moricet wanted to employ a supervisor. She thought of Ségué n'Di and talked to him about it.

"I suggest that you apply for an official recruitment. Many candidates would take part in the competition and you would not be suspected of being given preferential treatment."

The idea was written in a proposal that was sent to Geneva. The agreement, successful, was included in a memorandum stressing that the recruitment had "to be announced several times in the English, Spanish, French, Hausa, Kinokoroni, and Koufini language newspapers as well as the national broadcasting corporation."

The choice of the examination texts was left to the regional office of the consortium, "with the approval of the International Cooperation Mission, the Ministries of National Education and Culture, and the embassies of multinational member states."

Mrs. Keurléonan-Moricet borrowed books from the ICM library and photocopied a hundred pages kept in her possession, which tallied with the framework of the competition whereby at the end only one candidate would be recruited.

Applied geology, physical geography, geodetics, and elementary vector calculus, rough sketching of the rocky terrain, along with English, and French were the subjects of the program. The government had appointed four representatives for the International Cooperation Mission. During a working meeting, Dorcas asked them to propose suitable texts.

"This kind of work should be given to our African friends," the French envoy remarked.

"We are not experts in all the areas proposed in the competition," his counterpart from the Ministry of Culture and Communication said.

The envoy of the United Kingdom stated that the English texts should be taken from works of Anglophone African writers, of course.

"Given that the German language was not yet international—which is extremely unfortunate—notwithstanding, I think that the FRG could choose applied geography, geology, and geodesy texts. In that event, I would very much want Mrs. Keurléonan-Moricet to collaborate with me," the representative of the Federal Republic of Germany said.

"With great pleasure, Mr. Steinberg," the regional office adviser agreed.

"As for the texts in French, it would be right that there is at least one from an African author among them," the representative of the Ministry of National Education stressed.

"Since the competition consists of an orthography test and one of textual or thesis criticism, I suggest," the Culture and Communication representative said, "that a French author is—"

"Thank you very much, Inspector Kiriniofuki," the representative of France keenly conceded.

Dorcas glanced through the books in her area of specialization, presented the pages to Steinberg, which the latter scanned through, taking note of the figures, and accepted, sometimes adding others that he gave to Mrs. Keurléonan-Moricet for her opinion. The earth sciences overrode the key subject matters; the pages that the FRG approved were also those that Dorcas had instinctively photocopied. In French, Aragon was preferred to Camus for the orthography test, but a page from the Sisyphus myth would be the subject of the textual criticism. An elusive smile quivered on Dorcas's cold face from time to time.

"It seems that Africa is forgotten," she said.

"Oh no! It doesn't matter! Let us replace Aragon with an African author," France responded.

"Camus is already from Africa," the minister of Culture and Communication said.

"Let us retain Aragon then."

The choice of a Mongo Beti text was not a problem. Dorcas looked at it; she preferred Ata Kofi, but she had *Mission terminée* in her own library. Chinua Achebe went up against Mphahlele for the English test; the United Kingdom won it by supporting the Ghanaian Ata Ama Aidoo. The confirmed texts were sent to Vienna. Two months later, a large envelope with the center for the International Baccalaureate seal arrived from Switzerland.

▪ ▪ ▪

Ségué n'Di studied nonstop. He had "digested" a hundred and thirteen photocopied pages, made sketches, cuts depicting the inner walls with details on the stratifications, fractures, and a lot more that would prove that the candidate knew what he had written on paper. Dorcas had photocopied the two pages taken from *Mission terminée* before lending the novel to him, which he read and reread; the pages of Ama Ata Aidoo's *No Sweetness Here* did not present any unsolvable problems to him.

"How is it going?" she asked in a tone that hardly concealed her concern when they met in the forest.

"Everything is already in my head," he answered tapping his face with his hand.

"You learned everything by heart? It is not possible!"

"That would be unreal; anyway, not a proof of intelligence."

"So, what then?"

"I read them by translating them into Wanakironi, my mother-tongue, as you know by now. Thus, the main part of the pages anchored in what you would call my noggin was something I memorized, keeping their order, as if I narrated stories heard from our old folks."

"I do not understand."

An inaudible laughter cascaded through him, and then he explained the operation of the mnemonic process of griots in traditional African societies relating nonstop a day or weeks of historical narrations.

"It is like your Homer. I learned in school that he had not written the stories he narrated, but reported on old facts and wars in his country. He had a blessed memory, this good old man! The process used in Wanakironi would also be valid in Kinokoroni, our national language, but such recordings in my mother tongue come to me more easily," he specified, and then he started an oral account. Dorcas listened, catching moving rhythms in it.

"Translation! Translation!" She cheerfully exclaimed.

"*Odyssey*, book one, verses one to forty-three."

"It is impossible, let us see! Homer in Wanakironi—"

"I adore this man beyond all the other ancient Greeks."

"All right, but don't tell me that you translated the *Odyssey*!"

"Of course not; nevertheless, from now on, book one is alive in my head in my native language. My grandfather also knows it and likes it. One day as I recited it aloud in front of him like a herald from ancient times, he said: 'Again, child'; I obeyed and he asked again. A few days later, he reproduced the poem with a kind of jubilation; it is now a game between the two of us to sometimes exchange passages of this book one of the *Odyssey*, like table tennis balls."

"Marvelous, but hard to believe and also odd that your grandfather could retain so many lines of the *Odyssey*."

"Has it never happened that you remember the stories told by your grandparents, your parents or peasants, and villagers in France to relate them to friends in the evenings?"

"My poor friend! I am a city dweller; it is in Africa that I learned to interact with the rural people."

"Rural life, arborescent environments, still horizons, I would have an awful time doing without them."

"I notice them as soon as we are together. I will make you an immodest, even indecent confession."

"Oh, oh, Mrs. Keurléonan-Moricet!"

She blushed; her eyes were closed, and she lowered her head: "I blushed, too bad," she murmured, but already the young man's rhythm guided her in her suggestive appeals, made with dilated eyes and a fixed expression as if she had died without ceasing to look at him.

"You restore me; I confess it without shame, you knew how to awaken or revive, how do I explain this? The life that vegetated deep within me? Yes, that is it."

"Such a confession disturbs me," he said, beside himself.

"Why then? Are you embarrassed by the truth?"

"The truth? No, not the truth."

"You are thinking of my husband; you ask yourself why and how did he not know?"

"I sometimes find it difficult not to think of him, although I have no remorse; but your children are there in Europe."

"What can I do, Ségué n'Di, since you have captured my heart?"

"Honestly, I do not understand," he mumbled.

"How do I explain that, except by trying to honestly translate what has happened in me? With you—I can say, in spite of the fact that I feel myself turning red—I had, right from the first time, the feeling that love in terms of sexual contact between a man and a woman was not possible, even antagonistic, without the rhythm and harmony of movements. Something about you brought me toward the absolute. I do not know; in any case I am sure of getting there with you, not with him."

"Don't believe me if you want. I am becoming more and more disturbed, even sorry for him."

"Listen: It was as if you had entered with quiet but decisive steps a sanctuary ruled by a priest, whose authority you disputed."

"It is a provocation, and it is very serious: among our people, nobody, even the initiated ones, would behave in this manner, in a sacred place without the approval of a learned assembly of priestly dignitaries."

"However, it is what you did. You drove out a temple priest who officiated badly or who wasn't even an initiate. It is my belief right from the beginning," she retorted with a small laughter of a whispered dream.

"I am guilty of many things, instigator in your life of a disaster that I don't want and that I wish never happened."

"Beautiful words. I would rather like to shout my love, to cry 'long live' . . . ! Finally the end of my mineral straitjacket. I will add this, which perhaps will seem idiotic, absurd to you: I sensed you and even loved you as soon as our hands touched in the dense crowd—"

She stopped, unable to continue on this impetus, waited a bit, and continued in a calm voice that seemed to allow her thoughts to unwind: "Whether we are together or not, I am unable to control the boundless longing and desire that I have for you. Is it an impossible horizon? I want to reach it because I feel an insatiable desire for you."

He looked stunned as his arm stretched toward her, hand open like someone begging, but which she clasped, feeling, like the first day, the spontaneous poetic sentiments of friendship for a stranger that comradery alone infused in them, before desire suddenly bobbed up with its impassioned tender force. Standing on a slope of Mount Kiniéroko, they looked at the summits where the rays of the setting sun were dancing. It was in the blistering dry season where the lightning sometimes spouted out of a rock somewhere far off; the phenomenon occurred and its lightening shone in them. Dorcas flinched, turned toward him as he then looked like a frozen statue on the mountainside. But she clasped her arms around his neck, gripped him. Life was revived in the inert body and the heavy flow of desire rose to its climax.

"You are breathtakingly seductive," he said in a low voice.

"I have to go home," she murmured.

CHAPTER 10

For seven weeks, the International Cultural Center was filled with Africans between twenty and thirty years old; they read books, took notes, swapped them, got information from each another.

"What are your preferred courses?" Awa Tohégy, a pretty mulatta with sea-green eyes, was asked by a two-meter tall candidate built like a basketball player.

"Math and geography, and you?"

"History and languages."

"Aren't you perhaps on the wrong turf?"

"As a gym instructor, I like to rub myself with oil before competitions; you never know."

"I sell cheap goods at AKARAKA; I have my Basic Education Certificate, so, I can give it a try."

"Hush! Hussssh!" came from here and there. In spite of her height of one and three-quarters meters, Awa looked at her interlocutor with astonishment. Accustomed to the library, Ségué n'Di was there quite often. He signed up for three earth science works, skimmed through them one after the other as soon as they were brought to him, ascertained the contents of the chapters whose photocopies he had, and read the pages that preceded them as well as the transitions. The introductions revealed the authors' interests to him. The colonial reports on farming and the substratum held his attention; he read them without taking notes. The issues began to move away from the framework of the contest and alluded to politics. He read about details dealing with the lithosphere, the carboniferous period, and types of rocks and surveys of sections, layers, and the density of their growth toward the Earth's center; he was so fascinated by the compelling material and the training process that he reread it in Wanakironi. He was absorbed in A. von Humboldt when someone else who needed it came to take it. He had absorbed the essence and his brain crawled with undreamed of information. "Even if I bomb this competition, which I would not have taken on without her obstinate will, I will have learned a lot. My whole culture gains from it," he said to himself, thinking of the importance of geography, its rational use for the economic and social development of a country.

Dorcas had told him about the usefulness of applied geology, revealing to him what would become his obsession when he became aware of the problems: "The collection of information is a priority for me. Conveyed thoughtlessly to the companies whose task it is to evaluate it, to make the maximum profit possible from it, information of this nature would lead to an immense neocolonial exploitation of your countries." He fell back on the oral tradition to talk about the wealth of the substratum confirmed by the discovery of the gold mine. His ideas came to him during the preparation for the competition, as dreams for the development of his country prompted by the potentialities and their analysis by specialists excited him.

Suddenly skeptical, his thoughts raced, and for a good fifteen minutes, he saw himself again far from the library. He was then at the Kirinikimoja beach, beside Greenough when they spoke about the rise in unemployment and Western companies' reluctance to employ Africans. Without beating about the bush, the journalist had warned him against White people.

"Listen, kid! This group of people who claim to help Africans is a group of cuckolds!"

"Oh come on! Daddy Greenough!"

A Westerner in swimming trunks looked at the journalist with such contempt that it horrified Ségué n'Di.

"Who is this man? What did you do to him?"

"One of those mediocrities of the ICM; he thinks that his wife and I were lovers. What's wrong with that? His problem is that he believed that I targeted him in the article where I denounced the arbitrary racism of that clan of social climbers that fills up the international public office."

"I remember you exposed the method used to unseat Kirini n'Kororiyingy, in spite of his professional skills, university diplomas, and mastery of five European languages."

"Good memory, kid. They preferred a white man without suitable qualifications to an African in every respect over certain ICM bigwigs. I energetically highlighted it, and I'm waiting for them to file a lawsuit against me. The employee is none other than a son of the general manager of the ICM; his mother, one of the mistresses of the man who does not hide his disdain for me. OK, I will still cuckold him because he was in on it, supported by the secretary general. What made me angry is also the fact that, besides his native language, the illegitimate son chosen through the elimination of an African only speaks English and broken French."

"The ICM is alleged to be an offshoot of the United Nations system, but what a mess! I want many of its bigwigs to have to put up with the cuckold show."

They burst out laughing, slapping each other's hands like in a game played by African kids.

"Listen, good kid: it is not easy to guess the real age of an African straightaway, but you could not to have been more than five years old when I arrived at Wanakawa . . ."

"I am twenty-three years, going on twenty-four."

"My guess is pretty right. Well, I who speak five languages from this continent, I could have been your father, if he had also had the honor of being cuckolded."

"He did not live in Tigony. I was ten years old when he died."

"Sorry! Listen carefully to this: you must be wary of the white men, especially the so-called overseas volunteers, Africanists, etc., who scour your country."

Ségué n'Di's face looked like an astonished mask. Greenough noticed it and elaborated: "The environment is a peat bog; impossible to imagine what it is hatching and not to pay careful attention while walking there—"

"They cannot all be saints, but still—!"

"These new Westerners not only court your politicians, they also compromise those who are visibly maniacal government officials, and then are responsible for cascades of actions prejudicial to Africa; that enables them to deal arrogantly with 'big children.' Those people do not play the game of Black Africa, which should have already taken off. Those for whom they are their agents gloat in Europe: 'Negroes are incompetent; all the better, the continent should be exploited.'"

"Last year, after your report on the bribery scandal in the Brasil Terminal Portuário (BTP) company, rather heavy allusions were made to the Westerners' 'notably overseas volunteers'; none of them were questioned, but all the Africans were interrogated and—"

"It is only one ridiculous aspect of neocolonialism and the methods of these 'specialist' civil servants in whatever. They are a bunch of predators or sharks of a rare nature who look out for each other. From my point of view, their country should have handpicked them before dumping them on Africa."

"I heard about it. I guess that you don't like them."

"That isn't the problem. I know more than one of them and have heard of swipes against the principles of the 'club,' I kept this statement in my notebook: 'any absence for health reasons or family, etc., leads to intrigues, plots, if not a cabal to undermine the missing person. You insinuate yourself in the interim when you're taken on, cunningly digging under the armchair of the absent person the abyss into which he will be pushed on his return.'"

"Horrible! Cruel! The *Daily Encounter* should publish a report! They should draw attention to their activities and importance in the country. In fact, no one knows what they negotiate," Ségué n'Di said, and then he added: "It must be the same all over the world; it is certainly not restricted to the Westerners: people of this caliber are also in our country."

"With the barriers such as having a confidentiality agreement, diplomatic immunity that harms and protects at the same time, it is not easy to infiltrate their net. But that doesn't stop me from taking note of how they work. No morals among this association of men and women supposed to be in Africa to help the Africans."

"To help us, they ruin us, with the cooperation our leaders; the *Daily Encounter*, *L'Afrique actuelle*, *Karayinky*, even *Kahakiyingu* repeated it this week. If that is what you are stigmatizing, I completely agree with you."

"The 'Great White Men's' activities are also praised," the journalist said with a lively skip in his eyes. He kept quiet, then continued as if in a soliloquy: "'the Great White Men' raise hopes that they themselves dash, hopes of the fulfillment and evolution of Africa. I am dismayed at the intrigues of some Europeans, but they claim to work in accordance with the high-level official commissions. The bigwigs come, are acclaimed, are welcomed with dancing; they receive presents, offers, promises, enacting decrees in favor of your country and your problems; they appear to you like gods, new gods who fill you with 'wonder' after the wretchedness of colonialism. Sick."

"It is a blistering picture. It has the benefit of being objective in presenting one of the faces of reality. But high-level promises—"

"What promises? It is you Africans who believe that the 'Great White Men' like you by making you dream; look for the word 'lure' in an English or French dictionary. The 'Great White Men' scorn you."

"How can you talk like this, you an upper-class white man?"

"Me? White? Have you looked at me well? White! White! I am an African pachyderm! Hello, you have—no, you did not read *War and Peace*, right?"

"No, who wrote it?"

"Tolstoy, Leo Tolstoy, a great Russian writer. Without taking sides, I prefer James Joyce to him—"

"Russian, you mean Soviet?"

"The USSR is a recent invention; nobody thought of it. Tolstoy, and well before him Pushkin, a descendant of an African, was a great writer of imperial Russia. At eighteen years, I read *War and Peace*, an epic novel, when I came across a passage that revolted me. The scene reminds me of what I see in Africa: Napoleon Bonaparte among Russians of his time symbolized the 'Great White Men' of today, with their self-righteous conviction that their presence in the African countries electrifies the people, and elicits the madness of the worship of white men. At the time of the Napoleonic wars, focus of the action in his novel, Tolstoy reports that when you drew Napoleon's attention to the Poles' dedication to himself, 'the small man in grey frock coat rose, called Berthier, and walking with him along the river and giving him his orders, glanced inattentively and with dissatisfaction at the lancers who, drowning, diverted his attention from serious matters.' I knew this passage by heart but thought that I could no longer remember it; it came back to me exactly enough. That is a picture of the 'Great White Men' and men in high places."

Ségué n'Di heaved a long sigh, thanked him for having learned so much from him, for opening his eyes all the more by quoting a novelist but also by referring to the history. Then he exclaimed, looking at him from top to bottom: "Oh! Daddy, I forgot that you are in swimming trunks—"

Greenough looked at himself in turn and burst into laughter. "If the cuckold meets me, he would want to knock me out."

"I will not let anybody get at Daddy."

"Kid, perhaps I seem to be eccentric, but I bear witness, which does not mean I am indifferent. I observed and outlined the events in African countries, bedded so many women, but also blossoming girls, that I certainly have children here and there. How many? God knows better than me who will account for it. After independence, the old anarchist idiot would have liked to deal with natives conscious of their country's problems; no dice! You find yourself opposing fossils floating over the course of helpless currents, foreign forces moved by powerful wills that don't give a damn about your country's problems or bring any real change. Fossils controlled by long-distance tele-guidance."

"Thank you again, Mr. Greenough," Ségué n'Di had said in a very low voice.

"Good God! Stop thanking me and looking like that. It is sheer luck that made this encounter take place on this splendid beach where an obtuse man looked at me cross-eyed and will have to pay for it after he's become a plaintiff! Yes! Whether in life or in Wanakawa, he has nothing better to do other than be what he is. I would like it that you, Ségué n'Di, do something, see me as something other than a cuttlefish bone that the sea washed onto a beach."

"But I like this cuttlefish bone, the pachyderm too!"

They patted and shook each other's hands. The old journalist turned toward the sea. About thirty ships flying European flags of convenience waited offshore to move toward the port swarming with steamers and cargo ships, with about two thousand sailors in fishing boats that were spread across a crested swell of scum moving toward the coast with its noisy backwash. One meter sixty-five, tall like the forty years spent in Africa as special correspondent for the *Daily Encounter*, before becoming the "permanent one" with the curly salt-and-pepper tousled hair. Women liked his green eyes under the arches of abundant and black eyebrows in a long face with even features. Nimble, forthright, at the wheel of his white convertible Austin he seemed like a ubiquitous force in Wanakawa.

Always dressed in light blue jeans and a white unbleached linen Byron shirt, with the cuffs rolled up uncovering his wristwatch on one side, his gold chain engraved with his initials on the other, as soon as he started talking, humor, intelligence, and curiosity came alive on his face. Rumor had it that the paternity of three mixed-blood children with other men's wives belonged to him, and that he discreetly maintained each of them; every allusion to this situation made him laugh. His first meeting with Ségué n'Di who spoke to him then about his "unemployment status" had taken place during the strike, on the side of the

Kirinikimoja Bridge. On that day, he was also in swimming trunks. One of his victims, an African not far from them, had raised an angry fist. Ségué n'Di, not understanding what he had done, had pointed his forefinger at his chest. Shaking his head, the man had pointed a threatening finger at the journalist who had burst out before commenting that: "If this guy who, far from being a gentleman, really had what he showed off so noisily and knew how to make good use of it, by Zeus, he would never have been cheated on so much."

Ségué n'Di could not help but burst into laughter, but had had to ask if Daddy was responsible for his misfortune.

"His misfortune? He has two wives and mistresses; doesn't he need help in not spending too much energy? It is right that he is cuckolded."

Ségué n'Di had held his sides with laughter.

"I have to leave you, kid: these waves are like the women who excite me," he had concluded, and running like an athlete, he had plunged in before a wave crashed, with its noisy rumbling backwash heard on the beach.

A happy smile quivered on his face and his lips when his imagination brought him back to the library. As he returned the books before taking leave, one of the people in charge said without seeming to address himself to him specifically: "It is disturbing that there is no national library with works treating all the subjects of general culture in Tigony. They would willingly be read, without too many problems." It was his own remark made the previous year as the petty fumbling of one supervisor had annoyed him. Amplified, various comments in chancelleries got passed around: "employment appointment," "intelligent," "leftist," "political protestor," Ségué n'Di Niriokiriko Aplika was a "man who it would be better to be wary of."

To repeat without forgetting one word of the sentences in his report, at the time when he prepared for a competition, didn't greatly disturb him. Daddy Greenough had come to pick him up in a car. A sudden smile on his lips, he left the library, agreeing with the old journalist.

CHAPTER 11

Counselor Steinberg had pleaded the cause of his country by highlighting the importance of "global German investments" in Wanakawa, and then he hoped that the competition would be hosted by his embassy. The ambiguity of the word *globalization* had brought a discrete smile to the lips of several Europeans. The representative from the USSR had raised a flabby hand before giving up on expressing himself, after having squinted at his counterpart from the GDR, who had raised the thumb of his left hand resting on the table. This quiet diplomacy made it possible to convert the reception room of the embassy of the FRG. The competition took place there after several advertisements in the newspapers in African as well as European languages. Twice a week, radio broadcasts had repeated the academic disciplines that the candidates were to deal with on "the fateful day; alas, there can only be one successful candidate; the GGAG Consortium only wants to employ one officer."

The media had named the works from which the texts would be taken and reminded them that the candidates, "compulsorily Africans," had to register their candidacy with a photocopy of their national identity card and two photographs.

■ ■ ■

Seventy-six desks from Saint-George College and Jean-Jacques Rousseau Technical School filled the embassy's reception room. The supervisors' chairs were set, two in the first row, two in the last, and three on each side of the room, which the dazzled candidates discreetly peered at. Portraits of Goethe, Schiller, Adenauer, and Willy Brandt intercalated masterpieces and German landscapes hung on the walls. Dressed in a turquoise-colored skirt and short-sleeved houndstooth bolero, Mrs. Keurléonan-Moricet fell in behind the cultural attaché of Switzerland.

"You look good enough to eat, Dor!" Gaëtan said when she was leaving, and she kissed him, like when they were young."

The diplomatic envoys only made routine appearances. Seven African teachers were in charge of monitoring the competition. Candidates, some dressed in African and others in Western attire, settled in. The instructions announced in the newspapers and on the radio were reiterated: "surnames and first names, as they appear on the national identity cards, must be recopied at the given spot, before folding and gluing the gummed corner of each sheet intended for the tests."

They distributed special sheets for the draft, then those for the tests, which had the INTERNATIONAL CONSORTIUM COMPETITION heading. The formalities completed, in a crisp Prince of Wales checkered suit, the Swiss cultural attaché adjusted his oval gold-rimmed glasses. Of average build, with a round head, hair parted on the right side, he had a cold look, but a grin that resembled the outline of an evasive smile that quivered on his lips. He took out a large manila envelope sealed with red wax from his Moroccan leather bag, and raised it above his head. The candidates had goose bumps. A distressed silence followed when, with exact movements, he broke the wax, opened the envelope, brought out the envelope for the first test, unsealed it, and gave it to a supervisor who started the distribution of the exams with his colleagues.

"Ladies and gentlemen," Mrs. Keurléonan-Moricet said, "in the name of the Recruitment Committee, I implore you to please comply with the instructions: except for possible erasures, any other mark on a copy, however tiny it is, will have as a consequence the elimination of the candidate. In the name of the committee, I give you this signal," she finished, crossing the index and the middle fingers of her right hand.

Although impressed and intimidated, Ségué n'Di stared at her as she spoke, while she looked around the room. The competition lasted eighteen hours spread over three days. The copies were sent to the attention of the minister of National Education, and the corrections, for "secret motives," took place at the embassy of the United Kingdom, which had called African and European teachers together for this purpose.

CHAPTER 12

THE NEW WAVE OF DESTITUTION CASES LOOKED LIKE AN EPIDEMIC. IN TIGONY and in its outskirts, the No Hope For Work (NHFW) looked like a multitude of binary fissions; you could see them everywhere, haggard, gaunt, or they fell on you with sleeves rolled up, in colorless shirts and trousers pockmarked with holes. Women or unmarried mothers who did not want to expose their exhausted bodies, their malnourished children hoisted on their backs or on hips, carried their misery like a carnival mask, from the category of those who, in spite of the fear of AIDS, were able to prostitute themselves for money to live on. Kids in patched-up shirts sewed into patchworks, taking great care in their jobs as shoe shiners, anxious about not being suitably paid, winked at the customers for whom they worked like dogs to dust, polish, shine shoes and who, perhaps, would leave them out in the cold. The job finished, they sat up and raised a half folded arm. Eyes on the money put in their dirty hands, they looked at it, smiled at the tiny sums or suddenly turned sullen before running toward other customers. Scroungy men with no other guide apart from their knotty sticks. Unemployed beggars who used to beg for a living discovering unfair competitors. Mentally handicapped people in parks or in front of the department stores, places of worship, railway stations or roads, and on the pedestrian crossings of the bridges.

Among these categories of Africans, also shaggy white men in worn trousers, bare-chested or in indecent shirts, sitting cross-legged, a dog or a cat at their feet, head lowered, and who stretched their hand or begging bowl to the passersby, seemed to have emerged out of the blue. Astonished to discover Westerners reduced to depending on their generosity in their underdeveloped country, Africans watched them out of the corner of their eyes, while some, dropping a coin in a hand with filthy long nails, wondered how these white men in such a condition had been able to land in Wanakawa, if they were poor natives or—

"These are perhaps laid-off ex–overseas volunteers."

"You think so! Severance pay together with expenses of repatriation and all that crap—"

"If they are now as poor as ours who really lack money, it is perhaps that they had invested in shares, which they lost in our country—"

"Come on, Hatikini. Have you ever heard of a white man who invested in Africa, for example in building or buying a house? That was in the past in the colonial period, among the braver types who were attached to the beauties of our country; but now it is business, nothing more. No friends or personal interests before anything else."

"You are certainly right. For seventeen years, my parents had European tenants with luxury cars, house staffs, incredible comfort, parties, etc. They could have built their own homes to sell or rent out before returning to their country."

"Are you kidding? The 'overseas' villa? Wasn't it by investing nearby or by hoarding the CFA francs that you proved that you have lived well there?"

"You're tiring us out; let us work on the continent and live in peace with—"

"You say that because your brother, it seems, has two houses in Europe, but not one hut in his own country?"

"How come? Does he stay in a hotel when he returns to Wanakawa? And our parents' villa, did it fall from the sky?"

"Thus, Blacks invest with Whites; as for reciprocity, my foot!"

A dispute on the other bank of the Kiniéroko stirred up the crowd in the surroundings of the Méyingy district. Five African dockers in worn-out breeches surrounded a white man in trousers and culvert shirt.

"You tief us! The tourists yo' said we are doing, it bring only yo' money, not us, ne'er!"

"Yeeeah! it's fo' im 'lone! He said we work to'ether, but the money is alw'ys fo' im."

"Yo're White and a tief! Yo' came to ous to steal a'ain!"

"Yeeeah White tieeeef!"

"You do politics instead of looking at the world in the face! Who came up with the idea of this cultural tourism? Who has run the business for three years? Who among you is able to organize and make this small business that we run together as friends productive? Does it not bring us many customers from Europe, America, and elsewhere? Thanks to whom? You, Founkiya? Not you, Zinigy! You neither, Hatinikiyingy; or you, Susufuku, or you, Kiriokufuku? You owe everything to the white man who you call a thief and you crack me up, bloody feckless!"

"Yo're even insulting us?"

"Wot's dis tolk 'bout Afflik?"

"I say and stand by it: you are unfits, fuckers!"

"Haaaa heeee? Yo're also a dickhead!"

"And the dugouts? Heee, the dugouts, are they the property of the bugger White mother?"

"Haow? Yo' exploit us and insult us: niggers and whaaat now?"

The argument degenerated; the Africans engaged in fistfights, stamping their feet, close to engaging in a fight with their "partner" when a police siren sounded. Rémy Draguier seemed reassured; one and three-quarters meters tall, mean, muscular, round faced, crafty, he was bigger than the Africans.

"They have worked for me for a long time, and I pay them reasonably."

"Wot's re'sonable? He 'ves fife hundlet Flancs to each person eveli day!"

"A lot my brother," one of the officers said.

"Haow mush? The dugouts, we're de ploplietors! The man over there, he exploits!"

"What do you say, Mr. . . . Fraguier?"

"Draguier, Rémy Draguier, please."

"Agreed, excuse me, sir."

"Who does the equipment belong to? You or them?" another officer asked.

"I agree that the boats are their property."

"Is it because of that that each one of them is paid five hundred Francs per day?"

"Is it insufficient in a country where unemployment prevails? Officers, what do you think of the strikes that are being prepared?"

"Mr. Fraguier, are we talking about the social problems in this country, or yours with these men who are complaining about you?"

"Let me repeat to you, I am called Rémy Draguier."

"Your opinion, Police Chief Naifurini?" an obsequious officer said, touching the visor of his military hat.

"Mr. Draguier, since you want to be called that, in what capacity are you working here in the cultural tourism profession?"

"It is at the special request and on Mr. Turiéka's directives that I take care of the cultural tourism."

"Which Turiéka? There is a score of them in our country."

"Maurice Kufuni Turiéka; I am under his protection."

"Is it the minister of planning who allows you to work in Wanakawa?"

"It is because I contribute to the reduction of unemployment in your country; should I regret it?"

"Give me your papers, Mr. Fraguier—"

"It is provocation, officers! I will lodge a complaint."

"You are free to do so. We are doing our duty in accordance with the law. Give me your papers, please."

Drawing his zip fastener on his shiny maroon leather satchel, a men's overnight bag containing banknotes as well as his toiletries, his hands trembled. One of the officers threw an ironic glance at his identity card and his residence permit that had expired two years ago, showing it to his colleagues, and said: "He can always lodge a complaint."

"You know, in your country, someone of your caliber, but an African with your type of papers, would be seriously dealt with and thrown into a plane to be repatriated back home."

"I am—"

"Protected by Mr. Maurice Turiéka."

"I am sorry; I did not have the time to take care of it."

"You are so busy in your work in cultural tourism. Follow us."

"You will not arrest me! It is a violation of human rights!" he cried, red like a peony.

"Here is an arrest warrant for you, Antoine Culbouché; you're looking ashen," an officer said, taking a paper out of the pocket of his shirt.

"It is racism. You have no right to make a remark of this nature!"

"Mr. Culbouché, it is worse in your country where racism spares neither Africans, nor Arabs from North Africa, even if they have the same nationality as you do. I know what I am saying. Have I not got the right to say this? My apologies, even though you swapped yours for another; but tell me, when will we have the right to deal with you? You live under a false name; in the bargain, you are a con man of the worst type. A correction, Mr. Culbouché: I practiced my profession for fifteen years in France; I was a chief commissioner before returning to my native country. It means that I knew the face of racism, unlike what you are complaining about."

"He! He! Blothers, me I have a cetificat, I can speak the tluth, all the Turiékas, they are from my village, and yet so we're going to settle aour problem naow before the boat of the White D'laguié that is not at all who he says he is," responded one of the confused ferrymen, strongly supported by his other colleagues.

"We are going to see Turiéka. I know his mother who trades in the blig maket on the Kirinikimoja Bridge."

Antoine Culbouché seemed to have regained a bit of color, and supple, less arrogant, all of a sudden accommodating, he proposed to pay each of them one thousand Francs per day. An officer stared at him, and one of the ferrymen was suspicious.

"The D'laguié slay one thousand Flancs pa day. We have woked sinc, let uos first of all coun it makes meny yeaz and shome."

"And evly day, even Shundays."

"There ar' de oders, shince we ar' tlelve with six bloats.

"These are negotiators. You are wrong to have underestimated their intelligence," the commissioner said, playing with the handcuffs he had taken out of his trouser pocket.

"I realize it. But between you and me, would it be difficult for us to come to an agreement?" he whispered.

A police car, coming from a suburb where a suspicion that a "riot preparation" had circulated, stopped; two chief commissioners came out of it. Kakinigy approached them without turning to Culbouché.

"You have been followed for six months. Some people knew how to nail you down tonight."

"Me?" He was amazed.

A dazed hollow mask of questions showed on his face. The commissioner looked at him with a sardonic smile.

"Yes, you, Antoine Jean-Luc Culbouché, say Rémy Draguier: the real as well as the false name are in the police's sights."

"He will say that he is under the protection of Turiéka's chief of staff."

"Where did you pick him up?"

"The most stupid thing in the world because luck also does not like crooks."

"The man is involved with so-called cultural tourism politics, without bothering to get bogged down by the kufani ferrymen's plight for the past three years. They were nearly getting into a fight when we intervened. Culbouché was all over the place acting as promoter of cultural tourism."

Hunkering down, head bent, he looked at them without unclenching his teeth. Commissioner n'Guiyingy looked at Culbouché with disgust. N'Guiyingy had also worked in France as a police commissioner with Sigrid, his wife, who, born of a German father and Japanese mother, was mother of four children. Married to an African man, she found her status "rather nice." N'Guiyingy who spoke Japanese, did his training course in Germany, then England, and was promoted as the chief for international relations one year after his return to Wanakawa. He was the one who had cast the net Culbouché and his group got trapped in, in the district.

"Which African or North African Arab in Europe, more precisely in France, would behave with impunity for such a long time, like you here? The finance officers will inform you on the rest, but let me tell you that your funds transfers to Liechtenstein and Switzerland have been intercepted."

Staggering, Culbouché almost fainted when the handcuffs were put on him; he was made to get into one of the cars that drove off. The crowd dispersed; crying in anger, his "workers" threatened to go to Kufuni Turiéka, to his "old mother as well" who would not be proud to have such a son who had gone chummy with a "White hoodlom, even wic'ed, milking, gelding p'or Blacks and all the moni dat go to de Wite man over there!"

The rumor spread, crossed over the bridge, reached the other bank. The entire city soon knew that since his arrival in Wanakawa where he traveled through the provinces before settling down in Tigony, Antoine Culbouché, alias Rémy Draguier, had transferred ten million French Francs overseas, with the complicity of some ministers and high-level ministerial officers. "The plan was also to go to the rescue, using the chief private secretary as the footbridge."

"Weeee wee are going to shee the minista himself!"

"Dere ish always one of aour people in de cabinet, ho!"

"Deflitely, de lite man lipped us off, right?"

"A lite man lipping Blacks in dier own countly! Is that not shamelessness!"

They discussed on the way to the minister of Internal Affairs. On seeing them worked up, the guards discouraged them from venturing in at a time when the social climate in the country was stormy and electrified.

"Whot about aour moni theeen?"

"Your case will be announced. It seems as if the chief commissioner n'Guiyingy has already seen and listened to you. He would write a detailed report on this matter. The other departments would also do the same thing," they were told in Kinokoroni and Kaïnifuku.

CHAPTER 13

At the steering wheel of his Austin, J. G. F. Greenough saw the police R4, accelerated, put on the headlights, overtook the Renault, slowed down to its level, and made signs to the officers that he wanted to talk to them. The cars stopped. He saw Culbouché handcuffed, sandwiched between two police officers, gave a thumbs-up sign of praise, and cried, “Great! You finally nabbed him,” and then he clasped his hands together.

“It is true, there are certainly ten other Westerners of the same caliber as Culbouché. The net is closing in and it will happen quickly,” Chief Commissioner n’Guiyingy stated.

“Do you know that three of his partners were cornered on the eastern border?” the journalist asked.

“When was that?”

“I heard it on my cell phone about half an hour ago. An email was immediately sent to the *Daily News*, in London.”

N’Guiyingy informed the central police station.

“We have Antoine Jean-Luc Culbouché, alias Rémy Draguier, with us. Some of his partners include—”

He gave Greenough a satisfied look while listening to the police station's confirmation, and then informed Culbouché that the northern customs officers had detained his partner and friend Georges Marinet, alias Jean-Paul Serrefrein, as he fraudulently sent one hundred and fifty ton of oxen skins and tanned ostrich to Turkey.

Culbouché wept, vomited. With a smile on his lips, Greenough took a picture of the incident with the Minolta camera slung on his neck.

"I do not understand that their embassy was not informed of this situation: irregularity, false documents, and fraud. Wouldn't such people be detrimental to your country? It got a paragraph in my text dictated to London and Ireland. The *Daily Encounter* will repeat it."

"Would it perhaps be easier if all these men had the same nationality? I do not know. The police are not diplomatic."

"The one who calls himself Cyril Durville is Anatole Prebscjl or something like that; seven of the hoodlums are French. They have partners in the government and are linked to each other through dubious means."

"Oh la la! Mr. Greenough, you don't waste any time in quicksand."

"The seized documents—on one of the men that fell into one of your nets—mentioned transfers of considerable funds intercepted, destined for foreign banks. Seven million five hundred thousand pounds sterling; how much is that in French Francs and CFA?"

"The customs officers cooperate with the Internal Intelligence Agency and Interpol. They know that the funds belong to Culbouché's partner. As for what—"

"Your English is excellent, read the *Encounter* then, but the local newspapers will also repeat the problems," Greenough said, cutting him short, then took off like a shot, delighted to have obtained other information on the most important event on the eastern and northern boundaries.

His sources had informed him that Draguier had fallen into a trap where he had been lured by an informant, a ferryman who was threatened with being buried in mud. He called the police officers to confirm it.

"What accuracy! But affirmative: fire had been smoldering in this 'cultural tourism' for a long time."

"Tell me, dear brigadier, how people who do not speak any of your national languages could run a profitable business, enabling them to transfer so many funds to safe places?"

"That is a huge problem, but that is another matter, Mr. Greenough."

"I want to state that clearly: how have they succeeded in an area where the government ignores the potentialities, not even thinking of—?"

"It is all politics, Mr. Greenough. You should discuss it with people whom you have a better chance of approaching than us. The appropriate minister could grant you an interview."

Greenough burst into laughter.

"Juicy! Wonderful and savory," he laughed as he dropped his mobile phone.

The car returned home, entered the fine gravel driveway, and stopped in front of the brick villa painted in a mottled white, built ten years earlier. The lawn was planted with grass that was often well maintained. Northeast of it, there was a twenty-five by ten swimming pool with a murky bottom. Eucalyptus, coconut trees, mango trees, lemon trees, avocado trees, and a giant copaiba created the atmosphere of ease, relaxation, and sobriety in the calm that floated over the property.

He bounded up the pink granite path leading to the front steps, stretched himself as he heard his spinal cord crack and the cervical bone released. He felt as if he was being relieved of a burden, and blew a cheerful boy scout whistle as he walked through the hallway with its pink granite floor, past the white marble living room, to the old wine cellar. Iranian, Fez, and Afghanistan carpets seemed to be scattered in a disorderly manner. Séliki brought him a glass filled with pressed orange. A small, pretty Fulani woman with a willowy figure, fine features, and a calm gait, she had been his housekeeper for many years. Forty years old, with a nice bosom, a reassuring expression on her face, and in her glance reflected her nature.

"Thanks Séli, what are you preparing for me to eat? I am beat," he said, taking the glass of juice.

"You talked about roasted John Dory yesterday."

"If you do such a thing to him on earth, he will shut the door of paradise in your face."

She smiled, two dimples deepened in her cheeks and with as much curiosity as mischief, she asked where the paradise was.

"Oh sorry! I forgot that you did not know where it was. Me neither, it seems as if it is very far away, very beautiful, and that you could get there from all over," he said with his eyes fixed on her, and she felt as if he was undressing her.

She returned to the kitchen as she heard his voice, full of such tenderness: "Oh! Séli, I will be unhappy for the rest of the day if you shun me . . ."

"Oh by Shiva! I feel helpless when you talk to me like that! I do not want you to be unhappy," she said in a low voice, eyelids lowered.

They sat side by side on the Chippendale divan of hardened dark brown leather. Greenough's hair was salt-and-pepper; now he dropped his head on her knees with nonchalance, less studied than it seemed. Séliki's glance searched his face, as if looking for the reason behind it. Each time, she was so open to the inflections in her employer's voice, who all of a sudden became an unhappy child who could only be comforted by her, a wife and mother of three children, by immediately giving in to him when he needed her. He turned his head. Séliki's eyes rested on his face. He turned and saw the desire wandering on their faces like pale blue lampyris gleam. The mischief left his face, and he smiled.

"My soul shivers. Why is it like this every time you talk to me in this voice?"

"I do not know. I hear your heart saying something different from your question."

"Are these perhaps the whisperings of tenderness in me that I have to put in your life?"

He sat up and took her in his arms.

"Good heavens! I love this country, but I think that the Black continent as a whole would not have meant much to me, without the caresses and the tenderness of a woman like you, Séli. Why are you not my wife?" He said, breathlessly.

"Because I already belonged to someone else. Is that really important? Hush, we are here where life has meaning, I can feel its breath pass by."

▪ ▪ ▪

He went to put on his swimming trunks, crossed the room, then the courtyard, and gave a sidelong look at the bougainvillea arbor with the trellises full of white, red, orange flowers; he wondered if he would have lunch. Splashing in the pool, going down the pool like ballast, he climbed back up, swimming the crawl from one end of the pool to the other, turned over, swam on his back, alert to the movement of his muscles, to the suppleness of this "pachyderm body," to the mental relaxation when the first sentences of an article on the riot took shape. He knew the inevitable beginnings. Returning without drawing a breath, to the bottom from where he saw the sun's rays sliding down like molten golden wire, he stood upright, thrashing the water with his feet and hands.

Standing by in the doorway at the entrance of the hallway, Séliki saw James

G. F. Greenough, who walked briskly toward the villa like a child who enjoyed the sun dancing among tree leaves. He entered the villa and put on a pair of trousers and a white shirt. Séliki brought a whiskey decanter and a crystal glass.

"Still no drink?" he mischievously inquired as he served himself. She said no, shaking her head calmly.

"Drink some juice with me then; why don't you ever take a drink with an old man like me?"

"It is not in our custom," she answered, smiling, and, eyes lowered, she returned to the kitchen.

Greenough sat down in an old padded velvet Louis XIV armchair, sipping whisky while going through his mail. There was a tightly taped parcel of books. "That's just like Arthur," he grumbled cutting the sticky tape. Loosening the pack, he saw the edition of *Histoire*, loaned to his brother during the latter's stay at Tigony. Great! He was happy about it, but saw that Tony Lewis Arthur Greenough had, intentionally or by accident, marked some parts with a green marker. He opened the volume to one of the pages and read:

> If it is true that the wife too contributes to the seed and the generation, plainly there is need of equal speed on both sides. Therefore, if he has completed quickly while she has hardly done so (for in most things women are slower), this is an impediment. This is also why they generate when united with each other but fail to generate in encounters with partners who go with the same speed toward intercourse.

"My God! Dear Aristotle, how many in my race at the same pace . . ." he gloated while moving on to the other side marked by Arthur:

> Further, the woman emits into the region in front of the mouth of the uterus where the man emits too when she has intercourse. For from there she draws it in by means of the wind, just as by mouths or nostrils. For everything that attracts without using instruments is either hollow with an inlet from above, or draws by means of wind from its present place. . . . The way through which it goes is constituted as follows in women. They have a tube, just as men have the penis, but within the body. They let out wind because of this and by means of a small passage farther up, whereby women urinate. This is also why, when they

> are sexually excited, this place is not in the same state as before the excitement. Now it is from this tube that outflow takes place, and the region in front of the uterus is much larger than the way by which the outflow comes to that place.

"Well, Old Greatest, you've bowled me over," he said with a sigh, convinced that without the clues from his brother, he would certainly not have read these lines from Aristotle in a book from his own library, which "that bloody Arthur" had borrowed.

Séliki fingered his hair. It had been already eight years that she worked for him and this was the first time that she dared do such a thing. Her hand slowly moved behind his ear, slid down his neck, and gently pinched his cheek. He looked at the Fulani woman with a kind of sexual excitement in his blue-green eyes. He no longer wanted her, but she wanted him and was crying it to him in the silence that gripped him, as if she had also just read Aristotle again. He knew for certain that the mechanism whose workings he had discovered was in action inside this woman's innermost. Desire erupted and he was happy that it was she who had wanted him to want her again. He stood up, drew her against his body, then took her hand and led her into his bedroom. Later, seeing her nude, fast asleep, he admired her body, took a large sheet of Canson drawing paper and rapidly drew a portrait of her. Then, as if he had to send it to one or another of the magazines in Dublin and London in which he published his articles under pseudonyms, he wrote: "Whoever—male or female—is unable to appreciate the beauty of the body that is within his reach must be cuckolded!"

He peered at Séliki's shapely body, hips, and breasts. "My eyes feel, caress them, and inform me before my hands touch them. What a body! God, what anatomy!"

He took his pen and scribbled on the drawing sheet: "African artists must, without self-censorship, learn to sculpt a black woman's body, like Phidias and so many of the Greek sculptors and, closer to us, Michelangelo, Velázquez, Vermeer, Picasso sculptured or painted women radiating pleasure."

Séliki stretched at length, woke up, and cried, "Oh! Your fish, Mr. Greenough! I am really very sorry!"

"I am not hungry! I am no longer hungry."

"It is ready, see, Mr. Greenough! Please pardon me!"

"It is grilled John Dory, isn't it?"

"Certainly, it is what you wanted . . ."

"We have wanted so many things and were both even in paradise, so what? Hot or cold, we must also share this poor John Dory."

She was still laughing as she brought the food.

CHAPTER 14

WITH THE GENERAL DISCONTENTMENT A RUMOR CIRCULATED THAT THE government did not care about the people's silent march, or the unemployment growth in three years, and that there was a risk of an accumulation of tensions escalating into a riot. The supporters of the sole party argued that the rumor arose from "the vox pop radio gossip." Waking up two weeks later, the country found itself in an iron grip. The taxi unions, dockers at the port, railway workers, the Civil Servant Alliance, the Students and Pupils Association, and the National Federation of Public Transport started the strike following their warning reiterated to the government.

"It will continue as long as the government insists on watering down its never fulfilled customary promises instead of finding practical solutions to our just demands," Maïlidi, general secretary of the National Federation of Public Transport, had stated.

One meter sixty centimeters tall, hunched, apparently frail with his coconut head, he had a friendly look about him that would make him look like someone easy to manipulate, had it not been for the willpower and the resolute firmness that spread all over his face when he spoke. Neither the calm movements of his hands, the rhythm of his sentences, nor the quiet movements of his look at the crowd gave an inkling of his leadership qualities; but they listened to him when he talked and they loved him.

"I was not elected to speak for all the workers in our country. Notwithstanding, I am aware of the need to pass on the highly ridiculed wishes of our federation to you in which other organizations cannot help but hear the echo of their own demands mocked and trampled upon by a decisively autocratic government," he had asserted two weeks earlier, and the minister of Internal Affairs had suggested "to discreetly create problems for that Maïlidi." It leaked, the idea spread, and the Students and Pupils Association responded through Karl-Karl Kariyingy.

A level-headed man opened the debate with a high voice that no one could conceal, and the head of the police quietly murmured that he should be stifled. "Through what means, what method? They dare to reveal to us that they encourage us to take vocational training, while depriving us of the appropriate scholarships; they dazzle us with the possibilities of getting higher education, knowing full well that there will not be employment. Yes, they suggest targets for our youths, which adds to the numbers of unemployed people wandering about Wanakawa. The head of the police should take good note of this: our strike is also aimed at stopping all provocation and shedding of blood. We solemnly warn the government that it must dismiss its mercenaries, mainly made up of Westerners hired by those who foment coups d'état in Africa to assassinate those who they want to remove. These people, we are assured, would be here to train—still this verb!—and direct their Wanakawani counterparts. Does this country really need this mob?"

The unions that hardly approved Karl-Karl Kariyingy's confused recovery process did not dissociate themselves from students and pupils. The angry minister roared at the provocation, and summoned Karl-Karl Kariyingy, who disregarded the invitation. The fear of confronting a working-class riot for which he might be perceived as responsible concerned the central police station anxious to choke any zealous attempt.

Beyond the mountains, the moaning of traditional bullroarers and twisted buffalo horns could be heard the whole of the night. At the lower end of the country, traditionalists did not disapprove of the social movements bent on shaking the government out of its sleep and its state of inertia. Aware of the demonstration that was plotted, the police formed a high-level provisional crisis committee.

"This Internal Affairs minister is irresponsible!"

"Son of the soil and fundamentally irresponsible. The Western puppet he succeeded was no better; he had the excuse of not speaking any of our languages and not understanding any of our problems, whereas Kariyingy . . . !"

"He forgot where he was born. It is not by surrounding us with alleged highly paid foreign experts that he will create order in this country."

"Experts? Don't make me cry. The mercenaries and spies who tail all of us, police officers or cops who are children of the country and yet they are ready to lock us up and throw away the key at any time . . ."

"We will not go to advise Kariyingy; he only listens to himself!"

"Some persist in claiming that it is because he is a criminologist that the president made him his confidential agent. They forget too quickly that he is first and foremost his brother-in-law and that must please Utafirini."

"It is exactly my opinion. The president taken hostage, Kariyingy makes use of the family clan and perceives Wanakawa as the Haïnakogninifus' property!"

"A hardcore of the Special Branch and foreign police officers in civilian clothes erected a wall around him. This unit is supervised by you-know-who, himself, and by top-ranking mercenaries who infiltrate the hardcore. It is the typical organization of surveillance in our country since independence."

"These are the 'Masters.' It is worse than *1984*. Orwell produced followers in Africa. We are supposed to be happy about it."

"Possibly, but the traditional bullroarers' buffalo and impala horns are the fortresses and sure foothills that no government would have enough mercenaries to overthrow. The high authority does not underestimate this mystical power that would drop it, if we were stupid enough to arouse this human multitude that so far is exercising control and holding back latent anger."

"Even if the order came from the minister?"

"Better not obey so that the country does not experience a blood bath."

Invigorating sun; flowing from everywhere, the anguished crowd of people proceeded into Tigony's blocked main streets. Difficult, stifling, the march got stuck as the dense crowd grew with affluent sympathizers from the peripheries and the side tracks. From the monotony of the feet on the laterite ground rose dust similar to an immense, thin, horizontal veil, always in front of you, that took ages to go up to the sky. The Westerners riding in their cars attempted to wade through the crowd.

"What madness!"

"A provocation?" was murmured in the rows.

The leader of the demonstration stated in a voice whose firmness gave shivers: "It is depressing that the wealthy ones who have nothing to lose, no matter what happens, show their contempt for the cheated people!"

Several people turned back; those who could not go on or back out left their cars, locked the steering wheels, closed the doors, and left on foot in a bad mood, while others, putting on a brave face, joined the march. As before, the participation of Westerners reinforced by the arrival of some others, surprised but encouraged the Wanakawani people. The organizers' messages, circulated now and then, from the provincial towns, made much of this "foreign presence" of which the government disapproved, but did not use any means to stop it.

"Some white men understood the base of our demands. The government is exposed."

"Westerners abandon the government even though they exploit the country."

"If we wanted a revolution or simply to overthrow the government . . ."

Remarks erupted in the rows, the national radio gave appraisals, some asked in loud voices how the civil servants from the Ministries of Internal Affairs and Information, who dared not join them, could evaluate such a human swarm in the country. The elderly, men and women, taking up the cause of the strikers, seized their cane or a knotty stick, and joined the crowd; its pace suited them and they seemed to be happy to be there. One saw an adolescent or a man in the prime of life give an old man a hand and engage in a conversation with the elderly member.

"The olden days are the past. The old poverty of the past is nothing like what we are now enduring."

"We are happy to be independent! By the gods, wouldn't we be happier if all the assets did not disappear into the pockets that no one sees?"

"Isn't one of your grandchildren in this government?"

"Poor thing! He invests everything in women, money, luxury fabrics, cars, and a beautiful house like the White people here and there. Even us, his grandparents, we cannot reconcile the ungrateful child with his parents!"

"Do remember," the grandfather butted in, "in our time, a worthless hoodlum of that sort, you would have tied his hands and feet and disciplined him with strokes of the cane until he yowled kin'klin! kin'klin! mi kin'klin lôlôlô! Whereas now—tchio!" he ended, spitting on the ground with disdain.

One heard the clashes of the sticks and the dragging on the ground. The elderly members stopped a few times, sighed, said that they had done their best in joining in solidarity, then pulled out of the crowd. They moved away with dignity, lining up on the sidewalks, under the eucalyptus, jacarandas, or the flamboyant trees. There, scrutinizing the crowd, they pointed fingers at old acquaintances they recognized and recalled that they had last seen them during such events as births or deaths.

From the villages' crisscross roads rose occasional songs, and the crowds of people hummed, droning like a large wave that was driven by an unruffled force in its race toward the coast.

"We need not be sad; sadness does not bring victory; no, no resignation! Steadfastness and dignity must be the motor and the cement of our most lawful demand for our rights! Colleagues and friends, Westerners have joined us! That is solidarity; that is fraternity!"

"Hurrrrah! Hurrrah! Hurrrrah!" the crowd shouted with enthusiasm.

"This makes you courageous when you see the people react against the behavior of the upper-crust bastards."

"The so-called ministers!"

"Yeah, with more of their kind under their wings, in the cabinets . . ."

"Those guys, they only beg when they are presented with a document or a problem."

"Bribe," a white man explained without looking at his listener.

"Here, it is 'stones of the gods, snake droppings.' Wine, it makes you drunk; the stones of the gods facilitate a project," retorted an African.

"As a proof, well-furnished houses, three or four cars, a big car for each son."

"Not to talk of the Peugeot or Volvo station wagons, the inevitable Range Rover or Toyota for trips to the countryside."

"One comes back with quarters of warthog, pork, vegetables . . ."

"One understands that they all cling to their upholstered armchair in their air- conditioned office."

"A sinecure," another Westerner summed up, turning his face toward the person who had been talking behind him.

"Cine what? It is not the cinema, but real, authentic things, as a friend of mine, Zankorignidi, would say!"

"Vocabulary problem, Mr. Toupilly," an African dressed in native attire with a poppy-red camisole, her head tied with a bright Vichy blue head-tie knotted below her neck, intervened.

"Why! Do you know me, madam?"

"I am the pharmacist at the Falaise Pharmacy."

"This is incredible!"

"Why then?" Nayéni smiled, astonished. "The incredible is the presence of White people in this demonstration."

"I am sure the Westerners who have joined this movement have no interest in it."

"Is it because you are good?" Nayéni's neighbor inquired.

"No! Some among us work in private, without being knights of a hypothetical re-conquest of an old colony."

"It is a pleasure to hear that," an African said.

"It is sometimes necessary to make things clear: Africa is reasonably and humanitarianly exploited."

"That also exists?" another astonished African said, in a confused manner.

"Yes! Yes!"

"Except for three pharmacies on duty in Tigony, one in each provincial town of average importance, it also applies to the doctors; all my colleagues lend their support to this mass movement," Nayéni added.

"Counselor Séguéeniyi," a big-sized African said, introducing himself to Mr. Toupilly.

"Lawyer or public notary, one never knows?" acknowledged the latter, an athletic, red-faced man around fifty years old, his auburn hair full of bristles. His abundant moustache cut under his long nose made him look like a youthful old man.

"Lawyer at the bar of Paris, currently in Tigony."

"Terrific, sublime! Who would expect the upper middle class to support us!" Toupilly exclaimed, eyes sparkling with mischievousness.

"Isn't it from this country, this middle class, upper or lower? Categorizations and dissections deprive you of the best from our country. It is such a pity, because you will never understand Africa," Nayéni said, smiling.

CHAPTER 15

An association of traders of bean cakes, sorghum, fried yam or cassava, hard-boiled eggs, and peeled oranges scored to juice them up circulated in the crowd. The sun had left the mountaintop. Those who were hungry brought out money, but the traders smilingly gave each person what he wanted, saying: "Support from our association," "support from our association of traders."

"The common people understood us! See how they generously give us refreshments! We were accused of anarchy, of being used to dissatisfaction, concerned about using all possible means to destabilize the government! Are the Westerners present in our midst also anarchists? Are they in the process of plotting to wipe out the government of a country where the companies they represent are thriving? Colleagues and friends, the march and the struggle should continue with the dignity of which we are living proofs. The lovely snacks provided by the common people add to our courage and pride!" Maïlidi stated. Passing in front of the police headquarters, the crowd moved toward the Avenue des Jacarandas, to reach the Place du Ministère de l'Intérieur, and applauded keenly.

"Have you ever been to Mount Nariékiyingy?" Counselor Ségueéniyi inquired, talking to Mr. Toupilly.

"It is that volcano that has presumably been extinct for a long time, isn't it? What a beautiful place! A hiker took us to its foot," said Mrs. Toupilly, a big brunette whose hair jutted out from her large rimmed raffia hat.

"Mount Nariékiyingy means more than that to the natives . . ."

"It seems as if it is also a divinity with terrible centennial fatal angers," Toupilly said.

"Rather unforeseeable angers. As a sacred mountain, every Wanakawa child considers Mount Nariékiyingy as his property: you love it, you shiver, and you experience it like an amorous desire when you are at its foot."

"Exactly; I am talking less as a native than as a pharmacist," Mrs. Nayéni agreed.

"But! That volcano kills all the more easily because its anger is unforeseeable, doesn't it, Counselor Séguéeniyi? How can you revere a divinity that kills?" Mrs. Toupilly inquired.

"That, as well, is Africa, madam. Quite frankly, to admit the reality without Cartesian analysis, the endogeneity of things that one cannot understand differently," the lawyer said.

One glimpsed, either through the crack of the doors, the courtyard of houses and their inhabitants, or on the street corners, women and their babies on their sides, in their arms, or "carried" on the back, or heavily pregnant. With happy, astonished, or admiring looks, everyone made signs of encouragement to the crowd. The unemployed and vagabonds took advantage of the gratuitousness of the snacks and stuffed themselves, by taking it out on bigwigs "without qualms or shame."

"They exposed the good plebs to poverty so that they die of hunger!"

"Shame on this country! Dey whil all go to hell!"

"Yeah, if that village also exists!"

Toupilly smiled. An international consultant, he voiced his opinion of his one-year practical experience in the country, without beating about the bush: "Each of the projects developed, of which most of them are, alas, buried or nipped in the bud, would have been accomplished if the protagonists, above all the politicians, focused on a single point of application."

"The scams of politicians and Western experts stretch their African counterparts more and more; so what? Well, all this falls within the area of the dark forces," the lawyer said.

"Quite relevant, counselor" Toupilly exclaimed.

"Recently, in Zimbabwe, a thought crossed my mind, which I thought was without much consistency. To my amazement, it had become the theme of a long discussion: 'in the present fragmented Africa,' I said, 'the people we are supposed to be no longer take time for the real lifelong concerns that we should prioritize, instead of some short-term results saying "me first or only me"; to reach the target, the politicians trample on what is basic.'"

"You know the country, counselor," Mrs. Nayéni said, and she added: "My brother, permanent immigrant?—I dare not believe it, let's say temporarily, he went to Benin—was a member of the government. He left after making these comments to President Haïnakogninifu: 'Dear Mr. President, it is as a childhood friend that I want to share my thoughts with you: in our team, each person would find it profitable to make the ray of light in him bloom and develop, to the benefit of the people; it is my conviction after months of activities, observation, and reflection.'"

"What was the president's response?" Mrs. Toupilly asked.

"Scathing: 'Raïnifiki, I know that your intelligence is more than mine. I will nevertheless be as direct as you have been: my government is not a freemason's lodge! You can resign if you no longer like what it is doing.' My brother resigned the day after this incident."

"Edifying—unbelievably edifying," Counselor Séguéeniyi said.

"An outstanding well-wisher!" Toupilly exclaimed, seeing a naked man moving through the crowd.

Koudjègan walked around at his own personal rhythm without aim or sense of time. Shaggy, aged, gaunt, he had travelled about a thousand miles, and he blended into the crowd when he saw it because he went where his feet directed him. He stank and the crowd avoided him. He looked at his neighbor and asked out of the blue: "Yeah you have seen Kokolie have you seen Kokolie you know her don't you you have not seen her why have you . . ."

"Of course, I know her, I saw her over there," Ségué n'Di responded on the spur of the moment, not even knowing what it was all about.

"Ah yeah ah yeah she is dressed like on the Kouroufunifunkouhouhou bridge . . ."

"Well, like that, like you, and she was beautiful."

"Ah yeah Ah yeah you spoke with Kokolie aha aha yeah . . ."

"Just a few words; she left quickly, saying she was looking for you."

"Yeah yeah Koudjègan Kokolie is looking for Koudjègan . . ."

"Exactly: 'I must find my Koudjègan,' she said."

"Ah yeah it's me . . ."

"Without doubt, one cannot help but want to get to know you. Do you want a bean-cake?"

"Ah yeah no I want Kokooolie . . ."

"You must leave the crowd; go through that way, behind the crowd. Kokolie is at the back with her friends."

"Hahahaha with friends with friends I am going there, must see Kokolie Koudjègan's Kokooolie," he went off as he left, with his penis so erect that people noticed, and they were more surprised than amused by it.

CHAPTER 16

He took his Walkman, looked at it, blinking as though he had never made use of it, and then slid in a cassette. A sentence in his brother's letter danced in his head. He smiled, took a letter from the "Family folder" and reread it.

> Dear old Boy, the thought of this practical object, carved by these Japanese—who are out to do us in everywhere in Europe—was not produced by my old grey matter: I had seen myself face to face with our delectable aunt Cynthia in the Haymarket; she wanted us to go out together. I gave her my arm and we walked to the concert in Charring Cross, fought our way to Oxford Street. There, in front of those shops teeming with electronic appliances, Cynt stopped, looked at a showcase, pointed the ringed finger of her left hand at a Walkman, and exclaimed: "Oh Arthur, Dear! . . . why don't you buy this for Freddy? It would come in handy for his interviews . . . and his dreams as well."
>
> You remember, don't you, that she always preferred to call you Freddy? So, old sybarite, how you made use of this thing. Son of a bitch! From the grammatical point of view, the old lady thinks more and more in past simple and future perfect. There was a libidinous glow in her beautiful blue eyes when she talked about you, and I suspected that she had not been unsullied during the three

weeks spent in parts of your house; she even makes less and less secret her love life, alluded to forbidden areas; so, she did not hesitate to refer to your avuncular sexual relationships. I had an inkling of it, but that she herself spoke of it with such delight in her eyes, went as far as to quote Wilde was incredible: "There are moments when the love for sin, or for what this world calls sin, and every cell of the brain seems to be prey to inexorable instincts. Then conscience is killed or, if it lives at all, lives, but to give rebellion its fascination, and disobedience its charm." she added: "these were delights to devour my Freddy. Arthur, don't say or think that the age difference—seven years! What does seven years mean?—made my nephew an easy prey. What do you say of such a prey when it went into action, making a predator out of its victim, whom it swallowed . . . ?"

There, old lecher, that's what gets you worked up. Another thing: speaking of sex, I read in Herodotus that Ethiopians produced Black sperm; but that dear Aristotle, contesting the assertion, taunted the historian. It does not matter. As you are in the field, there should be possibilities that you, an excellent journalist, and me, no less an excellent biochemist, work together to send a message to the related Nobel Committee, if you could make Ethiopians ejaculate, whose sperm I would analyze. Right! I know quite well, it is not in your nature to go that far with men: according to Cynt, you prefer your delectable housekeeper and other African beauties. What a continent! What a town this Tigony! I'll make you a confession: my meeting with Myriam shook me, but that effect is in the deep past. As for science and the love for research, James my brother, good heavens, help! Record interviews with Ethiopians and take samples of their sperm in bottles. . . .

He burst out as at the time of the first reading, shook his head, and murmured: "That old devil Arthur, he is really my blood relation." Then he took his Raleigh, a bicycle with rectilinear handlebar, sat upright on it, pedaled at a walking pace, and accelerated as soon as crowd or a sign caught his attention. It looked as if a thunderstorm was brewing in the sky as the crowd approached the Ministry of Internal Affairs. Greenough wandered round the city, wearing a scarf, with the wonderment of an elfish kid that he felt was alive in him, the sophisticated Sony Walkman fitted with radio and recorder-receiver.

Mixing with the demonstration on the Avenue des Jacarandas, he caught sight of Ethiopians or Somalis and thought of the sperm samples; a silent laughter started building up in him. He put on the Walkman, and taking the handlebar with one hand, he recorded: "An innumerable crowd of nearly three million on the streets; the news correspondents of the provinces highlight 'the incredible abundance of people on the streets' take account of the numbers: the Ministry of Internal Affairs, the organizers of the demonstration, Reuters's assessment, Agence France-Presse (AFP) without forgetting the embassies of the United States and the Soviet Union. Stop; my reports as an observer for more than a quarter of a century: a conflict between the fierce race for individual happiness and the emergence of independent Africa paralyzes the initiatives likely to get the country off the ground; no emergence without good management also taking into account the sensitivities as well as the local realities. Politicians know it but flout it like their old G-strings, since politics is nothing to them but a springboard to achieve their personal ends. The West laces their crowns, thinking that they see in them people capable of being useful to their countries. Alas, these are lures more harmful than they seem. What could likely happen could be: whoever comes to put out a fire by coming too close to it to urinate on it, risks seeing the flame engulf the faucet. Korigoriky is capable of such an act: the Ministry of Internal Affairs suits him as the miter and episcopal cross suit a Fulani shepherd."

▪ ▪ ▪

He recognized Ségué n'Di chatting with his neighbors and beckoned to them to call him. He came, hurtling sideways in the crowd.

"What is new?"

"You see, Daddy Greenough: a well-organized march, a demonstration without problem."

"There are indications that it is not totally without some."

"Where then? From whom?"

"There are leaks: the dismissal of the minister of Labor. The rumor got to me less than half an hour ago; don't talk about it before they are verified. There is a ruckus in the palace; the minister of Planning is in a stinking mess. It would hardly be surprising if the president sends him to mediate in front of the Mount Nariékiyingy crater."

"It is a lot, isn't it? That goes far, all that . . ."

"If you say a word about it to anybody, unless you are a potential government lobbyist . . ."

"It is intolerable! I will not allow anybody to have the least suspicion of such a muck-up, or dream of it about me," he retorted dryly.

"Good reaction; a single word will destabilize the strike. It is important to note the amplitude of this odd gathering, before the people officially hear that under their pressure the government had to yield, constrained and forced. You are all walking on the edge of a volcano crater. Do you understand me, kid?"

"Certainly. Why confide so much information to a nobody like me?"

"You are like a son to me. In addition, you must get ready for the sales of the *Daily Encounter* as soon as things get out of hand, OK?"

"OK, Daddy Greenough."

A hectic feverish shiver ran through the crowd and the Supervisory Committee urged them to continue the subject: "We are in a place with extreme feelings, a place where unpredictable things can happen!"

A message from the Coordinating Committee passed on by word of mouth: "Take your neighbor's hand."

"Form a union chain!"

"No one should let go off the hand he his holding, whatever happens."

The crowd moving in the main roads and alleys of Wanakawa as if in chains gave the impression that suddenly aroused, Mount Nariékiyingy discharged its lava across the whole country, as one heard the cracking of machine guns, coming from only God knows where. The cohort instinctively stopped. Maïlidi's voice immediately rose in the loudspeaker: "Sisters, Friends, and Brothers! Nobody stop! Carry on with the march! The bullies and assassins on duty want to intimidate us! To give up is to fail!"

He had hardly given his orders when one heard the Forces of the Earth, their conch hands flattened on their mouth, cry out from the mountains, and in the eucalyptus forest, the thundering anger that rose to the skies. Their voices seemed to have come out of trumpets and one perceived sobbing, hiccups, and moaning of human beings, prey to tortures, or to what one was about to accomplish.

The distressed Westerners grasped the hands that they held. Their neighbors reassured them if they were fully informed Africans.

"It is a secret initiatory company. It looks after peace as well as the equilibrium within our country."

"Its demonstration is a warning. The government will not dare take any reprehensible actions."

"And the machine guns that these bent and schizophrenic people in power carry around?"

"Definitely, Minister Korigoriky's bullies."

"It is believed that White mercenaries train their Black associates; the West pays such a scum with special funds; that is called cooperation."

From the off-centered slum quarters where poverty was also strongly felt from a far distance, the community citizens waded into Tigony by going down the wooded eucalyptus heights with hurried steps. From the mass of their peasants', artisans', and outcasts' feet rose the dull chorus of steps supported by the breath of the deep country. The clock of the town hall, beautifully built in the neoclassic Mussolini style, rang four o'clock when the official loudspeakers, installed here and there in Wanakawa, broke the news that Greenough had informed Ségué n'Di about.

"We don't give a damn! They should all go away!" almost the whole of the crowd yelled in unison.

"The internal goings-on of the government are not our business: the solutions to our demands, those are our problems, the justification of our demonstration!" Maïlidi exclaimed.

Silence fell over them, heavy with anguish, and then it was broken up by the announcement of "the resignation of the minister of Internal Affairs" that the demonstrators greeted with dismissive indifference.

When the cohort came to the front of the ministry, it saw and burst into laughter at the broken-down colossus with this crumbling conscience of he who had been the paragon of the repressive force, and who, now deposed, sought, frightened, the official air-conditioned car that he didn't have any right to use anymore.

CHAPTER 17

THE COUNTRY WAS OVERTAKEN BY THE NIGHT. THE COHORTS DISPERSED WITH the obstinate will to "resume the movement if this government did not provide valid concrete solutions"; the crowd marched faster as at times flashes in the distance streaked the sky, which was already darkened. Raindrops splattered on the ground; a smell of sprayed dust was exhaled, but the street lamps, lit as soon as the false rain alert was made, were turned off because it was not the official time.

At home, Dorcas put her research notes in order, but watched the news on the television. In capacity as "respectable international civil servant," Gaëtan had caused a humiliating scene by attacking Malifiki, and she had not been able to join the demonstration. His arms laden with ironed laundry, the butler went to the wardrobe as Mr. Keurléonan told him to drop the laundry on the table. Hands behind his back, he watched Gaëtan who took one piece after the other as if he was counting them. Surprised and amused, Dorcas watched him out of the corner of her eye.

"I am sorry, Malifiki, you have to remove your smock as well as the trousers," Keurléonan said with a sharp voice.

The butler jumped. An average-sized Fulani man with long muscles, oval face, frizzy hair on his oblong head, he retorted, "The smock belongs to you, I can give it back to you; I had already thought about it when you did not want me to march with the strikers. As for my trousers, never, one does not behave in this manner in our country, but I believe you are mistaken in who I am as well as our times."

"What is this insolence, Malifiki?"

"You are talking to a free man in a free country."

"Your country is not in question. I want you to take off your trousers!" he howled, crimson, face contorted, his blue eyes suddenly hardened like granite.

"I repeat, do not be mistaken about Africans, Mr. Keurléonan. Even in the colonial times, as Whites had all the rights over Blacks, some Africans rebelled against their masters. We are independent. I will not accept any humiliation from anyone, Black or White," he stated in a calm voice whose firmness stunned Keurléonan.

"What is happening? Why are you having this confrontation?" Dorcas said, stunned by the turn this incident had taken, which she did not expect when, putting the dirty laundry in the washing machine, she had seen that in a pair of Gaëtan's underwear, the reinforced pocket meant for the genitals was stippled with pubic hairs. She had even laughed before hiding it.

"I do not know, madam. Married, head of a family, I would not be a handyman in your home if in recent years the economic crisis and the unemployment that it caused hadn't made it impossible for us to cope with life. But I will never tolerate disregard for me from anyone, African or Western. Please bear this in mind: for us, unless he is an insane dictator, one does not ask a human being to go naked."

"Your reasoning is an insult and idiotic! You have stolen a pair of my underwear; I am sure you have it on now!" Gaëtan foamed, head and hairs swollen with a rush of blood.

Wide-eyed with amazement, a sardonic smile ran on Malifiki's lips as he unbuttoned the smock, and then the trousers.

"Do not do that, Malifiki! I beg of you!" Dorcas cried, moving away.

"I would not be indecent, madame. Master claims that I stole his underwear; I want him to see what I have on under my trousers. I do not know the kind of underwear that you misplaced I don't know where."

He took off his trousers. For underwear, one could see a pair of faded blue sports shorts.

"Is it me you are making these remarks to, Malifiki? Never do that again!"

"Really? Well, I, Malifiki, son of Karanikirikikikididiki and Lamniki, I forbid you to address me using the 'tu' form again. Tomorrow, you will no longer see me here. The African slave does not exist in Wanakawa. I repeat, sir: I do not know where you lost the underwear I am supposed to have stolen. You can go to my home and look through my belongings and those of my family. I do not wear the white man's underwear."

Red with shame, taut as a bow, he did not know what to say, or what to do as he saw the sadness and disgust on his wife's face.

"Malifiki, I agreed with my husband to hire you. I was pleased that you had your elementary diploma and are a man whom we did not have to explain things to at length. And besides, I like your way of working; I also appreciate your discretion," Dorcas calmly said.

She was silent, looked at Gaëtan as if to seek his consent first, and continued: "I do not accept that you leave us; we will not sack you. A misunderstanding has given way to a bit of nervousness. OK, Malifiki?"

"Madam, it is nevertheless regrettable that I was humiliated. It will take some time for me to feel at ease in your house the way I was until today."

"I understand you," Dorcas said, leaving the room.

CHAPTER 18

"There have been tensions and discords between us for some time now. I do not understand what is going on," he said.

She did not unclench her teeth, did not look at him, and continued to watch the succession of scenes of the demonstration that was aired for an hour on the television.

"Dor," he began again with a lot of softness in his voice, "we have spent nineteen years together without any rift, two children who are doing well in their studies. Africa, life in Africa augments our happiness. What is happening? Are we not going to be happy? What was there before my clumsiness regarding Malifiki? Is our household drifting apart?"

She turned toward him as Ségué n'Di's picture in the crowd made a rush toward her, as if it was in close-up. Her eyes opened wide, neck stretched; she felt herself thrust toward the screen but reined herself in. Bringing her reflexes under control, she sighed.

"There would be nothing else for you in Africa besides supplements to be added to what you call our happi—"

"Dor, I hold onto the essence of my question: are we drifting apart?"

"Should you not be asking yourself the same question, Yvan?"

"Perhaps, but I'm asking you anyway."

"The easy life, your grandparents' restored house at Quimperlé, a four-room apartment in the Marais, a farmhouse at Isle-sur-La-Sorgue. Is that happiness even in capital letters, when the household seemed to break up or showed signs of doing so?"

He stood up quickly but felt faint and sat down again and yelled: "Our marriage, a failure? Our household, a failure? How could you think like that, you, Dorcas?" he said hammering the words, jaws contorted, his teeth hardly unclenching.

"My darling, I am interested in social activities; everything in you converges in you alone. I think of life, living it with you, and we both sink into the stone core of the reality of this country, since we are here. Admit it, whatever efforts I make, I find in you an invincible negative spirit, even a denial that underestimates many African problems."

"The so-called problems would not be subject of what you have cruelly called failure! Do you realize this? Are you really aware of what you said?"

"I agree, the hazards—which for me are continuous—of life in Africa have nothing to do with our marriage. Do you have to deny them when you live here? They would be parameters of the presence of all Westerners in Wanakawa. The fact that you are here as an international aid worker doesn't change what I am saying: I make no fine distinction between the bilateral and the international because you are too much of an expatriate, cooperating only with yourself, to bother about the misery in Africa."

"This is an assassination! You've picked up and handled a weapon I would never have imagined of you, but it is too easy to use it the way you are doing."

"The work of international aid would certainly be more difficult if, without exception, you had not related everything you did to your own selves by perpetually aiming for the long term."

"Please, be specific!"

"Well, I have observed cases in an organization like UNESCO, at the time of a meeting on tectonics. What a mess! Pettiness, injustices, and arbitrariness from one division to another; all of these protected by a hierarchy incapable of passing judgment on a 'sometimes racist low-ranking boss.' To such an extent that an African had stated in a packed room, this—I noted it so as not to ever forget it—'UNESCO is one of those rare sociocultural organizations where clannish problems and tribal stratifications, worse than in Africa, will never be examined.'"

"It is iniquitous and cynical to see things only from this perspective. I admit that my presence in Wanakawa must not transform me into a Saint Bernard. The picture you have painted of an international civil servant is nevertheless unthinkable."

"You do not approve of my social activities. I have no particular merits in behaving in this manner. You had known me like that; life in Africa only digs the furrow deeper. I watch several hundred natives racking their brains to develop their talents with as much purity as liberty. One feels like taking their hand, the pleasure of wanting to see them succeed in their country, but also to take part in their struggles. My darling, I spent a part of the day watching you live and I am nauseated; there was your assault on Malifiki; you did not listen to the radio or watch this mass demonstration supported by Whites along with Blacks on television. That left you cold. It's not normal; it's beyond the inhuman. Does being an international civil servant entail undergoing an amputation that would prevent you from being sensitive to the suffering of others, to express your sympathy for some actions in the country where you are working? You are readily unjust, swift to humiliate by trampling on other people's feet."

"Then?" he asked, hard eyes in a cold face, in an equally heavy cold voice.

She stared at him, stood up, lowered her head, and started walking around talking as if to herself. "To think that I have come to play Good Samaritan would be a grave mistake. The desire to help set up people who can and wish for it, on a base that is essentially their own, but not to get involved in hypocrisy due to my activities—"

"My poor Dorcas, professionally very competent, even an ace, but naive! Naive enough to make you want to bawl!"

"This is new! You impose your wish by resorting to violence; you proved it again today. Tell me, Gaëtan Yvan Keurléonan, of what use is it to be in the country, in addition to earning much money, if it is to remain trapped within yourself, incapable of thinking of anyone but yourself? You speak of African problems as 'alarming facts'; as for taking action, never. Remain open-minded, be helpful, especially if you have the means, are you capable of doing that? You are afraid of depriving yourself of extras by helping those in need of help, even the minimum tenderness or affection that one sometimes needs."

Tears ran down her husband's face, but she continued, affirming that she deliberately went into the midst of the Wanakawanis to understand them better.

"Their social lives? You make fun of them: the sociopolitical problems whose solutions will help some of them to become more than unemployed people, do you ever think of it? You live far removed, caught up in plans for your own future; the International Cooperation Mission is your springboard. It reminds me of those I observed with as much sadness as disgust in their wheeling and dealing, goings-on, and arbitrary actions."

"Dorcas! Dorcas!" he yelled.

"I'm through. You subjected this very brave Malifiki to an unspeakable meeting; his response, his dignity, and his pride made me cry hurrah in the quiet of my heart. I would have cried it out loud if you were not my husband. You were despicable. I still wonder why those lost underpants were so important and special," she ended, bursting into laughter.

Gaëtan nearly flew off the handle, but a false smile hovered on his lips. The congeniality that he also tried to draw into his conciliatory behavior lacked sincerity. He looked Dorcas up and down and noticed that her large, wide-open eyes were fixed on him as if a violent death had carried her away immediately after the laughter that had hurt him deeply. He thought of their happiness augmented by a common accords, by dint of much sacrifice. He gave a nervous shudder; his face turned purple. A thought and its picture quickly crossed his spirit with the force, like the violence of a meteorite at its fall: he was afraid and went to shut himself up in their room.

Dorcas went and took an old edition of the *National Geographic* from the library, browsed through it, and stopped when she saw the photographs. Two double pages of rock fascinated her with their beauty, the dizzying brutality of perspectives, the infinite poetry emanating from nature captured by the photographer's eye attached to the lenses of his camera. She remembered her first year in Wanakawa, when she inquired about the region, with the curiosity of a tourist anxious to know where to go, what to visit without a plan marked out with references that needed to be looked at from time to time, but to drift away, to find things out without having been informed. Also she did not bother herself with specifications, but with vague, hazy guidelines she moved toward horizons unknown to her and things she would not have read or whose descriptions she would not find in any book. She thought of one outing that Gaëtan described as "boring." They went all over some of the steepest areas of the south region; the cliffs exposing their sheer slopes to the walker's view. The suicidal attraction is all the more fascinating since reaching them and seeing their profile, one finds out in a dizzy environment, the water whose movements the creek contains and that seems to be of an unheard-of transparency, when it licks at the rocky parts that it knocks against.

"Boring, there are better ones in France!" Gaëtan had grumbled.

A page of the magazine showed a rivulet slipping among bulrushes and water lilies. She looked at it for a long time, sighed, and said in a low voice: "I did not come back to Africa solely for the geography. I would so much have liked him to make me come alive, feel the way he can feel; alas, he's turning me into a fossil! God, I am choking at his side!"

CHAPTER 19

GAËTAN QUIETLY TOOK THE HANDSET AS SOON AS THE PHONE RANG. HIS FACE went from paper white to crimson.

"When will we see you again, Mr. Malifiki?" he asked, gruffly, and then he added on leaving the bed: "I will put you through to madam."

"Good morning, Malifiki, have you got some problems this morning?"

The butler told her about the escalation of the strike that all the public transport workers also took part in. The radio did not stop repeating it, so he would not come to work. "Yesterday, I travelled thirty kilometers to and fro only to be rewarded with humiliation. There will never again be so much enthusiasm and zeal as now. In short, madam, I am sorry, but I want to be frank with you: I don't want to withdraw my support from something as important as this national strike. I am taking the day off to demonstrate with my people."

"I approve your decision to demonstrate. If I understood you clearly, you are not leaving us, right? Good; you know, things can be resolved if the people accept to work together. Till tomorrow? Okay, see you soon, Malifiki; I'll also be there with the crowd from your country."

Gaëtan gave a sudden start as he snarled: "He is taking revenge, the bastard!"

"A dignified man, proud, with a nature far from that of a bastard; you deliberately humiliated him. He has his own will and could resign. When will you understand the revolt rising from someone, who can't and won't tolerate any more oppression?"

His face suddenly crumbled; defeated and sad, he said in a very calm voice: "I don't understand you anymore. You prefer a nigger to me! Africa has taken my wife."

"'You prefer a nigger to me, Africa has taken my wife.' My poor Yvan, always about you and your refusal to admit the reality of a situation, your worries only center on yourself, and yourself alone. My dear, come with your wife to demonstrate with 'the niggers.' I'm sure the crowd will be more than what I saw on the television yesterday; no one will notice the presence of the secretary general of the International Cooperation Mission. There were Westerners, there will be some today again; only a liar could pretend to know who's who . . ."

"I do not see myself being like those Whites, or in the mood of a striker."

"What a pity! There is food in the refrigerator, but also rice, canned red and green beans, and soybean in the cupboard . . ."

"You will be sorry for leaving me to take part in this demonstration."

"Threats? You do not know what you are talking about: my freedom depends on no one," she retorted, stared at him with pity, and shrugged.

"I beg your pardon?"

"You don't know the bounds you went beyond speaking to me that way," she said, with a sarcastic smile on her lips.

■ ■ ■

Wearing faded blue jeans, a matching shirt with the sleeves folded up below the elbow and whose tails gently blurred her body graciously, a wide-rimmed unbleached raffia hat, blue tennis shoes, and sunglasses, she left with her Samsonite carryall.

At 8:00 a.m., groups of strikers from the provinces in private cars or buses as well as trains poured in, bringing Tigony to a standstill; groups of people rushed out of the houses, also near the mountain, and made the crowd compact. The Maryanika's stream, a populous area, flowed into the Hamkani Boulevard toward the bridge on the Kiniéroko as Dorcas joined it. An African on the same row recognized her, threaded through the cohorts, and came to greet her.

"Thank you, madam, for your understanding."

"It's the right thing to do; anyway, I do what my heart tells me to do."

"It's rare in this former colony; we can't end our dependence and become truly independent. Old mentalities persist and become resistant."

"You have to fight without giving up, so that things will get back to normal."

"I want to tell you something serious, madam."

"I'm listening, Malifiki."

"You're not meant to live in this country with most of the others. I repeat, the old reflexes of domination still continue with them. This is the reason why there are confrontations when an African shows his character."

"I'm only too well aware of it . . ."

"I thank you once more. Excuse me, my wife and our kids must be in front or behind, with our old parents. I have to find them."

"It is great to be with the family! Till tomorrow, Malifiki?"

"Certainly, madam, because of you."

To everyone's surprise, the loudspeakers broadcast some strange remarks: "You too are wrong! You will pay dearly for it!"

"I only carried out your orders, Mr. President."

"You badly understood what was meant to be done or have misinterpreted my orders! You are an idiot!"

"Certainly not, Your Excellency . . ."

"I say you are an idiot! Born idiot! Tell me that you are an idiot!"

"You will never get such a statement from me, Mr. President."

"What? Proud! You will be relieved from your duties! I am the one who made you!"

"No, Your Excellency, you inverted the facts: I brought you votes and the support of a sociocultural group that you would never have taken. I am sorry to stress it although you are aware of it: your party could not have had the majority in the parliament without my 22 percent."

"Well! Well! The minister of Information Accounts and Calculations?"

"Since you underestimate or misunderstand the contributions of some of your partners, would it not be right that each one recalls what he is owed?"

"That's the limit! You lack political direction. No matter that you have read, studied Machiavelli, de Gaulle, and François Mitterrand, your lack of flair and political tact is tragic. Thus, take what belongs to you and this as well in your poor brain: I AM THE PRESIDENT OF THE REPUBLIC OF WANAKAWA and you, Mr. Kirinikoïyé are no longer the minister of anything at all."

"Mr. Haïnakogninifu, I am far from being poor and will never allow anyone to treat me this way. Secondly, you cannot insult me by discharging me in the cynical way you have just shown—"

"Mr. Hamlikilini Kirinikoïyé, you are not above others. But yes, come to think a bit about it: you are proud and envious; you are organizing a coup d'état. My intelligence agency had already informed me about it and put you under surveillance; your office, your house, those of your two mistresses are being tapped. I could get you arrested, put in jail, and have you shot. I dismiss you and you do not show your gratitude? Idiot! Idiot! Born an idiot!"

The heavy silence that weighed on the crowd suddenly broke, and the cohorts burst into deep laughter. The "summit dialogue" gave way to the announcement of a "message from the president of the republic."

"Citizens, citizens, dear compatriots!

"Three ministers were forced to resign from their duties yesterday. The justifiable pressures of the people brought about by their sufferings that were also caused by the socioeconomic problems with which this country is confronted have led to these decisions taken a long time ago being carried out.

"Thus, I have just relieved another minister from his post and personally inform you that Mr. Dibiliki Hamlikilini Kirinikoïyé is no longer a minister."

Like the waves of the sea in its hurried course toward the coast, a flood of laughter spread through the crowds.

"I understand this approval of our people as a proof that my action does not change the decision—"

The laughter grew louder, degenerating into mocking cries.

"Silence! His Excellency the President of the Republic continues his address!" the protocol officer's voice intervened.

"Citizens, dear compatriots, I understood you, I approve of your demands; they will be quickly acted upon. Are we independent? I assert it. Are we not? I, too, say yes because for many problems as in a certain number of areas, we are still under constraints and have to depend on what's coming from overseas.

"As for what is happening with our country, I solemnly declare that I shall put a break on it that nothing will be able to undo. It's a question of, as you all know, an inert amalgamation, a number of unspeakable things that are happening, with many secret plots, teeming together, personal ambitions, small-minded worms called advisers, consultants, experts, representatives; all came from elsewhere, controlled from afar, and do not help us! They are the ones who are managing our affairs because our children have trusted those who do not speak any of our languages.

"You would retort with logic, and justifiably, that the responsibility falls on the president. I would admit this specious inference if the duties had not been delegated to the partners, ministers of whom some, crassly incompetent, have surrounded themselves with this clan of foreigners, and have all been bribed. I promise you, all these brotherhoods will be removed, sanitarily if necessary; we are going to find their diseases. They are sick, contagious for the nation. Citizens, dear Compatriots, I have finished. Your demands will be met. You can count on my word of honor. Long Live the Republic!"

The crowd that continued to march during this speech now passed in front of the Kinikifunkuyingy Palace protected by more than three hundred policemen and officers keeping their eyes open, armed with machine guns. There was a balanced mixture of Africans and Western aid-workers; others were notorious mercenaries marked out in the presidential guard. Instinctively hands clasped one another and the immeasurable unity chain of the previous day re-formed.

The sun had passed its zenith in the blinding azure sky, but through the layer of dust that the marching had kicked up from the laterite ground, its rays fell on the human flood with the same intensity as before the beginning of its sunset.

CHAPTER 20

Ségué N'Di threaded through the crowd for hours. He hastened to slip between her and her neighbor as soon as he saw her, but excused himself as if all he was doing was to elbow his way through the crowd.

"Are you going to demonstrate at this speed, sir? Stay here," Dorcas said, taking his hand.

He thanked her with a brief smile, and then looked in front of him as if he was looking for someone. Maïlidi's voice rose. A sigh of relief wafted from the crowd.

"The strike will get harder, but the demonstration must take its course! Some of the organizers of this movement were invited yesterday to a meeting to discuss the 'modalities.' It is yet another game to deceive us. Who would deny that the synthesis of our demands, drafted for the first time six years ago and reiterated many times, is at the core of the specifications given to the government? Let them be fulfilled and the strike will end; otherwise, it will last the time that it takes this government that counts on the dismissals to resolve a social and wage problem!

People passed comments, some on the slanging match between the president and his minister of Information and Communication, oddly spread through the country; some on the presidential speech booed because of the misunderstandings caused by the dispute with Kirinikoïyé and the message to the people."

"The one who was just laid off for refusing to accept being treated like a fool," said a European.

"He is right for being uncompromising," Dorcas intervened.

"I agree, madam; but he is the one who doled out the threats discovered this morning in the Westerners' mailboxes."

"The ultimatum was also sent to our offices. The minister wanted to make sure that the message came across," another white man added.

"To invite all foreigners, White or Black, to respect the secretive clause while staying away from these strikers' "completely unfounded demonstration,' what jargon!"

"And discriminatory at that!"

"He is wrong to reveal his vocabulary in a sentence with that tone . . ."

"I can't stand the summaries. Yesterday, I watched the strike on television; I was moved, even overwhelmed, as much by the enormous crowd as by the demonstrators' dignity. The abjection of this minister angered me, and I decided to join the crowd."

"It is the same reaction that drove me here," added a Somali who started speaking Italian with the person in front of him.

"Are you Italian?" a Frenchman inquired.

"Native of a former Italian colony, you can't hide your origins."

"I know that . . ."

"It is surprising that Westerners always liked to have colonies; doesn't that add to their domestic problems? I mean internal ones in their countries?"

Laughter could be heard all around.

"But I am very serious!"

"Who would doubt it? In my opinion, the drive to conquer and interfere in countries situated millions of kilometers from the European continent, is a disease. Did you read about the lecture given by an African in Stuttgart? The newspapers put it to good use this morning," Dorcas said.

"There are some truths we must hit hard with. After having opposed independence in the colonies, they are often riddled with incompetent advisers. The president just admitted it," a Senegalese said.

"In order not to speak of my country alone, it seems as if this disease is atavistic: the number of French people who criticize Africa but live there while behaving like their ancestors is growing. In my opinion, what shocks is less our presence than our behaviors," Dorcas exclaimed.

"Well, it is extraordinary! Bravo, madam!" Ségué n'Di jubilantly said.

"Really, bravo! It is a pleasure to hear something like this come from a European," the Senegalese added.

"There have been lots of claims, stormy debate subjects among us instead," a white man with a Belgian accent said.

"What I would very much like to know is, why live in a foreign country and impose decisions foreign to the interests of their country," Ségué n'Di intervened again.

"You touched the heart of the real problem. Your neighbor used the word atavistic. It is tough. She is French, but since the word is right . . ."

"What would you say if Africans in Europe behaved the way some of our colleagues in Wanakawa do? It is a question I have asked myself for years. I come back to this article signed by . . ."

"Héblé Atchi Kuynumoï," Ségué n'Di said.

"Exactly, I brought *L'Afrique actuelle* because it is bilingual, but also because of another article that I am anxious to read," Dorcas said, taking the newspaper out of her bag.

"What would be welcomed is for Africans to be able to leave their countries and return to work in the areas with the skills they acquired in Europe, the United States. It is naive, utopian; would it be forbidden to dream?"

"Madam, could you lend me your newspaper; I would like to read it," the Senegalese said.

"I did not finish reading it before I left," a European said.

"Here is the most important part; it is about the immigration, etc., in Europe. The lecturer was invited to Stuttgart, the city of the great philosopher, Hegel. He took it out on him, admitting bluntly that he had judged Blacks without ever having seen them. Here is a major part of it":

> From being haphazard after the Second World War, when it consisted of the desire to transfer African labor at a low cost, into Western countries in precarious situations, African immigration accelerated little by little, the numbers driven by those in economic difficulties or forced out of their homes for political reasons incompatible with the autocrats in power. If this has led to structures that are . . . unsettling? Subjects of sociopolitical debates, including areas where the immigrants, without creating unemployment, instead put efforts into becoming owners of their own homes; it is less because of European difficulties

> of integrating these people who do not want to lose their roots, or their cultures, than that Europe, strongly saturated, is afraid of having a lack of superfluous workers.

"That is difficult to swallow," reacted a Westerner.

"There are some truths that one must have the courage to face. You live here, do you know what is going on in France—I suppose you are French—where the repression against immigrants even strikes at Africans whose papers are in order?" the Senegalese asked.

"What do you have to say, sir, about these White people one sees begging on our underdeveloped streets? Are their documents in order? And what about the amateur cultural tourism man with an organized gang?" Ségué n'Di said with irony.

"Can I continue?" Dorcas said, smiling. "Thus, Héblé Atchi Kuynumoï declares again":

> You will tell me that such a reflex is just a syndrome of the consequences of Hitler's War, during which Europe lacked vital necessities. I agree, but our countries contributed to that War which levied troops from them although it was no concern of theirs. They really supported the Motherland, as they said when I was young. The War ended half a century ago. The number of those who dread the African, North African, or Turkish immigrants and want to bar immigrants who are not yet born or are still in short pants or skirts. The sociologist . . ."

"Ah, he is a sociologist! These are wicked people, despite sometimes getting it right! Sorry for interrupting you, madam!"

> The sociologist, used to studying human beings and facts objectively, has put his knowledge and intelligence into cross-referencing them, for the facts to come out could affirm without fear of shocking: integration is nothing but a synonym of assimilation, with the same connotations as those of the colonial era. Also, the difficulties that the integrationist policy meeting in France comes up against, mainly, is the fact that it forgets that it is dealing with human beings, whom, perhaps unconsciously, it asks to do away with their basic personality, to live and act like the natural citizens of the countries where they sought and found asylum.

> Fifteen years of research in six European countries, of which three had had colonies in Africa, proved that 53 percent of Europeans think or believe that nothing tangible can be achieved with immigrants, all origins mixed together, "as long as they are not integrated and will not live like them"; that they are not—far from it—more intelligent, more educated, or more cultivated than those they expect to be integrated.
>
> To try to undermine the immigrant's culture in the name of integration that would uproot him from his native land, to be a mere number on local taxes and revenue is an aberrant, unacceptable idea.

"It is disturbing to hear! But there is indeed evidence in this article! It must be read when you can reflect on it," a Westerner said.

"This article is rather kind. When I was young, I bragged about the fact that Senegal was the most French territory among the French territories; better still, a real French 'département' in sub-Saharan Africa. But after ten years of living in France . . ."

"Kind, these crushing blows by a sociologist?"

"Listen, he has handled Europe gently here and there: the reality in many of these cases is as wicked as nasty."

"I read this article completely. It exposed me to some of the problems of Africans in Europe. He evoked the possibility of Africans living in the West for a short while, etc. It is a beautiful dream that some of us would like to fulfill. I have no means to go elsewhere, not because I am unemployed or that the desire to escape does not appeal to me at one time or the other, but to leave my country, live far away from here, it is impossible," Ségué n'Di exclaimed.

"Why?" Dorcas inquired, holding his hand tightly.

"It is quite simple, madam: before reading Héblé Atchi Kuynumoï's article, I did not have a clue of what one would call the expatriation instinct; on the other hand, the newspapers do not hide much of the situation of Africans and Arabs in Europe, whereas here, the governments turn a blind eye on white men in worse shape than ours in your country. What would I go to look for in a place where even those who have lived there for years, acquired your culture, your way of life, experience a repressive policy, even rejection? In Wanakawa, flowers, plants, streams, springs, rocks, mountains, and fauna provide me with some foundation; my useless character feeds on them and recharges itself."

"You are a poet, sir," someone behind him said.

"It is also what is killing us in this country; I would not dare talk about the whole of Africa that I do not know."

"Our friend is right; he is pessimistic, but one would be wrong to leave one's home only to return to it. Someone had this idea that I feel isn't a bad one."

"There are, powerfully put in my neighbor's proposition, substantive points that should shape your conscience if you decide to take charge of what you have and what you are being denied," Dorcas said.

A demonstrator in front of her turned his head to look at her. A cheerful expression played in his bright brown eyes. It was a priest dressed like a clergyman wearing a small wrought-iron cross on the lapel of his jacket.

"Madam, it is a great pleasure to meet and listen to someone, I mean a Westerner, reason like you."

"I deserve no merit for it, Mr. Abbot, I was born this way."

"May God bless your dear parents: what you said is exactly what the Independent African Church does not stop repeating, but one accuses of being leftists those among us who support objectives like this, thought to be ideological."

"What brings the death of the church in Africa is conservatism. It supported colonialism, and its representatives wage an underground war against progress and the advent of democracy," another ecclesiastic said.

"The conservatives are more and more numerous today, playing an ambiguous double game, even obscure. At Tigony, we are about ten priests, in short thirty in Wanakawa, taking part in this demonstration right from the beginning. Of course, we have been given credit for Marxism and all the names of birds of prey."

CHAPTER 21

The death knell started to chime in Tigony. Priests jumped and looked inquiringly at each other; an anguished mask covered their faces. All the bells in Wanakawa were awake and ringing. The crowd held its breath.

"Oh Lord! What is that for?" a nurse in plain clothes said in a low voice, making the sign of the cross on herself.

"What is happening?" one wondered, asking oneself or a neighbor.

"Something is rotten in our country, never mind, nothing will reduce our self-control. A rumor is spreading: the ex-minister Dibiliki Kirinikoïyé may have committed suicide; he was discovered on his knees, head in the toilet bowl filled with water!" Maïlidi asserted.

Unrest that was difficult to bring under control made it seem as if the country stumbled. In Séikaniko, the stronghold of "suicide," a revolt sidetracked many of the demonstrators toward the county clerk's office that was immediately sacked, watered, and burned down with the gasoline containers taken from gas stations. In Mariénaoïje, the president's hometown, Molotov cocktails continuously landed on a wing of his family home that was under special surveillance. The flames took the palace by storm as the security officers shot, without warning, four people suspected of having "raised their arms."

In Katakaranigny, his mother's region of origin where, except for some hardliner opposition, a sort of referendum had made him a congressman for twenty-five years before his election as the president, a huge swarm of hairy caterpillars attacked the sorghum, millet, manioc leaves, and spinach for a week, leaving behind a disastrous desert landscape. In their moaning, the dismayed peasants attributed the incident to the "the president's lack of comprehension and his deafness to their complaints."

Taken by surprise in their siesta by the detonations, his parents saved themselves by fleeing nude; the old woman fell and her husband picked her up, and they ran panting with fear.

"They are not going to kill us! They will not finish off two old people!" she wailed.

"Shut up, Ichininguy! We are the forebears of a man who rules without sharing in this country that has gone mad! They will kill us without showing mercy."

They saw the door of a house ajar and quickly ran toward it; the inhabitants ran to shut it behind them. In Mariénaoïje, no one forced open a closed door. While crossing the courtyard, Ichininguy suddenly realized that she was nude, put her hands to cover her private parts, lowered her head, and tears fell from her closed eyes. They brought them a wrapper, an old shirt that they accepted while thanking their hosts.

Kaïninkinui, the president's eldest brother, ran in the bush like a deer, topless, wearing a pair of khaki shorts. The insurgents pursued him, yelling.

"It is his doomed soul."

"Don't lose him."

"Get him!"

"He enriched himself a lot!"

"He also siphoned money abroad!"

Three peasants coming out of the bush caught him. The pursuers came to their aid, took him by the hands and feet, pulled him toward a marshland not far from there, threw him in the water and crocodiles attacked him. As he shrieked. "A few runaways heard his cries and calls of a hoodlum in distress," a provincial tabloid, *Hodi Leo*, would write.

Heavyhearted, the voice of the president of the republic rose in the country: "Citizens, very dear Sisters, Brothers, and Friends from around the world present in Wanakawa, I promised it and I will keep my promise: the just demands that are the raisons d'être of this strike, unique in our history, will all be met. I made an announcement yesterday, but no one answered my invitation, which would perhaps have avoided the tragedy that we have just heard of. I reiterate my call by asking the representatives of the demonstrations, of traditional religions, those of monotheists officially practiced here in our midst, to come this evening to the reception room of the president of the republic. I also invite the group of heads of international diplomatic missions and three or four of their partners to join us.

"There was a suicide. A zealous death? I do not know, never having, I say never authorizing such a thing. Firm, intransigent when it is a state matter, I am not a criminal. Believe me; I deplore from the bottom of my heart the death of a man whom I regarded with esteem. The divergences of the last hour that occurred among us are the lot of any political life; they would not justify such a tragic end. I do not believe that my friend Dibiliki Hamlikilini Kirinikoïyé committed suicide. The assassins, whoever they are, will be found and castigated. My family home was prey to flames; my parents' lives were saved as they escaped nude. Nude! My brother was fed to the alligators; others were beaten without notice. Deeply affected by these facts, I sincerely deplore them. I would have liked the strike to end in an atmosphere of calm dispute, humor, friendship in which it started. It has gotten out of hand. We cannot help but become part of it; but I promise and I say: from now on 'You will draw water with joy from safe sources.' Long live the Republic! Long live the emergence of democracy!"

A man in the crowd with an anchorite head, Rasta locks, long sticky beard, and a fakir's loincloth, flabbergasted to have heard the president evoke "the emergence of democracy," pointed his finger toward the sky and said: "Yes, you are whining Haïnakogninifu, but Eliphaz de Témân said:

> "Can a man be profitable unto God, as he that is wise may be profitable unto himself?
>
> Is it any pleasure to the Almighty, that thou art righteous?
>
> Or is it gain to him, that thou makest thy ways perfect?
>
> Will he reprove thee for fear of thee? Will he enter with thee into judgement?
>
> Is not thy wickedness great? And thine iniquities infinite?
>
> For thou hast taken a pledge from thy brother for naught, and stripped the naked of their clothing.
>
> Thou hast not given water to the weary to drink, and thou hast withholden bread from the hungry.

But as for the mighty man, he had the earth; and the honorable man dwelt in it.

Thou hast sent widows away empty, and the arms of the fatherless have been broken.

Therefore snares are round about thee, and sudden fear troubleth thee;

Or darkness, that thou canst not see; and abundance of waters cover thee."

The crowd around him, not understanding his inspired speech, looked at him, wondered where he came from; some laughed, others cheered him. As the night fell over the country and the heaven gently opened its floodgates, the demonstrators scattered like a class on break.

▪ ▪ ▪

They ran toward the replanted forest groves dispersing their myrtle scent, and penetrated it, following a path that took them to the side of the mountain they preferred, where the native residents built their homes. Extraordinary snakelike dances of fire animated the area. The mountain transmitted its vibrations, prelude of a demonstration, as a violent detonation preceded by heavy thunder burst, and the lightning, like a fire axe, spewed somewhere not too far away. Dorcas pressed against him.

"We will not climb up more, one must be very prudent at times like this," he said, taking her hand.

They went down to the forest. There was a hut where he and his grandfather often rested; he had played hide and seek with his brother, Agniku, his sister, Foniasi, and their parents, who sometimes took part in their play, when he was between seven and nine years old. They had left; his married brother and sister had left the country. He went into the hut without letting go off Dorcas's hand. A tree trunk on three pieces of rock had been in the same spot since his childhood days. They stayed there as he used to do in the past, and they relived the day's events.

"It is pleasant, I feel as if I have taken part in our village palaver, as in the evening in the courtyard my grandfather evoked past events."

She put her raffia hat on the floor and pressed against him. He caressed her; shivers from her body filtered into his. She heaved a long sigh, curled herself up in a ball, her head on the young man's thighs. Ségué n'Di's fingers gently slid through her hair, imparting the feelings of relaxation and tenderness. She lifted her arm in a slow movement, her hand touched Ségué n'Di's face, and his hand exploring her body under the shirt touched the heart of her desire. She trembled, sat up, laced her arms around his neck, and felt lost, infinitely happy, safe in accepting her pleasure and her anticipation of enjoyment.

"I truly feel like dying like this," she murmured, panting while hugging him. Spasms exploded deep inside her. "What would I do, what would become of me if we can no longer see each other?"

"Ah?" he said in a low voice.

"Don't you wish it? Don't you want it?"

"The idea has never crossed my mind."

"I am much older than you, you . . ."

"Really?"

"You are kind."

His surprised question was seductive, and she laughed gently in the obscurity of the hut.

"This is not kindness; I love you without worrying about genealogy or age difference."

She overcame a burst of frank laughter, said that it was wonderful hearing him talk like that. "I will never forget the lesson."

The passing of light breeze across the forest made the branches shake; drops of water fell as if it was still raining. He made love to her again; her breathing was extensive, and she felt the fulfillment of a woman who basked in pleasure's rays, to her own surprise.

"I am alive, that's what matters from now on," she said in a low voice, then added: "I do not know if you understand me; what is going on inside me is like a mineralogical phenomenon."

"You pass it on to me, my lot is a happy one."

"Is this true?"

"Why should I lie to you?"

"I know that you do not . . ."

He held her by the waist; she kissed him on the lips. Tears ran down her face at the call of her desire, so that he also felt the assault of the pleasure that made her so happy after a union that shattered the straitjacket of marital dependence, so that the freed sensuality finally blossomed.

"I would so much like to spend the night with you, even here, but I have to go home. Why must I do so?"

She did not speak to him, and he did not answer. When they arrived at the outskirts of the woods, she looked left and then right and started down the road where he watched her moving away. The heavy pigtail of her hair oscillated under the raffia hat; she carried her shoulder bag. Snapping her fingers while listening to the Walkman, she moved discreetly; she inwardly danced to the rhythm of Wally Badarou's music on a cassette that her daughter had sent to for her thirty-eighth birthday: "Great, Mum, lovely and sexy. Continue to listen to Africa; he is Beninois and you will like him!"

CHAPTER 22

Sidewalk Lotharios slowed the progress of their convertible, hugging the side of the road to avoid the men who called out to her. Realizing that she wasn't "one of them" and was ignoring them, they went their way. Two short hoots made her stop on the pedestrian crossing when she reached the bridge on the Kiniéroko.

"I went to look for you as it started raining . . ."

In a relaxed manner, she took off the Walkman and said, smiling, that everyone had taken refuge wherever they could before going home.

"What a crazy idea to stay so late in this demonstration with all these cock-and-bull stories about niggers sleeping on their feet!"

"The strikers and those who supported them were not there for nothing," she pointed out, getting into the car, a metallic blue Honda convertible.

"Such drama would perhaps not have taken place without their recidivism."

"You're priceless. These people demanded their incontrovertible rights that the government refused to give them; constrained and forced, the government was brought back to its senses. Would they have been happy about their frustrated situation?" she retorted, shaking her head but smiling.

"There is a strange odor," he suddenly said, sniffing here and there. She looked at the soles of her shoes.

"What sort of odor?"

He sniffed around them, then outside, once more in the car, and said directly: "You smell of a man!"

She burst out laughing, and then responded. "I was among and with millions of men other than you."

"Dorcas, you know exactly what I mean."

"No kidding? What man, White or Black? Stop the car."

"No!"

"You will commit the irremediable if you move a meter further. I smell of a man! I will show you how to be one."

"Beg your pardon?"

"You heard me; if you do not stop," she said, opening the door.

He obeyed, and she walked back. The car sped off, and he parked it on the other side of the bridge and ran to rejoin her. Repulsed, leaning on the parapet, she stared at him contemptuously; he stretched out his hand to touch her, regretting his remark.

"I warned you, Gaëtan," she said calmly and turned, facing the river.

Death brushed by Gaëtan who panicked, suddenly deathly pale; head lowered, he returned to his car, incredibly sad. Dorcas left the bridge, walked quickly, crossed La Marina Boulevard, went into the forest, and without taking note of the dangers of walking alone at such an hour, she ran as if she was making an escape and that her husband pursued her. She took a path, climbed at a fast pace and came, breathless, to the foot of the village, turned, went toward two windows of a room that was still lighted with a hurricane lamp, gently tapped on the window, and whispered, "It's me."

"I am coming."

He came out, crossed the courtyard sleepily, and saw her, tired but serene.

"What happened?" he asked in a low voice, pressing her to him.

She did not reply; he did not insist and took her into the hut.

"I am and want to be a woman who elucidates her problems as a woman." This rebellious sentence came back to him like a warning, or even a threat as much for her husband as for himself, but he preferred to think that on the way, on impulse, she had decided to carry out her wish to spend the night with him.

He had had his meal and left the rest in the pantry, a latticed box where food remained sheltered from flies and ants; he brought out two heads of corn cooked in water, a slice of grouper roasted on ember, a quarter of papaya, and sorghum beer. He then brought water in a basin with a piece of soap and gave them to her.

"You must be hungry . . ."

His thoughtfulness was so natural, really gentle, and the tenderness in his voice moved her to tears. He understood then that there was something else other than her desire that made her sad. The city hall clock rang 10:00 p.m., and the sound could be heard on Mount Kiniyinka. After having washed her hands and eaten her food without cutlery, she told him what had happened and stated that she had nearly confessed.

"If he had been direct in attacking me point-blank, 'You betrayed me, even today, you did not deny yourself,' I would not have hesitated for a minute not to hide anything from him; but sniffing around me, then on me like a hunting dog, to throw this at my face, in a brutally calm but murderous voice, that 'you smell of a man' made me feel undressed on the road! Yes, I would have confessed without revealing who had come into my life and taken the place he did not know how to protect; I owe no one any explanations. Denying would have been an act of cowardice, a betrayal, the rejection of the young man that you are; that, never. Did I leave you this evening with the sensation of the birth of something I had been waiting for in me? I don't know anymore. It would have been rejuvenation, I would say: 'This is nothing but a passing affair.' Do you understand me? This is not easy: I am a woman who is certain of never having lived as fully, as sensually as since we met; I lived by proxy when, as luck would have it, I chose to really start living by crossing the Rubicon. That exists in love as well and my defenses were down when I met you, me who had never been with another man other than my husband. I confess, out of an anxious curiosity also arose, that evening, the irresistible desire for the unknown; should I blame our pleasure? I do not have any remorse . . ."

Her tears flowed. Ségué n'Di listened to her attentively, as in his childhood when his grandfather's voice permeated him with tales. She stopped talking, dreamily. He came to sit beside her, on the bulrush mattress covered with two fine-bulrush mats and enfolded her into his arms. His body oscillated to the rhythm of a mother's tenderness consoling her child eaten with sorrow. She caressed his face and then undressed, stretched herself, raising up her hands, and he discovered in motion the statue of flesh and bone that she was. One of the paintings within the framework of eucalyptus branches suspended on the wall caught her attention. He took them down, offered his night wrapper to her for her to cover herself with, but she preferred to remain naked and he gave her the paintings: "It is . . ."

"Your grandfather. Did you paint it?"

"I try to entertain myself."

"It is really beautiful. As for work, you are talented."

"That is my father and this lady, my Antinilie, that means mother," he said, with emotion making his voice tremble.

Taken aback by the paintings whose models seemed familiar to her, Dorcas patted him on the cheek.

"Did the models pose for you?"

"I work from memory. The paintings of my parents, I drew two years after their death; my old n'Ata changed positions when I wanted him to pose for me, laughed, or was stiff, if he was not being funny by doing grimaces. So, I used my discretion."

"It is incredible! Where did you learn to draw?"

"Nowhere. Only just like that! At first with coal."

A nude person lying, seen from behind with an opulent matted ponytail made her jump.

"But it is me! It is my body!"

"There was the same lighting when you were here. I tried to restore the basics, a week later."

Stupefied, she looked away from the drawing to Ségué n'Di who showed her another one of a nude sleeping on her back: the head held in a hand whose fingers touched the matted hair arranged in a half-hitched knot below the neck; lips gently parted as if the person, eyes half-closed, murmured; finely curvaceous body, well-proportioned, relaxed, whose belly movement seemed like the rhythm of the breathing of slack water; a leg shyly reclining, the other in an obtuse angle; at the hip-bone, a thick pubic hairiness filled the delta; the fullness and tone of her breast exuded a discrete sensuality, and its intensity made you want to stroke the drawing.

She recognized her face, features, mouth, her small golden earrings, and her body, which she sometimes saw through the mirror in the bathroom while asking herself questions about her body, trying to figure out the reason why Gaëtan was unable to give her what she expected from him for many years. She moved her head gently; that someone she did not know was an artist who had produced these charcoal paintings that so much looked like her gave her goose bumps; her nakedness on the cheap drawing paper made her blush vehemently. She heaved a long sigh, put her arms around Ségué n'Di, and scrutinizing his face that a nice smile brightened, she changed the position of their bodies without loosening her pressure.

An offering; harmonized rhythms as she kept her eyes closed; her eyes opened slowly, then suddenly opened wide; a cry of despair made her open her mouth, but nothing came out; breathless, she sank her nails into Ségué n'Di's back; spasms and reciprocal effusion; she clung to him to scream; there was only a long exhalation and he heard "My God! My love . . ." Everything in her slowly relaxed. She caressed his face; he saw that she was surprised and happy at the time. They lay on their sides, in each other's arms.

"What will become of me later? I know you do not like this question," she murmured.

He did not answer; a mischievous smile danced in his eyes.

"I think that I would have the courage to commit suicide," she added.

"I don't like analyzing what I receive but I know that you are aware of what you give, with your rich natural authenticity; your offerings are full of generosity, tenderness, but tell me: why do you sometimes have these negative ideas?"

"I don't know; without doubt because I love you and I am afraid."

"What of and why, ti n'Fiéna Dorcas?"

"How do I explain it without shocking you? The sexual desire in me is a force that I do not know how to control. I do not know why it is like this, or why my husband cannot satisfy me; it is a situation that killed me, but I remained faithful to him. Two pregnancies and a miscarriage without any other satisfaction or joy other than that of being a mother. You have to be a woman to understand the nature of such a frustration. With you, thank God, I have the certainty of being a desirable woman, capable of also wanting to be made love to by a man whom she loves and feels also loves her. Let me confess something else to you: for a woman, the worst frustration that can even make her revolt is to live with a man who is unable to anticipate her sexual needs; it starts with the drying up of all sensation, then the sclerosis of pleasure in the sexual act; death is knocking at the door. There is the need to react; I have chosen to take action."

He listened to her, translating the sentences into his mother tongue so that they became fixed in his brain. When she stopped, he waited briefly and said in a voice so quiet that that she shuddered and snuggled against him, her head on his chest, "I repeat, you have an authentic nature that I like. You will leave me whenever you want to do so; I will not stop loving you. I would have preferred not to tell you, but I am and I would like to be loyal to you the way I am to myself."

"Leave you? Come what may!"

"If you love me too, please stop thinking of our separation, or death. Promise?"

She replied, nodding her head the way she did as a child when her parents comforted her by asking her if she knew that they loved her.

Astonished to be in love and, for the first time in his life, to be in a situation whose precariousness he measured by making a resolution not to do anything to spoil it, he regarded her, calmly.

"It is really me and it is really nice to be here with you like this."

"It is a situation that I love; its reality and beauty are admirable."

"All the better. I also love this reality. I see myself in it; I feel myself in it with all my heart."

She looked at the paintings again before returning them to their respective places where she had seen him take them down. The harmony, equilibrium, and movements of her body captivated him. He came behind her as she was hanging the last drawing, enfolded her in his arms. No sooner had she turned toward him than she felt a slow collapse within her and wept with pleasure.

"Are you feeling hot? Would you not like to take a shower? What you might have wanted isn't here, only a jar full of water in the bathroom. Should I take you there?"

"No, I want to smell of a man, sleep filled with your odor like a sponge."

He laughed gently, gave her his hand, and she felt as if they were taking a walk, naked in the dead of the night. They came back to the bed and covered themselves with the wrapper.

▪ ▪ ▪

Waking up at 5:00 a.m., he took a bath before waking her up. She did the same, got dressed, and took a half-formatted beige envelope, sealed and glued, out of her bag.

"Please keep it for me. You will give it to me when I ask you to do so."

"Okay, madam," he said, and put it in the metal box he used as a wardrobe.

CHAPTER 23

He usually picked up his sales bundle from the newspaper depot early in the morning. They left the still sleeping village.

"Better on the rack," he objected when she wanted to sit on the crossbar of the bicycle. "We might come across him looking for his wife. No scandal."

"At the stage we are in, I do not give a damn about what anyone will say and about the scandal."

"Nevertheless, be prudent. One has to be on this slope that we'll be rushing down."

"I was clear enough. Make no secret of it if the question is asked with careful speech. You know, if you have been given freedom, all eyes are on you. It means something else if it is the result of a conquest."

"Before independence, many of us were of this opinion."

"My father said: 'One should never lose one's freedom, whatever way it has been acquired.'"

"I agree with him."

"There is an infinite pleasure in living in freedom," she said, sitting on the crossbar.

The northern mountainside was less rugged than the others, but he pedaled with a methodological prudence, sometimes looking right in front of him, sometimes at the woman with the raffia hat whose personality intrigued him a little; he also thought of how much was extraordinary in her independence that her husband would hardly like.

"You are not talking, yet I hear your heart . . ."

"And what is this small machine whispering?"

"Damn woman! What did I come in quest of—a good old French verb—with her life and her problems?"

"Not really, but instead: 'Hell of a chick!'"

Dorcas burst out laughing.

"Watch out, you are making the bike move too fast!"

"So what?"

"Hell of a bird! She is earning a lot in her forte, but could drop the consortium for another one; freedom without bounds! That will kill a Negro, even a high-level civil servant!"

"Good analysis, except I never make such reckoning. Certainly, I like the independence that my profession and my remuneration and my premiums give me."

"That puts you at ease, as much with life as in your skin. If our relationship becomes known to your husband and the scandal gets worse . . ."

"The worst for me, my love, would be when you would no longer love me; as for the scandal, hold it! I am getting down here."

"I was going to suggest it to you."

They parted ways in the goings and comings of the lighted boulevard still hectic with all sorts of cars. She went into a bar, ordered a cup of coffee and a croissant, took them, and went out to sit on a bank of rock, along the pavement of the timber forest. The coffee in one hand and the croissant in the other, her body gently shook to the rhythm of Wally Badarou's music playing on her Walkman. A flashback to the times of her studies in Rennes crossed her mind; it was at a time that she and her fiancé planned to meet in Thabor or at the Catho. She dreamily smiled, as Gaëtan caught sight of her on the opposite side of the road. The Honda went round the roundabout, overtook several cars, and braked in front of her. She did not react. Without saying a word, he took the cup from her hand and finished the coffee; she gave him the rest of the croissant, which he took. Despondent, grave face, like a mask hastily etched, he seemed to have aged overnight. He took her hand and she stood up. He threw the cup in the dustbin, opened the door of the car, and closed it as soon as she had settled in; she moved her shoulders, the rotations of her spinal cord stretching that made her bones crack in her back.

"I looked for you everywhere—"

"Even on the sidewalks."

"No, certainly not."

"You found me there."

"It is sad, deeply lamentable; I am sorry, Dor."

"What do I smell of this early morning?"

"Euh, eucalyptus."

"Your sense of smell is refined; I like the fact that they spray the night with their essence."

"I am sincerely sorry. I do not understand that you take everything more and more tragically."

"I certainly need a holiday and a shrink."

"I have never had such a thought, but I made the mistake of a jealous husband," he said, hardly controlling the trembling in his voice.

"Jealous of whom?" She inquired in a quiet voice, but her eyes fixed on him, then she turned her eyes on the road that was becoming more and more alive.

"I searched. I do not know what came over me; I rummaged through your things."

"The Quest of the Holy Grail? 'The birds go in quest of grain.' Did you find some indices of the man whose odor I was carrying?"

"You are cruel; I am truly sorry."

"My poor dear, you spend your time being sorry. Would there be a day, an action, even what is called sin, that you would not regret having committed?"

He wept with jerky sniffles. Surprised, struck with pity, she slipped her arm around his thickening waist and put her head on his shoulder.

▪ ▪ ▪

He had spent hours going through not only her clothes as well as her toiletries in the wardrobe, but also the drawers where she filed her working papers, letters from Dorothy, Charles-Yvan, and her parents. His mania for arranging or his pedagogical psychology prevented him from having respect for his wife's "mess," which he took forever and a day to put in "some order," stopping her from finding what she knew was in a precise place. There was not the least sign of anger despite "the intolerable, abject intrusion" in her privacy. The incident of the missing underpants came back to her; the idea that the loss of such a piece of laundry had justified an anger followed by horrid scenes in the house of an international civil servant, who lost sleep over it, cast her husband's personality in a different light.

"Have you already had breakfast?"

The quiet, as well as the mild tone made him feel as if a dagger had been quietly stabbed into his back. He shuddered before saying no, shaking his head several times.

"Would you like oatmeal, with coffee or tea?"

"With coffee, please."

"Me too, and two fried eggs."

"I would like that, too."

She changed her clothes, slipped into a dressing gown, set the table, and they had breakfast, watching the television from time to time; the demonstration continued to be the highlight. Gaëtan changed the channel to news from France and the West in general. After breakfast, Dorcas listened to Africa n°1; humor, laughter, lively expressions, intelligence, and allusions to friendly countries were on. "And where are the friends elsewhere in Africa, who could have perpetrated all that without blowing up with hemoglobin, pillaging huts, stealing here and there from their brothers? Big news!"

A news flash on the radio broadcast announced "the temporary suspension of the strike, accepted by the organizers."

Dorcas jumped to tune in the national channel: ". . . the leaders summoned by His Excellency the President of the Republic all went to the Kinikifunkuyingy Palace at 7:00 a.m.; the president of Wanakawanijé has bemoaned the fact that none of his guests accepted the friendly breakfast offered to them. Nevertheless, the negotiations took place with equanimity, the will to reach reasonable solutions, pragmatic, and susceptible to be accepted by all. President Halilinikili Haïnakogninifu stressed that the demonstrators could continue their pacific demonstrations, if any useful solution did not result from it before 3:00 p.m. or later."

As usual, Malifiki brought the mail thrown into the mailbox. The *Daily Encounter*, borrowing its front page from Elias Canetti, ran as a headline in crushing print MASSES AND POWER, and J. G. F. Greenough wrote with extreme joy: "The pressure made by the masses in the country, studded—something unheard of—with courageous Westerners, who, surely, all being democrats, had understood the workers' demands, has got the better of the injustice of an autocrat and repressive government. Suicide or assassination, it doesn't matter which! Let us show sympathy for the parents of the deceased; the world, alas! Has seen and will see others."

For their part, *L'Afrique actuelle*, *La Nation aujourd'hui*, *Karuiroyoko*, *Kirainiwaifumi*, *Hoka m'Bihaya*, whether in national or Western languages, recounted the events without nuances, with precise details, which proved that the country stumbled, that signs heralding democracy were outlined, and the press did not want to remain on the edge.

The telephone rang; Gaëtan hastened to answer. Dorcas continued to flip through the newspapers, a dull grin at the corner of her lips.

"Let me pass you on to her; don't mention it, sir."

"At 10:00 a.m.? I will be on time, sir; see you soon."

She ran a bubble bath, opened the chest of drawers, saw that the drawers had been rummaged through, and drew an irritated breath as she took a bottle of eucalyptus bath gel; drops came out and the smell filled the whole room. She undressed, looked at herself from head to toe in the mirror, stretched, and got into the bath with the feeling that she was drowning. The idea and image of suicide surged through her mind and she murmured, "He would not understand; would he agree to understand? A coward's treason? I would have done it if I did not love him, but I want to live for you and my children."

Motionless as if weightless, she remained like that for a quarter of an hour before washing. She dressed in a pure silk dress, buttoned to the top of her breasts, whose pattern had pleased her as much as it had intimidated her; a belt matching the dress emphasized her waistline without being too tight; discrete makeup, a Spartan local production. She kissed her husband. The metallic blue Rover left for the Center for the Examination Commission for the Recruitment Competition.

Toward midday, a short news release sent to the newspapers, the national radio station, and the television announced: "Mr. Ségué n'Di Niriokiriko Aplika had won the competition with 18.75/20; his challenger, Mr. Jamhalika Nikiriyo Faa got 13/20." It was made clear that the latter would not be forgotten, if the Applied Geographic and Geology Studies office looked for another assistant.

The radio stressed that the award winner was unknown to the program. Another journalist insinuated: “Is this Niriokiriko Aplika not from the same tribe as those of the granite soil, and other constructible lots to be abandoned? Aha! These small landowners are poor although they have everything to be proud of in a country where there is a crackdown on unemployment!”

CHAPTER 24

Usually brightened by background music, chattering, or cursory comments about articles in the regional and international newspapers, dinner was gloomy; conversation was nonexistent or monosyllabic. Even when he quickly took a sting out of a judgment passed, Gaëtan resorted to an understatement; thus, that evening, he said in a voice that seemed to be nothing other than a supposition, "The association of workers would be targeted in *One*, like at Plato's."

"Not bad! Not bad at all."

"Am I mistaken, Dor?"

"I read a confidential report on the state-owned companies, private foreign firms, and aid-worker volunteers . . ."

"You did not tell me about it; are you becoming secretive?"

"Should the secretary general of the International Cooperation Mission not have been aware of such reports? As for being secretive, you know that it is not in my nature—"

"So?"

"The report stresses the observations that don't contradict mine, when it says that a number of the aid workers go abroad, notably Africa, 'covered with theories'; this is normal, even necessary. How many among these technicians and technocrats, once on the field, think of adapting preconceived theories and grids? Do they worry about verifying them, to detect at what extent specific and local realities, imposing their law, require the modifications of the theories and models? Make use of wrong tools when one has a mission to succeed, to help the people to overcome some of their difficulties, it's a crime," she added.

"Are you sure that you are not generalizing too much?"

"Also the Enquiry Committee? I am unaware of its project, but the facts, I had also seen them and kept them in my 'mess.' Discreetly, I had mentioned it more than once in your presence. We could have talked about it in private, so what? The aid workers' group, sure of itself, strong in its 'reputable experts,' is imbued with such reliable theories that it forgets about their objective and political applications. Are errors committed in that way? Committed on purpose, the faults of stubbornness are prejudicial to the country where one 'aids'; it doesn't matter, one is no less highly remunerated."

"What aggression! What hatred, still so controlled, despite the tone!"

"My dear, rather sadness than hatred."

"And someone has to pay for it."

"Can we deny having a part linked with the group?"

"What would we do, what would our children think and say, if misunderstandings, a failure took over our whole lives as a couple?"

"Here you are! You bring that up again."

"You think it is abnormal?"

"You are still your same old self."

"That is to say?"

"There are fibers or genes in me that are against everything antisocial; on the other hand, in terms of being a social player always on the ground, my observations add to my conviction of having obligations to the people of the country where I earn my living to a large extent," she said.

As he did not respond, she got up and left for the regional office.

▪ ▪ ▪

The ambience surrounding the demonstrators continued on the roads. The scattered groups talked about the events, the future "if the government got itself entangled in not honoring its obligations."

"The Westerners hurried to fill up their cars' petrol tanks."

"By all the gods, they have all the means!"

"The well-heeled and other wealthy ones from here fall in behind them."

"The white men had emptied the supermarkets; there was nothing left in the local corner stores: rice, milk, sugar, sardines in oil, household products, all snapped up!"

"It is because they have the means. Even our divinities are perhaps on their side."

"Yeah, and then, what is a Black going to look for in those shops? Me, I like our local goods better."

"Okay, one must not refuse everything coming from the outside. I work as a servant at Wlafshaft's house and it's so much better. On the eve of the strike, he and his missus yelled: 'Moïginguiii, we are going shopping!' We left in their big Volvo. Jesus Christ! There, a White crowd with their wives and households, as well as wives and the ministers' help; official cars and panel vans. What is happening to them? What is going on in their heads? Are we going to have a revolution? I put the problem to myself."

"Damn, those people who have too much dough."

"Me, I was happy like a god in the Kounioko main market: my old lady, you know she sells everything. So, in the morning she had said, 'they will inclease de plices of all de goods.'"

"Aha, our traders! Mine also categorically hurled that: the toubab, women, and ministers' harlots and oth'r crooks, they are sold things thlee, four times more explensive than normal: the crooks in the government cabinet steal the people's moni; de people, we are the ones. No mercy! Let 'em dlie of hunger if they can't pey!"

"My old lady also said the same of the fishes, big shrimps, and crabs: if these crooks feel that they are too expensive, well, they are smoked and sold later. This morning, she poured libations for the divinities. The strike supposedly made her rich for a month; she cannot slow down, even sleep for a week. Aha, our old women!"

There was a sort of price inflation. Customers who normally bought without paying much attention to price felt that the prices of foodstuffs were too high, whereas the drudges, day laborers, shopworkers, and slouches spent less on the same products. The guys gathered in small groups for black market, going off in search of anything they could turn up, shuttling between the immense Kounioko and the pavilions used by the administration's upper echelons. "Vigilance against the black market," the antenna of the trade union for food and commodities, trapped the members of the "catfish clubs," apprehended them, seized the provisions that they carried in their jute, raffia, or rush bags, scolded them or beat them severely, and they even sometimes exchanged blows.

Witnessing one "of the new errand-boys born of the strike," Greenough described in his report a fistfight that was a sensation. He was all over the place: telephoned London, Dublin, Paris, Nairobi, Harare, and Dakar; the telegrams in which he did not openly blame any European country. His allusions and references to the history, like his ironies, did not pull the wool over anybody's eyes. In his shorts, seated before his electric IBM machine that, despite his colleagues' gibes, he preferred to "those restive PCs that throw you off gear, and make you unable to flirt with even the sexiest woman in this country," his ten fingers ran on the keyboard like those of a genius secretary.

Efficiently organized, the strike sparked off by the unions, workers' groups, high-school and university students' groups currently on break will last a long time if the government uses its dilatory tactics. Although they are part of it, contrary to their custom, the high schoolers and university students did not take part in the sit-in, or the anarchist demonstrations full of noises and furor; one is also taking part in an event that will make history.

The dismissal of ministers—three in a day and a suicide, it was a lot—did not seem likely to change the determination of the corporations of strikers to profit from it. What is it about? As a matter of fact, the country is 'independent,' like almost the whole of Africa still interspersed with people, marked by devices that helped weave its history and modern psychology, detrimental to its development.

The consequence? An almost systematic sabotage operation that does not facilitate the economic and social takeoff of a former colony with considerable potential, but whose future seems to be blocked; the youth have no bearings, gradually affected by unemployment and drifting, reduced to begging, sponging off their parents who 'will have succeeded,' if they do not succumb to alcoholism. Delinquency opens its arms to embrace young people.

Like elsewhere on the continent, the high levels of administrative hierarchy, even political, are transformed into panoramic viewpoints, where their occupants look indifferently into the heart of the social, economic, and cultural life of the people of whom they do not worry about, or hardly, of improving the lot: these men—and women as well, who, like Tom Thumb's pebbles, sowed the seeds of the arcane mysteries of the administration and African politics—first and foremost, worked for themselves, only themselves. They don't care what happens after they are gone.

Thus, with rare exceptions—because those well-off defend and protect the interests that are not for their countries, but belong to the forces that keep them in power without building defenses against the people if they rebelled—the top brass of the administration is nothing but an fault of nature; the State, a gigantic fiction, the government, a delusion; both unpopular and despised.

A number of actors of the first decade or two of independence have disappeared from the political scene. Have the interests that motivated their actions essentially faded? The reproduction by fission works; so, Africa on its knees, made impossible to develop, is contented with quick jaunts.

The foreigners, all Europeans, have natives in their employment in a country where they do not speak or understand any of the five languages; I write languages, not national dialects. Although they have the same diplomas, the same competences, received the same education as their African counterparts, the experts, advisers, consultants, and all those Europeans, undoubtedly remunerated by their countries, still occupy the positions where the Africans would have done the work equally well, if not even better than them, and this with less expense. The idea may be stupid, but it is because this country would never have the means of paying its children educated in Europe, in the United States, and in the USSR their full worth.

Fewer among them are those who augment the unemployment ranks. Present during all the sit-ins, they took part in the demonstrations. The government that despises them, but pretends to be looking for solutions to their problems, would have publicly expressed its gratitude to them: in order to avoid any loss of control that could lead to bloodshed, these misfits amused and channeled the infuriated strikers, ready to turn their anger and debase it into violent explosions.

No erudite theory is necessary to filter the structures that divide the country: two years of investigations into this and that among about two hundred experts, consultants, all excellent Westerners, as they are called here, exposed the strategy belts of transmission between the latter and the holding trusts protected by the government, and the foreign consortiums supported by the African governments infiltrated by Western lobbyists as well as advisers or official representatives. The circle is locked. Africa is knocked flat on its back, or tied up in bundles, wriggled, eyes turned to an insolently empty luminous sky where no sign of hope seems to be outlined.

CHAPTER 25

Relaxation movements freed his neck and he cracked his knuckles by twisting his interlocked fingers together. The radio broadcast whirred that the public transportations did not yet know if the demonstration truce was for tomorrow or later; the country seemed paralyzed. Accompanying her husband yesterday afternoon to support the strikers, Séliki had felt that "this thing would not turn out badly"; she did not go to her place of work the next day. Driving in his car, Greenough made a detour to the Kamsin quarters to tell her that he did not disapprove of her absence.

"The situation could deteriorate; the negotiations should have ended by 3:00 p.m. It is 5:00 p.m. Stay at home tomorrow without worrying yourself sick, if there is no agreement between now and 8:00 p.m."

She thanked him. Her husband told her to "bring a glass of sorghum beer." Evoking some of the outstanding points of the day before, he watched, through the gap in his long lashes behind his horn-rimmed spectacles, one whom he resembled so closely that one might have suspected him of having assumed the paternity of one of his children. He did not find him too ugly not to be cuckolded, but for the first time he was surprised that this woman who loved this distinguished man with his ostrich-egg head could not deprive herself of debauchery with a watermelon-headed journalist, with a scholiast monk face, hairy legs, and badly tanned skin. Point-blank, he inquired if Mr. Abdou was Ethiopian.

"No, why?"

"Nothing urgent, it is Arthur, my brother, who wants me to pass on some information to him."

"I have acquaintances who are Ethiopians, perhaps . . ."

In order not to burst out laughing, Greenough pinched himself on the nose as he sneezed.

"We will talk about it if he asks his question again; it is perhaps to urge me to travel to Ethiopia."

Mr. Abdou bowed slightly to shake his hand when he took his leave. Eyes lowered, arms across her chest, Séliki also did the same, but her look crossed Greenough's and immediately provoked a rush of desire for her in him.

"I am really sorry, sir, but if a bus happens to pass by, I will take it so that you do not have to take care of yourself alone."

"There won't be any if the situation turns bad. I told you already, do not worry yourself sick. Oh, Mr. Abdou, what do you think of that lot? I would like to know your point of view, as well as that of your wife."

"I approve of the strike a thousand percent and support it."

"The proof is that we were there," Séliki added.

"I am talking about the politicians, those in their entourage who behave badly."

"The politicians, one needs to give them a lobotomy and then bury them alive!"

"Good heavens!" Greenough yelled as shivers ran up and down his spine.

"The Whites who swarm around in their digs and do too much evil should be sent back to where they came from. If they are treated the same way as the politicians, perhaps their countries will go to war against each other, and we do not have the means to make that happen. As for the African accomplices, they should be shot dead."

"I did not think you could be so violent," he reacted, his thumbs in his waistband, hands flat on the fly.

One eye half closed, the other lash raised like that of a hunter observing prey, Mr. Abraham Abdou moderated. "Perhaps it would be more humane to castrate them." Greenough gave a jump.

"My husband is not a drop wicked. He talks like that when he doesn't feel up to par, when something puts up his blood. His violence is always verbal," Séliki said, preferring that the politicians and their close associates, Whites or Blacks, were imprisoned or sent to the penal colony near Mount Nariékiyingy, for twenty years.

Greenough eyed her through his lashes drawn together. The beauty of this face, this body he had caressed many times; the freshness and pleasure in the rejuvenation, in the sharing.

He left them. The couple standing at the threshold of their house raised their hands to say goodbye. The car took off and Greenough soliloquized: "He made me afraid with his cynicism of a castrator! There were accidents, even a son? I ask the question again: what is the problem since no one is complaining?"

He burst out laughing, put on the car radio, and started singing a popular song from his childhood softly: "Ay! Ay! Ay! Tralalalala!"

He was interrupted by the classical music program on the BBC channel, bringing a different tune; the rhythm touched him, brought him as if toward an offertory as it ran up and down him, and he adjusted his movements to his driving. He thought of his father whose beautiful tenor voice moved him when he modulated "A te, fra tanti affanni"; tears of remembrance ran down his face fixed on the road, when, in a fraction of a second, he saw what looked like a phantom of his father's image on the windscreen as soon as it rose, superb, "Se vuoi puniscimi, ma pria." "Oh, no! Why *Davidde penitente* now that I left them? Mr. Abdou has nothing of the wretched Uriah about him; could one help but not love the Hittite's wife? Beautiful Fulani with seduction and charm, Séliki has nothing in common with Bathsheba; agreed, should one have done without her? And who am I, a mere hack beside the King David who was more womanizing than any other human being?" He drove at a tempo to the Mozart tune while keeping an eye on the comings and goings on the sidewalks where European prostitutes who had passed their youth but spent a lot of money on face and neck lifting strolled by, their female Black colleagues with reptilian eyes, dressed in African attire or slinky dresses that barely covered the parts they offered; all drew attention with the swell of their butts. Beggars, layabouts, pickpockets, the physically or mentally handicapped, and the categories of lumpenproletariat, who were integrated in the flow of the flood of strikers, had found their usual territory.

CHAPTER 26

SHE WAS UNABLE TO SLEEP A WINK; NEITHER COULD GAËTAN. THERE WAS no more sexual intercourse between them. Irreparably allergic to his presence beside her, she thought of making a bed in another room. That night, she stood up naked, threw her old gold-colored dressing gown over her shoulders, without tying it round her, went through the living room, put on the lights, and glanced round at the geometric layout of the static figures that her husband liked and imposed with quiet authority. As she watched them, she saw the indications of his introversion, and his uptightness, characteristic of pettiness and stinginess. Stiff natured, anxious, withdrawn into himself, and unable to take the plunge spontaneously, which she had known already at the time of their courtship and engagement, returned like an image on a screen in a movie theater. She felt like changing the places of the furniture, knick-knacks, some mirrors, thus creating a disorder that would cause him to lose his bearings and start screaming with rage.

"It is sui generis like his smell; nothing like such an upheaval will change him," she murmured, leaving the room. Tapering fuzzy flakes drifted slowly to the stars scattered in the sky where, round, beautiful, the moon rose with crushing serenity. The sea air coming from the southeast momentarily caressed Dorcas's face and naked feet in the whitish light of the remote daybreak, as she slowly paced up and down the driveway of the grass court. The cockcrow staved off by the splendor of the sky came to her from beyond Mount Kiniyinka like a call, and she shivered, confused. A steady light, like a trail of a comet at the end of its path, put dents in the horizon, accentuated by the nocturnal summit of the tall trees at the foot of the mountain.

Daydreaming, Dorcas walked fast, quickened her pace, almost ran as soon as she came to the three-hundred-meter steel and concrete bridge spanning the Kiniéroko now like a gloomy oily glum; the river winked at the twinkling stars. She crossed the road, entered the forest exhaling myrtle where the light of the evening star obliquely penetrated the glade. Out of breath, but plagued by the desire that yoked her, Mrs. Keurléonan-Moricet did not stop; she climbed, leaped, clung to a side of the mountain overhanging the timber forest, carried by the force born of her desire to be up there, in the pure air of this altitudinal space where desire and pleasure without hindrance would have every right.

Suddenly, a burst of pleasure whose force shook her gushed through her; it was as if Ségué n'Di was in her residence and she had given herself to him without being afraid of the scandal of such a liaison. She staggered, felt insane, and saw a giant white rabbit cross the lawn. Instead of moving faster in its warren because of a strange presence, the small beast landed on its hind legs before fleeing; curving its spine that was bent and distended in an amazingly efficient run, it also seemed to attack the mountain, guiding Dorcas in the lukewarm air and chiaroscuro sequined fireflies aiming their beautiful pale blue lights at the sides of Kiniyinka.

Gaëtan's silhouette appeared on the front steps. He moved forward on the lawn that another rabbit crossed. Terrified, he jumped, returned to his tracks, and then moved once more toward his wife.

"What are you doing here at this time of the day?"

"Breathing the early morning air."

He looked at her from head to toe, hardly containing his surprise and disgust.

"And naked! Really! What exhibitionism! It is unimaginable!"

"Exhibitionism in front of whom? Unimaginable for whom? For the first time since I've known you, you make me feel as if I had been born with clothes on."

"Please! We had a small spat; rather a misunderstanding that is not rare in all families worthy of this name and you, Dorcas, you are exhibiting yourself in the early morning air, as you say! Thank God it is not yet broad daylight."

"I am inoculated; let it pass. There is not one disagreement but many disagreements between you and yourself . . ."

"Certainly not; I like myself as I am."

"—between you and yourself, between me and myself; in short, between the two of us. I want the part of the lion. There is also a disagreement between your brotherhood of aid workers and myself. Brotherhood is global; you are free to break away."

"What a speech! The quarrel between you and me exists mainly in your imagination."

"Really?"

"Absolutely."

"Will I scandalize you by only taking care of the imaginary conflict between us, of which a large part is my fault? Not exactly; between the imaginary and the reality, yes. I know it and you are going to cite theories. Can one understand that sexual pleasure cannot be analyzed when everything is based on theories? You could not understand and you will never understand what it means to give pleasure to a loved one, to a woman.

"It is horrible, deeply humiliating, and vulgar!" he yelled, red-faced.

"For whom then?"

"For the man who has been your husband for nineteen years that you are talking to in this way? Damn! Am I your husband, yes or no?"

She shrugged and smiled, but he asked the question in a way that angered her.

"Tell me, my dear, is there someone else in your life?"

"Other than whom?" she quietly asked.

He was suddenly fuzzy-eyed, a feverish shiver seized him, and he felt as if he had been stabbed in the back. A brisk movement like whiplash made him lower his head, but he took her hand and they went into the villa, as if they were coming from a walk.

CHAPTER 27

NIRIOKIRI APLIKA SÉGUÉ N'DI WORKED ALONE IN A TWELVE SQUARE METER office; geographic, geological, and geophysics maps and the relief depicting Wakanawa to the letter and the entire African continent were fixed to the rough-cast walls painted white; industrial draftsman's instruments, block-notes, and letterhead paper from the consortium's regional office were arranged on the mahogany table. Posters, technical maps squeezed between the geographic ones, revealed the rocks that caught his attention, aroused his curiosity, and he spent a lot of time admiring as well as studying them. Neither the photocopies that Dorcas had given to him nor the illustrations and sketches the International Cooperation Mission library had offered him had as many realistic perspectives as what he now had within arm's reach.

His contract stated that he was, among others, "responsible for the rough sketches and designs completed on the quarry sites, to work and/or to explore; if necessary, he will take on the role of supervisor or the technical construction site head." The explicit notes, without the inevitable set language or the obscure jargon of international or administrative files, which entrap the officials, specified the related details of each paragraph of the contract. When they were together in private, Dorcas told him about others, which put him at ease. In that state of mind, he started thinking of his future as well as the granite terrain, a subject about which a journalist had made fun of his family.

▪ ▪ ▪

Although it was late in the night, the strike stopped on the day of the negotiations in the Kinikifunkuyingy Palace; 55 percent instead of 65 percent of the demands were met, provided that the situation would improve before the beginning of next year, so the demands no longer presented worrying problems. Everyone was aware that for many, unemployment was not close to diminishing. The social climate in the country was back to normal; Tigony had recovered its relaxed, almost carefree air. Those whom the strike had convinced that Wanakawa would continue to be ruled with authority by a dictator and his inner circle managed by the foreign experts and advisers, did not give up their "plan to breathe other air elsewhere, even in Africa." Within the framework of the consortium, Madjita's "resignation," shown in the form of a "leave without pay," made Ségué n'Di the "technical site foreman;" he would have liked it that this nice fellow citizen, with his open yet irritable character, would become his colleague, but the positive response to his application for a job in Zimbabwe had made Madjita Minoucodjoyingy's decision to go into permanent exile irrevocable.

The clearing of the mine had created temporary jobs for another group of day laborers. Armed with baskets, the unemployed workers who were hired went down the underground tunnels, a kind of underground prison at more than two hundred meters where the light of the acetylene lamps made the miners look as though they were wearing lugubrious masks. The humidity was 90 percent, but one breathed siliceous dust with this auriferous quartz. The use of wooden pillars to prop up the walls and the vaults made it look like some ghost ship's corridors, with the keel in the air.

Happy with this job, even though it was not forever, the recruits went into the mine and came back up with baskets that some diggers filled with stones, which they spread here and there; siliceous ground monticules were lined up on the ground. Ségué n'Di supervised the work, rapidly outlined mounds on a Canson drawing paper, and indicated with a Kinokoroni word those places where he knew large quartz pieces were hidden; he sketched the surrounding landscape with the entrance of the mine, accumulated rubble, and silhouettes of people moving. Dorcas was in the middle of around ten of them, going down into the mine tunnels, preceded by the head of the building site.

At the end of the day, when the laborers left, he went down to check the progress of the work. The air was bearable there thanks to a ventilation system. Mrs. Keurléonan-Moricet had had it installed at the end of heated negotiations for which, when confronted by the consortium, she had been able to win on her side the authorities of occupational medicine who supported her "more scientific and hygienic," and not merely humanitarian, ideas. Thus, the atmosphere saturated with humidity was humanely bearable; in the underground, Ségué n'Di walked around, looked approvingly, even with admiration on the walls and the vault, gradually moved the light of the acetylene lamp that he held by the handle. The wood reinforcements sometimes made him feel as if he was being sequestered in a complex machine from which he could not escape, but he moved on without fear and without knowing where he was going.

▪ ▪ ▪

"My hearty congratulations, with warm support of the consortium," signed Jean-Noël Janheinz, chairman of the board of directors. He kept the fax made up of one line sent from Geneva, as if it had been the diploma of the Commander of the National Order of Wanakawa. After Dorcas, his revered n'Ata, and the members of his village, Greenough was the first person to congratulate him. His warm, overwhelming spontaneous letter had given him such a pleasure that for his first ever use of a telephone, he phoned his dear and good Daddy Greenough. The old journalist was moved, but his humor and quick-wittedness of snapping at the opportunity prevailed and he said: "Well, Daddy would very much like to devote an interview to the success of the kid that he had not been able to father on the top of the Kiniyinka because there was a better and more handsome man than himself. But in short, since the offspring he loves a lot has achieved the success that all Wanakawa knows, an interview or an illustrated report carries weight doesn't it?"

Ségué n'Di, kindly declining the invitation, suggested that the *Daily Encounter* propose his job as a newspaper vendor to Jamhalika Nikiriko, if the latter was unemployed, if such a job, that he had never regretted having, would please his unhappy rival. A short article in the English-language daily that highlighted Ségué n'Di's modesty, and his sense of solidarity, at the same time launched a discrete call to M. Jamhalika Nikiriko: "The *Daily Encounter* would like to meet him."

Coming back to the matter, Greenough changed objective, wished to obtain "specific technical, economical, and political information as much as possible" on the consortium and the progress of work in the mine.

He did not hide having caught wind of a state project contract that the government may have sent to the consortium. Ségué n'Di promised to acquire more knowledge of it from authorized sources. Could he prepare the ground for a report on Mrs. Keurléonan-Moricet? Greenough asked. The kid, Ségué n'Di answered that he did not know his hierarchical superior enough to undertake such a move. "Hey! Why could Daddy, great reporter, permanent correspondent for the *Daily Encounter*, but also a known personality, not telephone the regional representative? The kid would intervene, very favorably, if one were to talk to him about it."

As a preamble, the daily rapidly wrote a broadly illustrated report on the Mount Franakiniriyo mines, but without a photograph of Mrs. Keurléonan-Moricet or Mr. Ségué n'Di Niriokiriko Aplika. The illustrations showed the site, laborers who went underground or came out, and baskets of excavated rock on their heads, which they emptied on the dunes; describing the fine scales of gold in these dunes, he raised without detour a fundamental problem:

"Where would the excavated rubble of siliceous quartz piled up on the foot of Mount Franakiniriyo be crushed? In the West where would the bulk of it go missing? Italy does not produce petrol, but the National Hydrocarbons Authority refines thousands of tons, which made Mattei, a very intelligent man of whom I had even published a long premonitory interview here, disappear in a plane that exploded during the flight. The petrol of a small country, such as the former Dahomey, today the Republic of Benin, is processed in Norway, although in Togo, a country one can no longer call a neighbor, there is a refinery destined to rust forever. Where will Wanakawa's tons of auriferous quartz go?"

A number of the other newspapers followed the *Daily Encounter*'s suit, as, first of all, its permanent correspondent had gotten an interview from Mrs. Keurléonan-Moricet "which only had to do with problems of a technical order." Carefully, she would nonetheless evoke the economic perspectives of the mine and its national contributions. To a question on Mr. Niriokiriko Aplika's work, she responded that "after a rather difficult examination, alas, the admission of one applicant out of seventy-seven, who has become one of my associates, had been very well received and recruited. In the current phase of his employment, the consortium is testing his practical competences and he is succeeding properly.

In addition, I say that such a position can only be occupied by an African; in a country bogged down by unemployment, the creation of jobs, even precarious ones, would not be a favor."

The journalist was enthused by such a conclusion; the photographer dazzled Dorcas with rays of light. For personal motives, but also to take account of a clause in the consortium, she wanted that not more than two photographs of her should be featured in the report; they would "even make her happy if they could be left out." The Polaroid enabled him to produce about ten pictures; she chose one bright one: her forearm straight on the desk, the Mont Blanc pen between her fingers, her left elbow on the desk, and her forearm upright. The movements of her fingers showed that she gave instructions to her listener.

The vivacity of her points was obvious in her look and on her face; she would prefer this photograph above others where her beauty and charm could not escape her readers' attention. Greenough stated that she was seducing; to have that in addition to political direction added to the admiration that he felt for her. The first words of his compliments made her tighten all her reflexes and she did not blush; the journalist nailed her:

"This intelligent lady, competent, and beautiful to the tips of her manicured nails, seemed like a garden spider to me; on the other hand, she is capable of not allowing anything to touch her sensitiveness before the most seductive praises. Having discovered a gold mine or spent hours near Franakiniriyo, surrounded by big auriferous stones, seemed to harden her character and cure her of any itches!"

"Well done," Ségué n'Di said in a low voice, his finger on the last lines of the interview, when he came to put a file on the representative's desk.

"It was necessary; he is a great journalist. I often asked myself how to act if he came to interview me."

"I have known him for a long time."

"I suspected it. After several retakes, he skillfully slipped traps into his questions, which is not abnormal, but I succeeded in avoiding discussing you."

"I was personally opposed to it. Your ideas regarding the future of the 'mines,' as one begins to say, and their impact on the country's economic development already provokes discrete comments, but which hardly conceal some people's annoyance."

"I was not unaware of where I was putting my foot; I had anticipated Mr. Greenough's question and had thought a lot about what I was going to say."

Ségué gave a thumbs-up sign and left.

▪ ▪ ▪

The activities progressed at an intensive rhythm; the reports piled up on Dorcas's huge desk made of mahogany, covered with a veneer of glass. Two Europeans, a technician and an administrator, transferred to Tigony, studied the notes, the rough sketches, the drawings, the photos, and the stages of the job. Their predecessors, who were also Westerners, weren't up to coping with the growth of the tasks, although two new typists, to whom Mrs. Keurléonan-Moricet assigned the functions of secretaries, had been hired to assist the original two, often running all over the place. The new recruits benefited from the "time credit training" administrative clause, which allowed them to attend the introductory courses on the computer, as well as to acquire a "good knowledge of English and French" at the IBM Technical Office. Ségué n'Di applied for courses enabling him to learn the secrets of a computer as well as to improve his English, along with his knowledge of French and Spanish acquired thanks to the courses broadcast on the radio.

CHAPTER 28

Both in the office and on the site, nothing hinted at any specific attachment between them. A report on technical activities brought thirty international key figures to Tigony; the presence of two South African representatives drew protests from the representative of the consortium, who threatened to resign. She was called from Geneva, Paris, Bonn, London, and Tokyo. She was unaware of the fact that Pretoria was part of the nongovernmental international venture, in which she invested her intelligence and energy, and that racism had taken root there; they assured her that the analysis of Nelson Mandela's character and his unambiguous standpoint, increasing the international pressure, accelerated the process of the end of apartheid in South Africa.

This jargon put her in a murderous mood: "The idiots do not shrink from any deal; all they know is money, even tainted with human blood," she said, without raising her voice. Her associates looked at each other. Summoned to a "staff meeting," Ségué n'Di could hardly recognize her and looked at her quizzically. Inviting them to sit down, she made a brief distressed pout; no one else apart from him understood the meaning. From the onset, she informed them of the presence in Tigony of an "international delegation including representatives of racism in South Africa; these key figures are not in Wanakawa for the problems of its population, or for cultural tourism, even less to look into the aftereffects of the strike. What are they interested in? Mount Franakiniriyo's auriferous quartz mines. I am talking of these people in this manner so that there will be no secrecy regarding my disapproval, but also so that you know that—everyone has his convictions and his political opinion—that by working in Wanakawa, we are supporting racism."

Struck, deeply sad, the Africans frowned; the technicians and administrators remained immovable except for Dugratin, a lively redhead: "I am a socialist, catholic born Freemason and am ready to go back to France. I would earn less money there than in Africa, but I would not have made it unethically. To fight for human rights by accommodating racism, in South Africa and elsewhere, no!"

Dorcas made her own position officially known to the consortium hierarchy, as well as the assuaging explanations given to her, and added: "The country will suffer if we abandon our jobs; I would not want them to be punished; the people are not indifferent to the government's activities. What I would like is for everyone to know that before everything, it works in the interests of the country where the gold mine is, which I am—and will be, come what may—proud to have discovered. We are associates of another caliber. Will the future judge our labor and/or us? But I believe that we will not have been detrimental or completely useless to this country and its people."

The secretaries stared at her; Ségué n'Di looked at her, quietly, contemplatively. He remembered a book from the library of the International Cooperation Mission, of which entire pages were translated in Wanakironi and that was dormant in his memory. He timidly raised his hand and started talking.

"If you allow me, I will first of all make remarks here that are not of my own invention, but deserve that one states them by taking them into account. It seems that economic geography, specifically commercial geography, draws up inventories of resources or production potentials that prepare companies for conquests or land speculations. Economic geography and statistics, preparatory disciplines with the businesses compile all the inventories. Mrs. Keurléonan-Moricet and others besides myself can give a presentation on these problems, and I understand your reaction concerning the presence of the racist South Africa in the delegation that came to Tigony.

"Among the ideas that I have been able to glean from reading this book, can be found those of military geography that uses above all the cartography, utilizes the results of diverse forms of geographic research, to assure strategic positioning and ground tactics. I think—by opening the brackets here—that the discovery of the mines drives the Wanakawa to act in the context described in the book. There is also the question of applied geography just like applied geology; in this case, it would be used to focus the factual analysis to report on the topics likely to contribute, within the shortest time, to the information of departments or the companies whose labor is used or to give value to a portion of the territory.

"I do not know if, like me, you see the analogies between what I have been repeating and what is building up before our eyes. It will be informative, for the nonspecialists that we are, that Mrs. Keurléonan-Moricet gives explanations, if there are some inaccuracies in what I tried to report. The press made numerous allusions to design offices and analytical laboratories that are being set up; to contracts made or to be made between public services and/or private companies; to the creation of lobbies of geographical experts; to projects for organizing colloquiums; and even to a large conference on applied geography.

"The question that is presented to the rest of us, natives of this country, but also to friends and Western sympathizers who understand us and who even take part in some of our struggles for liberty, the advent of democracy, economic development, cultural, and social, is—I refer again to the reading of a book that had traumatized me—for the geologist, as well as the geophysicist, to guarantee the scientific objectivity of his research, should he shut himself off from all the external solicitations?

"Despite my young age, the mediocrity of my knowledge, my ineptitude on the subject, I say no. But 'how can the goals of geography resist the fundamental changes that represent the passage of the thoughts free of constraints, often organized along rational criteria, to action subordinated to vicissitudes of conjuncture? What can be the geographer's contribution to the improvement of the conditions of existence of the human communities?' These are some of the authors' questions; this is where the real problem lies.

"Except perception error, Madam Representative, you seemed to have alluded to terms that made me think you were angry. In short, please excuse me for having discussed my thoughts at length, which I did not modify or add to, but which I approve and made mine. As for my own point of view, here it is: the children of Wanakawa should not be absent in the organizations involved in Mount Franakiniriyo. Create an African company in which we, Africans, will have the majority of more than 51 percent and in which all the Westerners who would like to and who were allowed to could also be shareholders," he ended, eyes on the impassive Dorcas, although he had read signs of approval on her face. The secretaries applauded keenly; Dugratin also. Grudgingly, his associates clapped without energy in the palm of a hand, with the fingers of the other hooked like a predator clutching a prey in its claws.

Dorcas seemed to listen, as if they also spoke in their turn. She approved "Mr. Niriokiriko Aplika's propositions," said to have "relieved the conscience that a Wanakawa national working for the consortium regional bureau could outline such ideas. The economic, social, and cultural future, quite often neglected in this country, will gain much from the mining that would not be a windfall only for the Westerners."

Analossokirioni, one of the secretaries, said that if the dream of an African mining company developed into a real objective, she would like to invest a part of her monthly salary, instead of keeping it in "these banks where our money brings us nothing."

"There is the need to know how to differentiate a current account from a savings account and a frozen account," Galopin, an accountant, intervened.

"All the banks in this country depend on the West; none allows an African to own a savings or frozen account. Our traders deposit billions of francs that these buildings there work with, without interest for their owners," Anari n'kosi, another secretary, responded.

"It is the government, more clearly, the state's job to set up a barrier against such abuses. But the people also, with the same determination as the strike, can have their own say and play their own role," Ségué n'Di said.

"Do you think that a strike of this magnitude is enough in a country like yours?" Thèse, one of the new technicians, said.

"It seems that in France, and also elsewhere in democratic Europe, the governments are not conscious of the reality of the problems that the workers or the people have to deal with," Selinio, another secretary, said.

Dorcas smiled. Thèse blushed vehemently and said, "You should have the means needed for succeeding at any strikes that you start."

"Certainly spontaneously as well as graciously, small traders and sellers provided food for the crowd during the strike, although their means are poor. In Africa, united efforts can lead to achievements, without one begging elsewhere," Ségué n'Di said.

Dorcas laughed again and then announced that the international representatives had decided to "hold a roundtable meeting. This is not our business; the report of their meeting will make the essence of their debates known to us. For the time being, I tell you that they will visit our offices, especially the mining site."

CHAPTER 29

Somebody had spread Ségué n'Di's speech, distorting it. He was suspected, since the briefing in the regional office, of having political aspirations that the management did not think favorably of.

"Let the dogs bark, the dead bury the dead," Dorcas wrote on a post-it that she stuck on the back of his hand, one morning as he brought her a file. Such support really made him happy, so he stuck the piece of paper on the secret package that she had entrusted to his care. Shocked by the denigrations, Greenough called him for an interview, which he declined, but directed him toward the "competent and empowered technicians and administrators to address certain problems."

The thought of seeing their names and photographs in the *Daily Encounter* led those involved to succumb to the crossfire questions without having first notified the hierarchy. Dugratin checked his watch right from Greenough's first words; under the pretext of urgent calls to his wife in Montpellier, and to a colleague in Geneva, he disappeared with the promise to return. Instead of their opinion on work in the mines, which they admitted they had not visited, and its impact on the country's socioeconomic development that the journalist invoked under different modes of questioning, Dugratin's colleagues, while declaring themselves "born free in a democratic country whose rule of law respects human rights," dwelt upon "Mr. Niriokiriko Aplika" and distorted his points and ideas that they interpreted by detecting who was "leftist," who "projects anarchy and subversion" or "despite appearances, anti-Western positions."

They overlooked comments made by Dorcas, who, recalling Ségué n'Di's works as well as the texts he had quoted from, had congratulated him for "refreshing her memory," explaining that she had been Yves Lacoste's student and that she knew the *Herodotus Review* journal to which she contributed. The analysis of the secret recording made during the meeting "revealed to them a potential political agitator in the person of Mr. Niriokiriko Aplika, hidden behind the idle chatter of researchers ignorant of the objective field, but who aired his own convictions."

As usual, Greenough avoided all censure but stressed that "the pitch-black portrait brushed by my interlocutors, the anti-Western ideas by a budding agitator and other factors of this nature, still astonish me about this kid whom I have known since he was only fifteen years old."

As soon as he had the opportunity, Ségué n'Di whispered that he only had a steely contempt for the interviewed people, greedy for money, of whom he did not fail to notice hostility toward him. He was not angry that they had been so stupid as to be led, head first, into the ambush toward which he had drawn them. For her, in the interest of the office and the work to be done, he would continue to behave as if nothing had happened. She advised him not to worry about "people without foundations and other dim-witted experts."

▪ ▪ ▪

His grandfather's state of health worried him as he took a walk with him on a Sunday afternoon. The Old Man enquired after his activities, the development of work in the mines, his relationship with his colleagues, and his "dreams for tomorrow," and he replied precisely, his remarks sparkling with anecdotes, which amused his "good n'Ata." He even talked of the granite grounds and family plots readied for construction; evoking memories of the strike, he spoke in praise of its effectiveness and made allusion to informal contacts, to "affective relations or friendship that such popular and nonviolent demonstrations made possible among individuals who did not know each other before their meeting in the crowd."

They were on the bank of one branch of the Funiarikinio River, along the eastern side of Mount Kiniyinka; limpid water, flowing blithely over the mossy stones, whispering its endless melody among the masses of reeds that leaned on one side or another of the canal's banks like foothills for the rivers. Old Nakinokofu stopped and leaned on his knobbly stick that had served as a walking stick for generations. Ségué n'Di saw a block of wood and went to take it, alternately carrying it in his arms and pushing it with his feet. They sat down on it facing the river, listening as they translated its whispers, commented on them, or conversed. His grandfather talked to him about his parents, his sister, and his brother, who without being sent abroad would not come back; his old n'Ata's sadness bore down on him. He cast a sidelong glance at his profile, choked with anguish, although all ears and happy to be side by side with this octogenarian to whom he was so attached that he thought that he could never die. It brought him such happiness that he was there, seated on the same dead stump as his grandfather. The picture of Dorcas as an intruder swished in their privacy, and he wished that she would appear like a ghost, even with her husband, and saw him with this excessively thin, frail n'Ata she had found handsome in the drawing. He wished that he did not have to hide from his Old Man his relationship with the woman who sometimes came to the ancestral village in the middle of the night!

He turned toward him, smiled, put his arm around his shoulders, and drew him against him; the good Nakinokofu perceived his emotion, sadness as well as fear, and gave him affectionate taps on the cheeks. Ségué n'Di lowered his head, clenched his teeth, repressing the tears that swelled up within him. Raising his head, he saw among the pebbles and bits of stone on the bed of this running water a golden brown object, almost entirely covered by the sand. He looked at it; he pointed it out to his grandfather and stood up.

"Don't go into the water; the depth sometimes is treacherous," he said in his tired voice.

He lay down flat on his stomach on the grass, stretched his arm, and estimated the distance between the object and his hand in the water. Prudently, cautiously as if this fine shining spot could grab him and bite him, his hand sank deeper into the water and closed on the object with the stone on which it lay.

"It is gold, my lad, the river always brings it," the Old Man told him before he stood up to take a closer look at it.

"Yes, n'Ata, it is! It is as big as your big toe! It is strange that it is so . . ."

"It is good. I wished and wanted you to find it before I leave you . . ."

"Do not talk like that, n'Ata n'Nakitani."

"Ah, you call me your great-grandfather!"

"Because you are, it is the way I feel and want you to be."

"I accept this gift, but do not be sad. I dreamed three times that you had found it and then I wished and wanted it for my little one. Keep it safely for the woman in your life, when the time comes for you to take a wife. You will have a woman worthy of us, won't you?"

"If n'Ata n'Nakitani wishes it, will I act differently?"

Laughing as if he was whispering, he stretched his long muscled, tapered arms toward him, still strong like a wooden club made from an iroko tree that had long weathered time. Ségué n'Di took them, holding them in his. N'Ata stood up and gave him back his stick. The Old Man looked at him; it could be said that he saw some sign on his face, and then he lowered his head sighing.

"Hmmmmmm, even in your speech, you are the carbon copy of my poor son whom I will go to join. It is not right to bury your children."

CHAPTER 30

THE COOPERATION MISSION OCCUPIED SIX HECTARES PLANTED WITH COPAIBA, combretum, flame trees, and jacarandas often blossoming; there were also the clumps of selected mango trees that yielded abundant fruits one could pick standing up during the mango season. Along the three-meter-high granite fence, at the covered top of a thick carpet of bougainvilleas, were arbors that were conveniently far from each other. Cuttings erected there over a quarter of a century ago had become architecture with interlaced and tightened branches, flowering in any season that protected against the sun, sheltering lively, debated meetings. The ICM Park was the venue of a huge reception in honor of the international delegation at the end of its assignment. Dorcas had insisted that her partners be invited there, and each had received a card. Ségué n'Di told her during the comings and goings on the mining site that he was not going to attend it.

"There will be such a crowd that it will be difficult for a cat to find its kitten," she had retorted.

"Certainly, but with Daddy Greenough, we would start to talk in Kinokoroni which he speaks well. He wouldn't leave me alone, except for a brief moment to talk to a high personality or some girlfriend. Our countrymen would join us. It would become a meeting of the clan."

"It would be wonderful to be with that good old Greenough who loves you so much and speaks an African language with you!"

"For us, Greenough is not a white man."

"Great! In fact, you would not like that some colleagues . . ."

"Yes, there is that as well," he avowed.

A smile was outlined on his face, and then he nodded slightly as if he had received an instruction from her.

▪ ▪ ▪

The opportunities to wear a tailored-made suit were rare. Gaëtan had tried on his white smoking jacket and had had difficulties with the zipper of the trousers; he patted his belly, clutched the padding around his hips, and grunted: "Shit! Got to be methodical. I've got to diet to get rid of this ugly fat." Two weeks later, he put on the evening wear without squeezing himself too much, but the jacket did not completely conceal his paunch. A well-built man, he stood upright and drew in his stomach from time to time. The unbuttoned jacket, the silk shirt with mother-of-pearl buttons, white silk bow tie, and matching shoes could not go unnoticed. Dorcas wore a midnight-blue velvet dress; the sleeves, discretely flared on the elbows, were trimmed with an old-gold ribbon similar to the oval low-cut neck; the color of the embroidery merged with the tan of her bosom and her neck. The ends of a five-centimeter-wide old-gold ribbon of floppy bow tie followed the soft curve of her hip as it highlighted the slender size of her luscious body; a real pearl at the end of a chain of fine gold, a present from her grandmother at the time of their marriage, rested on her bosom; two gold-wrought earrings bedecked her ears. The mirror in the den reflected the picture to her. She repaired the hardly perceptible makeup; the hair gathered at the nape of the neck in a voluminous supple chignon that discreetly revealed the neck and the necklace decorating it.

When she got to the living room, Gaëtan, breathless, could not hold back a whistle of admiration.

"Dor, I am proposing to you again, and I'll marry you immediately!"

She wrapped her arms around him and kissed him with tenderness.

"Hey, you also look great! You did well to lose a bit of weight."

"Is it noticeable?"

"Do you think I don't look at you any longer?"

"It makes me happy to hear you say that."

"Do we take the Honda or the Rover?"
"Oh, the Rover."

▪ ▪ ▪

It was a full crowd; nobody noticed their arrival. They moved forward as if with the drift, greeting those they recognized or who gestured at them with their free hand; they moved toward one of the long buffet tables teeming with people. Gaëtan succeeded in getting two goblets of champagne. Someone beside him recognized Dorcas and greeted her.

"Oh! Herr Hoffstein, let me introduce you to my husband," she said, and explained that the gentleman was an important member of the international delegation.

"I'm from Stuttgart. Your charming wife is radiant! We had a very satisfying high-level meeting with her."

"Stuttgart? Our son is studying there," Keurléonan said.

Straightening his head, he gained a few centimeters, stuck out his chest. Noticing the ribbon of his decoration of the Cultural Merit, Hoffstein craned his neck toward the lapel of his jacket. Gaëtan smiled; so did the German.

"What a beautiful decoration!"

"Mrs. Keurléonan-Moricet praised the excellence of the international delegation that came specifically for the Mount Franakiniriyo mines."

"Cheers!" Mr. Hoffstein said, raising his glass.

"Zum Wohl! Und bis später!" Dorcas said, raising her champagne goblet. Eyes sparkling with joy, Hoffstein bowed and they left him. "Oh! Mrs. Keulouamaurish! It is a great pleasure!" a Japanese man exclaimed.

Dorcas murmured that it was impossible to bypass him when he waited for answers to his questions and that Japan would not be an easy partner for the Westerners; then, smiling, she welcomed him and made the introductions. A fine smile of desire appeared on Mr. Fujiwara's lips as he ogled her; they nevertheless struck up a conversation, which revolved around the mines. Gaëtan saw an African woman; their eyes met and they winked at each other. He wanted to move away toward somebody who had made a sign to him, when the Japanese caught sight of a secretary whom he found attractive and left them.

"It would be better to dive into the crowd. I have the impression that gregariousness is holding the delegation in one place."

"We must find out where the dinner-buffet place is before we split up."

"According to the program, there are to be fifty stands for the two thousand guests." They moved forward, jostled a bit, chit-chatted, relaxed, and were happy to be there. They came across colleagues from the consortium or the International Cooperation Mission and greeted them without stopping; they also did the same, only raising their glasses, sometimes giving Dorcas a broad smile.

"Who is this halfwit, as my late father-in-law would say?"

Dorcas, moved, turned toward him with a face full of tenderness.

"It is Mr. Galopin, the accountant. You know, Yvan, you should visit us at one point in time or the other."

He put his arm around her waist, and there was more than affection in his gesture.

"You told me and I don't doubt it, you are going to ask for my hand again in marriage . . ."

"Absolutely, Dor, because I love you!"

Laughing, they gave each other light pats on the shoulder as a big, off-colored blond in a black satin evening gown with plunging low neckline approached them.

"I read your interview in the *Encounter*, very good, excellent, my dear!"

"Thank you very much; I am glad you liked it, madam."

"Ah, that old James!"

"James? Who's that?"

"But Mr. Greenough! He has three Christian names; didn't you know that?"

"I had never seen him before he asked for an interview."

"He laid into you; it was nothing malicious."

"We know about the press, especially the journalists since they are the ones who do it. It would be boring if they were full of praise for people they go on to torture a bit." Gaëtan looked as if he were being hustled as he drew back from them, taking small steps; two other guests walked up to them, and Mrs. Nakebone said, laughing, that he could leave his wife without fear to a hen party.

"No cock will touch her. We will find you again after our conference."

When he took his wife's half-empty glass, Gaëtan noticed that she rubbed her temple gently with the tip of her finger and her face was slightly tensed. He inquired in a low voice, "Is something wrong?"

"The signs of a migraine, and I have forgotten my tablets," she murmured.

"Do you want me to go and get it? I saw the tube on the table in the living room."

"No, no, I hope it will go away. Otherwise, I will go to the closest pharmacy, or quickly go home."

"Oh no! My dear, you are not going . . ."

"But no, but no, I'm still here. Please, leave me the keys before leaving us, if I do not find a pharmacy nearby . . ."

"Can we help you?" Mrs. Nakebone intervened.

"My wife sometimes gets migraines," Gaëtan said, worriedly.

"It'll work out; we will find what she needs, bye!"

He gave her the keys and went to blend in with the noisy cheerful crowd.

CHAPTER 31

About ten women, meticulously well dressed, formed the hen party. A man passed by, pushed about by the crowd—a nicely bald man in a burgundy velvet suit and matching floppy silk necktie. He kissed Mrs. Nakebone's hand without stopping.

"Ciao! Gianfranco!" she greeted him with a sweet voice that made it seem as if she followed him.

She turned toward the others, sighed, and announced, regretfully, "He was my centaur in the backroom. I had to get rid of him as he became cumbersome. Ah, that good old Gianfranco who made me frigid with my Tony! Then, I freed myself from him like an overripe fruit that fell from a tree that no longer bore fruit."

"It is unbelievable," Dorcas murmured, her finger on the temple that she did not stop rubbing.

A beautiful woman with a black chignon on her right ear, with her beautiful ochre satin dress with blossoming black orchid prints, said that a centaur as a lover wasn't particularly sexy.

"Better to have a centaur on you, even on the ground with a four legs session of lovemaking, than a Doberman," Mrs. Nakebone said.

Suddenly pale, Dorcas sighed.

"That should be great if one vibrates in stages with him, otherwise, what pleasure can you have in reality?" Mrs. Garnier, a big Russian in a gold-lamé organdy dress, asked.

"Some animals bring more sensations, even more joy than the human beings that we are," Mrs. Nadier, with an average cut, auburn hair, and darting eyes on her chubby face, asserted.

"Only me, I said to myself, I have free movement and take my life to the other end of these valleys as I like, happier than these torrents that fall from the mountains in order not to climb back again," Dorcas said in a soft voice, chin and cheeks in the hollow of her hand.

"My dear, they say you are a geophysicist; but you are rather a poet!" Mrs. Nadier exclaimed.

"I'm sure I had read that in my youth. It's . . . ah, this very emotional Breton, yes! Maurice de Guérin! Isn't it, my dear?" Mrs. Nakebone exclaimed.

"Bravo! This passage of his prose poems started to tinkle in my head, as soon as you spoke of your centaur," Dorcas said.

Mrs. Nakebone laughed heartily.

"My dear, if it has not yet happened, you will have at least one sexual adventure in this country," Mrs. Karlfield, a beautiful she-wolf with a natural fairness, intervened, devouring with her eyes.

Dorcas closed up, did not blush, and smiled with an ironic expression.

"In this land, it is better to have a good native wine than an imported centaur, be he the handsomest and sexiest!" Mrs. Nakebone said.

"Between us women, I would readily confess that I go hunting when I feel like doing so," Mrs. Nadier said.

A crawling redness in Dorcas's neck reached her ears.

"Who would be wrong to indulge herself, when our husbands hardly miss an opportunity to get loose?" Mrs. Karlfield said, with a quiet circular glance at the others.

Dorcas's big black eyes opened wide with stupor, but she smiled again and started rubbing her temple gently again. Mrs. Karlfield watched her and, shaking her head in a dubious manner, added, "Yes, who would be wrong? My dear, I see without doubt that you have not yet tasted any ripe fruit in Wanakawa."

"My first experience with what you lightly labeled local wine," Mrs. Nakebone said, "it happened with our butler, one day as he brought the pressed laundry into the bathroom. I was as nude as the day I was born when he knocked. 'Come in.' The door opened; he saw me and closed it as soon as he mumbled his excuses."

"'Come in, Haki, have you never seen a naked woman?' He entered; head lowered, opened the drawers, put away the laundry, and departed as if I had driven him away. Then I put my hand on his shoulder; he straightened his head, but kept his eyelids lowered."

"'Haki, do you really not desire me? You have never thought of me—how do I put it?—like a desirable woman?' He finally looked at me and said in a tired voice: 'Madam, there have been so many traps in Wanakawa, problems regarding men in domestic service . . .'"

"I didn't listen to him as I unbuttoned his overalls. The evidence in the trousers made me acknowledge formally what I suspected; Haki was in a position to be useful and I gave myself to him. Disastrous liquor! His flame of pleasure ran through me like a will-o'-the-wisp. He then made love to me again as he wanted. What woman would regret such a pleasure and such a sensual pleasure?"

Dorcas felt as if she was caught between two fires and blushed despite herself.

"Dear geophysicist, you are crimson like a young virgin! You have not yet dived into such a river, you who have read and know by heart the passages of this sublime Maurice de Guérin: 'my lively sides fought against the floods that they were internally pressed against, and tasted in these storms the pleasure that is known only on the sea shores . . .'"

". . . To contain with no loss of life raised to its heights and aroused," ended Dorcas, adding she was unaware of all morals in the country, local or imported.

"You are wonderful; it will come! For the time being, I'm delighted to meet someone who has read and likes Maurice de Guérin. Some write dull pieces called poems, ineptitudes that do not make even a butch happy," Mrs. Nakebone said.

"Maurice de Guérin was my adolescence; with Roman elegies, Goethe opens other doors. I have not yet read anything that measures up to him."

"Roman elegies? Where can one find this work?" Mrs. Garnier avidly asked.

"James has written about you: 'Competency, professionalism, work, elegance, and charm; she also made me think of an *apeira*,' what does one call this spider in French?" Mrs. Karlfield said.

"*Épeire*—garden spider, quite stupidly; it is a surveyor spider that measures out its web before weaving it," Mrs. Nadier stressed.

"My goodness, Mr. Greenough got it right; my husband—please excuse me for using the word—treats me like someone who is '*bordélique*'—a slob."

"Oh!" many of them exclaimed.

"It is a good French word that is not nasty; in fact, I never take that badly: the chaos is the disorder in my papers. In fact, I'm a sort of surveyor spider."

"Who reads Goethe! Splendid! Your husband is a happy man!" Mrs. Nadier exclaimed.

"Why so much rejoicing? That should be rather boring! I prefer the mess," Mrs. Karlfield said.

"My dear, the spider derives a great pleasure from the prey that it causes to fall in its web, and the male is not deprived of it. They share and every couple worthy of this name does the same. But beyond such a feast, how much pleasure there is in the extra joys!" Mrs. Nadier exclaimed.

"I will register for entomology to study the behaviors of the spider," Dorcas said, and then she asked about pharmacies in the area.

"There are two before the National Boulevard; are they still open? It would be better to go back home to take your medication," Mrs. Nakebone advised.

"Could you tell my husband that I'll be back without delay, if you . . ."

"Do not worry about your husband in a reception like this," Mrs. Garnier laughingly said.

CHAPTER 32

She heard it like a call in the night, went through two red lights without feeling as if she was driving, and like an eagle soaring up, an impulse took her to Mount Kiniyinka. She took a rising side alley. In a badly lit part of the northern slope, she saw the silhouette of a man whom she recognized, standing at the entrance of the steep path leading higher up. She braked and made him get in.

"Are you waiting for someone?"

He admired her, lowered his head, and said in his quiet voice that rarely allowed anyone to know his feelings that she intimidated him, added that he was waiting for no one but her and would have stayed there until 3:00 a.m. before going back home, if she had not come.

"I am sorry I could not get away quickly; did I promise to come earlier?"

"You did not promise anything. The radio said that there were more than two thousand guests."

She turned off the engine, put her arms around his shoulders, and looked at him with a touch of sadness in her eyes.

"I am still confused at seeing you here, at this late hour."

"I am going to say something absurd, too bad if you do not believe me. I felt a great need to see you this night. It is beyond idiocy, but I could not stop myself from coming down this far," he said and clasped her in his arms.

She snuggled against his chest. The quiet and regular beatings of his heart made her relax, and then her head fell on his shoulder as if it were suddenly broken; she sighed deeply and looking at the chiaroscuro area they had before them through the windshield, she said in a low voice, "What a beautiful nocturnal landscape! I feel as if I am in a secure and cozy nest where I am watching it from."

"It is one of the facets of this country, especially in the mountainous areas."

"If my father were still alive, he would have said that I am fiercely in love; he would be very far from being wrong, my charming Paul-Louis."

He kissed her on her neck. The car started again without him being worried about the destination. A few minutes later, he noticed that she was going toward the bridge over the Kiniéroko. Dorcas touched a button on the automatic driving board; the electronic door opened, then closed behind the Rover. Two of the lights in the courtyard came on. She did not take him to the main building, but instead she took him along to the bottom of the court, to an arbor next to a three-bedroom flat where some of their guests were sometimes lodged. She came back shortly to join him there wearing a dressing gown. There was an elevated flagstone furnished with a mattress in a slipcover. She snuggled close to him with such a longing and such a need of him that something broke down in her; she wept, murmuring that she would readily run off, "go far, no matter where with you, you'd like to, won't you?"

"The scandal," he said.

"Oh Ségué n'Di! What scandal? Do not leave Wanakawa, stay in Tigony even if there is what you call a scandal; a scandal for me would be that you . . . What would become of me? I would sink into madness."

He enfolded her in his arms; she surrendered herself to him, gave the entire depths of herself over, and the pirogue of desire carried her beyond the desire where pleasure released her innermost feelings. A long hour later, she went to take a shower and dressed up as before for the evening, and felt something radiating within herself like a soft ray of light at daybreak.

"You are superb. There is something in your face. I do not know how to translate it," he said taking her hand.

CHAPTER 33

She dropped him off not far from his place and came back to the reception that was no less crowded than before and had music in the background. A number of the guests were still eating; some had moved on to the dessert. Dorcas took a plate and served herself shelled lobster with watercress salad. Greenough reached her, took her plate, and led her to a table where he sat beside her among the other guests. Their abrupt change of subjects avoided all allusions to the mines. Happy, very relaxed, she also preferred the general conversation style to the spider's approach.

Although he had tried to create a diversion, Greenough had seen Gaëtan and Mrs. Myriam Haïlé-Haïkouni as they moved away from an arbor. Beautiful in her forties, her jet-black hair cropped short, she did not look her age. General Secretary of the Ministry of Economy, Finances, and Budget, she had a fifteen-year-old son, Ronald, who would have looked very Ethiopian if not for the square chin, the green color of his eyes, and also his appearance, which was similar to that of the Irish journalist. Speaking cursorily, like a telegram, Greenough provoked the reception by mentioning the cost, made allusion to the women's attire, the hen parties as well as the stag parties that "in this kind of conviviality, stick together like tribal clans. Their conversations are rather nasty."

Dorcas laughed frankly. The picture of the group where she had heard eyebrow-raising stories came back to her, and she said that perhaps people of that kind of group were in need of affection.

"Don't you believe it!"

"Why, to their attention, would you not also suggest some pages of Freud or Groddeck or Wilhelm Reich?"

"Great! Good subject, we are not going to get bored!"

Looking around at Mrs. Nakebone and her teammates in the vicinity, Dorcas discovered, as if with a telescope, Gaëtan face to face with an African woman whose right hand was placed on his shoulder; there was a glimmer of a small smile on her lips. She turned toward the journalist, who said, "You are right, your idea is pertinent; I will use it. To avoid any problems over copyright, I will state that it was graciously given to me during this excellent reception of more than two thousand guests. OK?"

Dorcas put the napkin on her mouth, burst out, and then cheerfully begged, "Oh please! Don't go on ahead so far!"

"OK, darling Keurléonan-Moricet."

They laughed heartily; Greenough brought her passion fruit and mango salad. She stood up a little later, took her cup of coffee with the saucer, and conversing, slaloming nonchalantly through the crowd, they were a few meters away from Gaëtan and his partner. In a discrete, no less languorous movement of her sculptural body, Mrs. Haïlé-Haïkouni drew away from him a bit. He understood that there was an awkward situation and, keeping quiet, did not make a gesture that raised suspicions.

A member of the international delegation came to greet Dorcas; she introduced the journalist to him. Remarks on the reception, the nice atmosphere, and the conviviality came from everywhere at the same time. The sound of the music in the background created an atmosphere that could not be more international. Mrs. Haïlé-Haïkouni followed Gaëtan elbowing his way toward them.

"Oh, hi! Myriam!" Greenough exclaimed.

"Hi! Good James, I haven't seen you for years!"

"Good joke, I was off to Zimbabwe for a week, and Ron didn't want to be my guest."

"Really? Nice kid! Well, sorry for him."

"Are you feeling better, dear?" Gaëtan asked.

"Well yes, I have even had something to eat, thanks to Mr. Greenough," she said, beaming.

For the past three years, he had spoken to her about Myriam Haïlé-Haïkouni with whom the International Cooperation Mission sometimes had meetings. Dorcas, who did not know this "distinguished, very beautiful and efficient woman," eyed her as Gaëtan made the introductions. She noticed that she was not his mistress but that their relationship was not platonic.

"Nice to meet you in person; my husband often talks to me about you."

"Badly, I hope!" she said, bursting into laughter.

"Not at all! Although it is hardly easy to relate at all levels, in terms of finances."

"Ah! Here is someone who understands us!" she exclaimed, then turning toward Greenough, she added, "The *Daily Encounter* described you . . ."

"It was not badly written! I loved its style, but also the scrupulous precision with which my remarks were brought across."

"Good heavens! Here is finally someone who is intelligent as well as loyal. Phew! An interviewee who does not complain that her ideas were distorted, betrayed! Thanks a lot for that, madam.

"Even for the garden spider?" Mrs. Haïlé-Haïkouni said.

"Why not? My husband ascribes other attributes to me," she said, taking his hand. Gaëtan blushed and retorted light-heartedly, "My God, certainly, I know that there are some investigations, even some charm in the disorder . . ."

"If it is on purpose; for me it is rather sui generis!" she said, laughing.

"It is even better, isn't it?" Mrs. Haïlé-Haïkouni said.

Dorcas found her a charming, really beautiful woman; it also seemed to her normal that, as long as sampling the local brew was concerned, her husband had tried his luck with such a beautiful African woman.

The background music changed without transition to a tango.

"Oh dear, would you leave him with me, please?" Myriam said, and she was so very attractive that Dorcas yielded.

"It is one of the dances that we dance well together, but since I have him at home," she said, seeing that Gaëtan hardly wanted to dance with her.

"Well, there is nothing Irish about this dance, but you would not drop me for one of the international delegates—me who would like to walk into a garden spider's web?" Greenough suggested, with his arms opened.

They were still laughing when, with Dorcas in his arms, they danced, keeping a convenient distance between them. Flexible with her sense of rhythm, she surrendered herself to his faultless guidance. On their side, Gaëtan and his partner betrayed themselves as they tried to disguise what was happening; the gap between the top of their bodies narrowed toward the bottom where there was none. They talked, smiled, moving from thigh against thigh to intertwined legs. Gaëtan had a hard-on; the couple danced the tango. Dorcas and Greenough seemed ethereal. The orchestra announced a break, many exclaimed, "Oh no!" but he started an Argentinean tango.

"You can have your husband back, my dear," Myriam said as she promptly embraced Greenough.

Gaëtan's sex still turgid, he held his wife less closely than he had held Myriam.

"She is gorgeous," Dorcas said, her eyes exploring his eyes as he was avoiding looking at her.

"Certainly, she is not bad; I know you to be quite objective and I would also say that she is gorgeous."

"When I was in Rome, they called Ignazio Silone's wife, whom I met twice, 'the she-wolf.' She was a beautiful woman, but Mrs. Haïlé-Haïkouni is even better, very beautiful and seducing," Dorcas added. "Why don't we invite her to dinner one of these days? Perhaps with that delightful Mr. Greenough?"

"Excellent idea, Dor! You ought to tell them about it."

She tried in vain to get closer to him. Everything in her rebelled against the nature of this man who fought not to betray himself. She was not taken in by their bellies' interplay. It was not he that had "bashed the bishop"; he was so aroused that he had been unable to loosen his "taut bow" before dancing with her, when he discretely passed a hand on his fly. She loved dancing the tango and had given proofs of it during a gala evening, in the arms of the best partner who was her father. She thought of him when the movements with her husband were developing into a fiasco, then she quietly took the initiative to impose her own rhythm. Eyes fixed on Gaëtan's lowered eyes, her arms, her feet, her whole body was nothing else than this tango. The couple was not far from the orchestra that had noticed her talent and played for her.

Red as a peony, Gaëtan smiled, although the tension seemed to him to be less hard than when he was intertwined with Myriam. Dorcas knew that it was not because of her that he was like this.

"My God! Look at that, Myri!" Greenough exclaimed.

"She is a beautiful woman, lovely, very talented, even stunning and knows it."

"She has above all a sparkling intelligence; she succeeded in putting me at an arm's length during the interview. Ah, these women, we men are always their victims!" he said in a mournful tone.

Myriam laughed as she moved closer to him.

CHAPTER 34

THE DELEGATION LEFT TIGONY WITH A CANISTER OF DUST AND STONES TAKEN from inside the mine; anticipating the tests that the samples would undergo, the press wrote that "they would be ground up, analyzed, processed on the computer and in the blast furnace. No matter how small they might be, the gold found in them would not come back to Wanakawa. Thus the recolonization of the country would start: the brain drain due to the government's errors, because of the richness of the soil and the subsoil, all following the complicity of the lobbyists' payoffs and bribes.

The instructions from the consortium's headquarters had been distributed to everyone in the regional office. Ségué n'Di's more important responsibilities often made it necessary for him to be on-site, and he had acquired a moped with a more powerful engine than that of his second-hand Solex. Wearing a security hat, happy with his new machine, glad to be alive, he went to Mount Franakiniriyo, crossing the main town, the inner suburb, and a few important villages that led to the savannah, toward the mining site. Proud in the vastness of the savannah trembling in the sunlight, a remote flight of meadow titlarks made him feel that space moved under the effect of their movement; then he felt as if he was also taking off, taking flight into the blue sky.

A Honda with an international public service plate number overtook him; he recognized the head and the outline of Mr. Keurléonan. The car passed him on its way back, before his arrival at the site; the tire marks showed that he had stopped about twenty meters away from the underground entrance and had made a U-turn before starting off again. Ségué n'Di noticed the imprints of Wellington soles in the siliceous dust, looked at them, and guessed that they should be size forty-four. His own were forty-two; he only used them for the site. In town as well as in the office, his locally made sandals were the shoes in which he was comfortable.

Mr. Keurléonan's solitary rides surprised him. He informed his wife as soon as he had the opportunity to do so: he noticed her husband's "excursions" in the area, three times in less than a month. She was unaware of it all, but had smiled; under no circumstances would Ségué n'Di affirm yes or no whether the general secretary of the ICM knew him or not. The rare times that he had visited the regional office, he had hardly paid attention to the employees whom he had greeted absentmindedly. The secretaries had felt him look at them out of the corner of his eye and perceived the womanizer side of him; more than one of them peered at him, whispered to another one that he was not bad looking, that she would hardly complain if he made a bold move. The employees were amused that he made the same gesture each time he visited: raising his eyes to the ceiling and sweeping the panoramic posters representing the mountains, valleys, caves, lakes, rivers, and geological sections before leaving as if he were chased away from there.

On the night of the gala, two secretaries conversing with the Westerners had greeted him when he moved toward the arbor in the company of a woman. He had seemed astonished to them, as if he did not know them. None of them had ever understood his behavior, which they interpreted as his contempt for everyone with a status below his. When Myriam drew his attention to them, he grumbled that they had to be his wife's associates, whose relationships he didn't know.

▪ ▪ ▪

The feeling of harmony that she thought she had observed between Dorcas and him during the gala had not made her suspicious of discordance in their home. When, responding to their invitation to dinner, she arrived with J. F. G. Greenough at the wheel of her general secretary's Rover 10 CV, with the rank of a plenipotentiary minister. Taking Dorcas's hand, Myriam asked herself if this woman, whom she instinctively thought to be straightforward, could have affairs that her husband did not know of. Very French, Dorcas kissed her while taking her hand but had to repress a burst of laughter.

When they had gotten back from the gala, Gaëtan, somewhat tipsy, had hastily undressed. When she put the shirt and the laundry he had dropped on the bathroom floor in the basket, Dorcas remembered the humiliation inflicted on Malifiki. She had taken the underpants with two fingers; there were still some pubic hairs on them. That Gaëtan could not do without such a souvenir amused her. She quickly hid this undergarment and replaced it with another of the same brand and set the washing machine.

Happy to have them to dinner, she laughed as she heard Myriam or Gaëtan talk, or because of Greenough's humor, or thinking of Myriam's hairs. They congratulated her on the dinner. She gave most of the credit to Malifiki, who had chosen the live lobsters, lamb shoulder, and barracuda rather than monkfish.

"He is right: those of us from here are tired of monkfish. The meat certainly has better quality than that of the barracuda; but as for the taste, the latter is ahead of it," Myriam exclaimed.

"Such a claim would not be made in Brittany!" Gaëtan retorted.

"I am used to the Nile perch, grouper, and barracuda. But that gentleman, better to have it on one's plate than to meet it while swimming," Greenough said.

"Swimming! Swimming!" Myriam enjoyed herself.

"Why not! I prefer the sea and the river to the Monomotapa hotel swimming pool; everyone plunges there, drinking the polluted water."

"Oh James! You will not put the people off this Olympic pool! It is not everyone that has one at home," Myriam complained, feigning discontentment.

"I am not the one who would scorn it; even for a Breton, relaxing in such a pool is a pleasure."

"My preference lies in the sea or the river. I like the immensity of free space," Dorcas said.

"On the condition that Brittany is not too far from you!"

"Certainly, certainly. Reims does not open to any sea."

"You are Reimoise? Ah! I love the high-quality brands of champagne!"

"My native Ireland does not have such a privilege. Never mind, some people are starting to be interested in the great Médoc vintages and even acquire old castles there."

It was a dinner with champagne for the diplomatic contingent. Malifiki served Fixin premier grand cru classé to go with the lamb shoulder. Myriam and Greenough—although the latter had tasted many good quality wines—had never heard of Fixin and wanted to know which region of France produced it. Background music, sometimes Bantu, sometimes South African with Myriam Makeba, added to an atmosphere of friendship and cheerfulness.

"I love that man! His music for the bicentenary of the French Revolution moved me a lot," Myriam raved when Dorcas played Wally Badarou's cassette.

"It is a present from our daughter, Dorothy. She is in . . ."

"I think he is Daho—Sorry, Beninois. It is odd that he could produce such music! After all, the world is so mixed that one should no longer be surprised; so much the better and a plague on the racists of all calibers," Greenough said, listening attentively to the music.

"Oh, dear James, why is it odd?"

"I don't know! The admirable late Gordon, I mean my father, was a tenor. Purcell, Händel, Cimarosa, Haydn, Mozart, etc., had made a great impact on my childhood and youth; I mean, despite the Negro-African sediments of the Beninois music, there are the movements, the shaking without analogy, that mark African creation, which draws me back a lot in my life."

"It is beautiful! Really significant! It is that which is terrific: remain yourself while making use of glories already won by others," Dorcas said.

"Absolutely, my dear, and bravo, my old James, for your analysis."

"What would you say to a Breton digestive?"

"Let us move to the living room, please," Dorcas said, standing up.

▪ ▪ ▪

Taking her leave, Myriam congratulated Malifiki before moving toward Gaëtan. Greenough also made compliments, adding briefly in Kinokoroni that his employers were very kind, to which the butler said in a low voice, "She, she is very, very good; he is disgusting."

Right behind them, Dorcas heard him. Without the knowledge of her husband and her associates, she had learned Kinokoroni since she started seeing Ségué n'Di who helped her to learn the vocabulary, master the basics of syntax, and practice when they met. Little in this national language that Africans used eluded her, but she remained the white woman who understood nothing and reacted cheerfully: "Is it in French, English, or Spanish in the text?"

She admitted she was improving her "knowledge of Kinokoroni, certainly to be on Ségué n'Di's wavelength, but also to understand this Africa better where my skills seem to be necessary and for which I want to fight and win."

"And what about walking around the courtyard?" she asked.

"Great!" Greenough exclaimed.

She told Malifiki to go home, leaving the dishes, which she would put in the dishwasher herself.

"But no, but no, madam, it will hardly take time; my family had been told that I would not get home before one or two in the morning."

"Thanks, you are very brave. Take something home to eat."

"He likes you a lot," Greenough said.

CHAPTER 35

"NO ONE UNDERSTANDS YET, OR CAN IMAGINE THE MOTIVES OF THIS BASTARD assassin who committed this criminal act," Greenough wrote, repulsed, at the same time in a state of shock and trance. The suspicions of the African-language newspapers, aimed at the "neocolonial lobbyists," "bully-boy mercenaries who prowled in the mazes of Power," "those that did not have to like the false remarks made about Mr. Niriokiriko Aplika, by his jealous colleagues, consumed with hatred that an African held a post that he could reach thanks to his culture, knowledge of the subjects of the competition, and intelligence."

Leaving the mine tunnels, the African and the representative of the consortium still had their security helmets on and walked side by side. The laborers came up, loaded with baskets full of fragments of quartz. A shot suddenly came from behind the siliceous rubble, making Ségué n'Di's helmet fly as it tore his right ear. Dorcas only had the reflex to throw herself flat on the ground shouting, "Oh no! Lord!" before yelling at the assassin. She sat up at once, raising Ségué n'Di soaked with blood. The sketchbook in which he drew the details was nothing but a horrible watercolor.

Thrown into panic, the laborers bolted from all corners, ran, yelled, and shouted at the criminal assassin. The women cried. Those who remembered his parents cursed "the white man who wanted to kill the orphan"; "his n'Ata, he woul die of glief, if his lituation lorsens," said those who knew his grandfather. A number of them claimed to have seen "a big Western man with a beautiful car"; "he fled walking down the curb"; "he wore trousers and a blue-jean shirt"; "the car was like dark blue"; "no grey a bit bright"; "not at all! It is dark blue that seemed even a bit black"; "we cannot say exactly what brand, given that White people, a lot of people also have the same type of powerful cars—Peugeot, Honda, Nissan, and Volvo."

They had taken off the victim's shirt soaked with blood to wrap around his head; a thin layer of skin about four centimeters wide hung under his jaw where the bandage held the ear separated from the temple. Carried off to the Range Rover, he was laid on Mrs. Keurléonan-Moricet's jacket, among the newspapers scattered on the back seat. Since her car was equipped with a telephone, she had called the hospital, the emergency services, and the police, then had come back to the site of the attack. The security helmet was there where it had landed as it flew under the violence of the shot. Taking short steps, eyes wide open, and ferreting here and there, she saw the bullet cartridge. Her heart was beating wildly and her hands trembled when she picked it up. She breathed deeply, put the cartridge in a handkerchief, tied it, and hid it in the back pocket of the fatigues, her working equipment on the site.

Getting back into the car, she drove on as the emergency services arrived followed by the central hospital's minibus. She made them look at the wound, stressing that he had lost a lot of blood. The medical service acted right away; they transferred the victim in the appropriate vehicle where they immediately started a blood transfusion. The police already on site asked Dorcas questions; the medical assistance had to set off without her. There was a continual coming and going of interrogations and explanations of the witnesses. Dorcas showed where she was "with Mr. Niriokiriko Aplika; he held his workbook in his hand and enumerated to me the problems in the mines, from where we just came out." Her hand shook when, arm stretched, she pointed at the direction where she thought the shot seemed to have come from. They saw the helmet; looking carefully, scanning the ground like hunting dogs, they followed the marks of ricochets to the place of its fall, describing its trajectory with contradictory gestures.

After having been informed about the victim's functions, they took note of his colleagues' names and surnames. When they inquired about their appointments, the representative of the consortium replied that it would be much better if they came to the office to interrogate anyone they wanted. Annoyed, they left, turning around some dunes, interrogating the laborers who said some of them had seen him, others glimpsed a white man and his car when he fled.

Dorcas followed them to the Nariyekiyingy central hospital. In the emergency station, Ségué n'Di was under general anesthesia in the surgery station's operating block. The police completed their official report as the anticriminal squad came; they conferred separately, after which the police officers took their leave. Shell-shocked but in control, she went home. Her clothing bearing marks of the accident, she was assailed with thoughts of falling into emptiness, which she refused to accept, but as she suddenly saw as if in a dream a revolver that pointed at her, she went to put on a pair of gloves, took Gaëtan's pistol, wrapped it in a tablecloth, and hid it under the bed next to the room that abutted the arbor. When he saw her collapsed on the flagstone of the arbor and started stating his "surprise and indignation," she sat up, looked at him straight in the eyes, put her arms around his shoulders, and asked crying why he had done it.

"Really, Yvan? Why?"

The nerves in his body, calmed after the gala, left him; he suddenly grew heavy, and they had to sit down.

"Tell me, Yvan, why?" she insisted, her chin trembling.

"I don't know, I swear, I don't know what got into me," he muttered.

"I have hidden your pistol in a safe place . . ."

"What reason would there be for them to suspect me?" he asked confidently, and then added, "Have you forgotten that we have diplomatic immunity?"

It was as if a mask of sadness, disgust, and revolt was also pasted on his wife's face, when she discovered in him a man who had been able to premeditate and wanted to kill someone.

"You are jealous—" he heard as if it was not his wife talking to him.

"Yes, I am certain that you slept and sleep with him."

"At the point where we are, there is no more use in hiding it."

"You admit it, so calmly?"

"Would I have or should I try to kill Myriam Haïlé-Haïkouni and others?"

"You are mistaken! You cheat on me with a nigger, and you are highly mistaken in regard to my relationship with Myriam!" he yelled, blushing crimson.

"Unbelievable! You do not even have the courage of satisfying your desires and you lie; you always lied. I responded without hesitating because I like to bear my responsibilities in my life, my profession, my feelings as a woman to whom you have rarely succeeded in giving what was needed."

"Enough of this idiocy and hysteria, please!"

"Let me get to the end of my thought, if you don't mind. You flee from reality, you are horrified by realities, but I am going to tell you one thing: you have never been capable, in any case not with me, to anticipate my desire so as to give me the pleasure that I would very much have loved to get from you; you lack generosity even in love; you do not know what sensual pleasure means. Is it only with me?"

"And the nigger brings you all that?"

"Bring? He satisfies me, gives it to me absolutely. But tell me, is it really out of jealousy that you wanted to kill him, or because he is what you call a nigger? You insist a lot on this description of him. Myriam, the Ethiopian, is she not a negress?"

He did not react, seemed not to have understood that she had used the word negress while talking about Myriam, sighed at length, and shook his head, with an obtuse expression. Quiet, eying him, doubting that jealousy alone had made him decide to come to such a point, she felt a real allergic reaction to this sometimes brilliant man whom she had loved.

"What do you find in your nigger, sorry, your African, and that is lacking in me after so many years of marriage?"

"I would have preferred that you do not ask me such a question."

"I ask it nevertheless."

"You already know my response. You wouldn't have listened to me."

"The exact details would not have bothered me."

"Caressing a block of marble sculpted by time or by man gives a certain pleasure. You are raw stone or dead wood, a cold creature that does not exude any human feeling, unless it is with Myriam and the others."

"I think we should look for a solution."

"What do you suggest?"

He did not respond, left for the courtyard, came back, and suggested dining in a restaurant. She declined the invitation, telephoned the hospital to inquire about developments, pronouncing without embarrassment the name and surname of "Mr. Niriokiriko Aplika Ségué n'Di," and asked if the operation had gone well, if he was awake, and if she could talk to him. In the name of the consortium, she had given instructions that a single room should be given to him. The anticriminal squad had left formal instruction that no one should visit him, "except members of his family whom the victim of the assassination attempt knew and the director of the regional office of the consortium, in her official capacity."

At Dorcas's first words, Ségué n'Di had the feeling that something was amiss on the phone and answered in monosyllables, in a drained, sluggish voice. She heard his breathing, imagined his embarrassment, his distrust as well. She restricted herself to telling him about her sadness, to passing on their colleagues' greetings and that of the deeply moved laborers on the site; she promised to pay him a visit the next day, to inform the headquarters of this unacceptable act. "I would make sure that the accident report and the administrative formalities are filled out accordingly," she ended.

▪ ▪ ▪

She trudged into the bathroom, ran water, and lay down in the bathtub where she spent an hour. Coming home toward midnight, Gaëtan saw her lying on the leather settee in the living room where she reread "Christ Stopped at Eboli." He thought for a moment before bending to kiss her on the neck. He had gone out to look for someone to have sex with; the smell betrayed him. Dorcas smiled.

"Do you have any suggestions?"

"Divorce seems to me to be the best solution."

"On friendly terms or . . ."

"With lawyers."

"Very well; you are playing a losing hand."

"Me, Gaëtan Yvan Kervin Keurléonan? I would even say KERLEONARD, to correct the horrible deformation of illiterate niggers—them again—who damage the origin of my name."

"Alas! With all your forenames, even the correction that neither your parents nor you have not been able to bring to your family name . . ."

"We'll see about it."

"I don't understand why you're getting worked up like that."

"I am hotheaded, in spite of being a dead wood in our bed, since your discovery of the nigger who saturates you in sensations and makes you come, you, a cold-blooded monster!"

"You are aggressive, lamentable, vulnerable, but you know that I neither fight with an adversary lying on the ground, nor against a loser."

"It is me you are describing like that? What do you want to take away with you? Say it quickly so we can bring it to an end."

"We have come to the serious issues and I am going to express myself with equanimity. I shall keep our property at Isle-sur-la-Sorgue; it is still being restored, but it is of no importance. I'll add the apartment in Paris to it."

"The four rooms in the Marais? Are you crazy? Never!" he yelled. Bloody, red-faced, he gnashed his teeth.

"I will not ask you to be reasonable, but a bit loyal, a bit honest, if you can be."

"That is to say?"

"I like neither calculations nor apothecary accounts."

"You are very generous; I am sure the nigger will love it."

"It will be difficult for you to make me angry over your allusions and references; let us continue clarifying things since you are against my choice regarding the apartment."

"I also have good taste and I am attached to this apartment, since we bought it jointly. Dorcas, it would be better to put it up for sale."

"I do not have the private means to buy it back, neither do you; here is your small calculation."

"And so?"

"Decidedly, you lack generosity, but I am going to refresh your memory: I financed the whole restoration of your inheritance in Brittany, I mean your grandparents' property and the renovation of the contiguous three hectares of woodland; perhaps it will go to our children. I didn't want to have to talk about my actions; they were done with an open heart. I do not have any regrets, even now."

Arms crossed on his chest, head bowed, white, as if emptied of all his blood, he looked like a badly polished statue. Dorcas stood up, put her arms round his shoulders, and said that she was sure they would come to an understanding, "as in our youth, after the small tiffs."

"I sincerely count on it, Yvan, don't you? I would like it that as long as we are able to see each other, to talk, even about this rather short life, that it would be idiotic, a lack of intelligence not to live, relaxed and flexible. Listen to me carefully: I do not care about your chasing after women. You already cheated on me while we were engaged; I knew it. Your parents also felt that I was kind, very courageous; now, I want to live my life. Do you understand that?"

"What pains me and pisses me off—call it what you want—is that you are leaving me for a nigger."

"I made a choice."

"The day will come when he is going to dump you! Fed up with the white woman!"

"You are not God. My future will never depend on anybody's predictions. No matter what happens, a line is drawn. I shall not go to Canossa."

"Where did you put my pistol?"

"In a safe place. I will say nothing to our children about the man you have become."

"Oh, yes! Again I acknowledge your generosity," he said sarcastically.

"I don't worry about the problems of those who don't have any."

CHAPTER 36

The squad was made up of two Africans and two Westerners. One would think that their measurements had been taken before they were appointed: they had the same size, same muscular build, and same athletic gait. Had it not been for the obvious pigmentary difference, they would have been taken for quadruplets because of their balanced oval faces in which the Negroid features of some didn't contrast much with their colleagues'.

From the onset, they took turns asking Ségué n'Di questions concerning his relationship with "his colleagues in general, notably the Westerners, taking into account the corroborating opinions of the witnesses that the person was a white man seen from the back and dashing toward his car." He was shocked by an allusion riddled with a persistent vulgarity, but unruffled, he responded with a weak smile on his lips that such an idea had never occurred to him. They strongly insisted that his social situation that was "not bad at all for a native" put him "in the position to have needs, high ambitions."

His hardly accentuated smile became sardonic, and he retorted without lifting his still weak voice: "I'm not a pure spirit; who could be, in our country that is so subject to poverty? An endemic unemployment plagued Wanakawa for a decade; you are too far from the people to be aware of it . . ."

They held their anger in check when Ségué n'Di asked in a soft voice if they thought that the issue that seemed to concern them so much had to do with the competition in which he was successful.

They made signs to each other out of the corner of their eyes, some scratched their heads, and others rubbed their cheeks. One of the Africans wanted to know if he knew the husband of the director of the regional office of the consortium.

"Know, no. Like all of us—unless he came back when I was on the site—I saw him there three times. He didn't seem to me to be interested in the employees. He only looked at the posters and other sketches hung on the walls."

He had talked a lot and seemed tired. About to take their leave, the squad said that they would like to visit his home. The chief consultant took part in the questioning and keenly intervened.

"Because of the precariousness of my patient's health, victim of an attempted murder, he can't go out; deeply traumatized, the lack of balance due to damage to his eardrum, which could result in hearing disorders. On the other hand—since that is not part of my area of competence—the situation in his home demands a good measure of decency."

Suddenly intrigued, Ségué n'Di turned his eyes on the general practitioner who left with the squad, as if he had abandoned him. But he made a sign to him, and he understood that he was coming back. Some minutes later, he gave him the message that his grandfather had sent through his cousin, Kaïrofugningy.

"Since it is early in the morning and you were still asleep, we felt it was better not to wake you up. Your cousin had come to tell you of your n'Ata's great sadness; he encourages you to hold on tight. He stated that: 'N'Ata prays to the spirits of the ancestors and to those of your own parents as he is thinking of you.'"

"Doctor, I beg of you, I have to return to Mount Kiniyinka. I will not stay long there since I need your treatment and many things that are not available up there."

"Your condition . . ."

His look became unbearable and, with a tragic command of himself, he said in Wanakironi, the mother tongue that they both spoke, that he would be prudent because he held on to life. He lowered his head, crying quietly, saying in a quiet piteous voice: "My n'Ata's message is beyond the grave, my good Old Man is dead; I have to go back home. You know it as well, doctor, I have to spend some time beside his body before he is returned to the earth."

Awestruck, the doctor looked at him with compassion, then, teeth clenched, hands on Ségué n'Di's shoulders, which he pressed, he then gave him a series of traditional praises.

"I will make the necessary arrangements for you to be driven home; you will tell the driver at what time you want to come back to the hospital."

▪ ▪ ▪

On her arrival at the office toward six o'clock, a secretary informed Dorcas of the anticriminal squad's visit, commented upon with indignation by all the employees. She listened, reckoning that it was "normal that the squad did its work in line with its methods," then she telephoned Ségué n'Di who told her about his grandfather's death, "probably brought about by a cardiac arrest. I regret," he said with tears in his voice, "that they told him too soon, certainly making it clear that it was an attempted murder and that his grandson had been shot at. The man who was my Old Man could not understand that; he could no longer bear the shock, I have to get out; I have to see him again and touch his body before the bur . . ."

He broke down in tears. Dorcas cried silently. The conversation was being listened in on; they had no doubt about it. She would inform his colleagues and asked him where he lived, if she and they could also be at his side; the undercurrents made him feel as if she was near him, and he replied that "according to the custom, no stranger, no matter the color of his skin, can take part in the burial of an initiated."

"My grandfather is . . . My God! . . . was the head of the artisan guild."

She wiped her tears and went to break the news. The secretaries cried, talking in Kinokoroni. The Europeans did not hide their grief; they went out into the garden and, hands behind their backs or in their pockets, walked back and forth on the grass, under the azure bright sky.

▪ ▪ ▪

He went into the deceased's hut. The car had climbed the mountainside east of Mount Kiniyinka with a thousand precautions and had dropped him at the foot of the village. He knelt down with his face against the ground; he remained like this for a while before getting up to caress his grandfather's face, knees, and feet; then he sat down, huddled up on the ancestral tripod, and gathered himself with his face hidden in his hands. An hour later, he went into his room, took down the drawings depicting Dorcas, took the envelope she had given him, put everything in a carton that he taped, returned to his n'Ata's side, and put the package under his bed.

▪ ▪ ▪

Dressed in a discreetly open, polka-dotted, marine blue sleeveless dress and a linen poncho, Dorcas went to the hospital the day after the burial. As much sadness as fatigue was printed on her face, which did not totally leave; afraid that a third party could come in any moment, as soon as she sat down on a seat beside the bed, Ségué n'Di gave her an envelope with business cards that she put in her handbag from which she brought out four books borrowed from the library of the regional office and put them on the night table. He smiled with recognition, taking one after the other: *La Condition humaine, La Ragazza di Bube, Dubliners, Géographie humaine.*

She took a look at the temperature sheet at the foot of the bed when there was a knock on the door. The same men from the anticriminal squad, accompanied by the head doctor, came in. They greeted the representative of the regional office and gave their best condolences to Ségué n'Di, the Africans in Kinokoroni or Wanakironi, the Europeans in French, but Dorcas recognized the Belgian accent of one of them. She wanted to take her leave. They begged her to stay; they were paying a routine visit.

While one inquired about the patient's discharge date from the doctor, another took the books and passed them to his colleagues who shook them; a calling card fell from one of the books. They promptly retrieved and read the notes of a reader on the pages, perhaps to reread it. The agent referred to it: the description of people, populated and animated places, psychological reflections on war, etc. At the time of their departure, the highest-ranking officer reiterated the question concerning "the number of days that the patient would still require to be hospitalized."

"Eight days, maximum ten," the practitioner responded, annoyed.

Ségué n'Di stood up, moved, dragging his feet, opened the cupboard, took the key to his hut out of his pocket, tendered it to the agent, and said in his voice of a man at the same time exasperated and exhausted, "I live in a family village; it is Block 7 on Mount Kiniyinka. Here is the key to my hut. The rituals were performed for my grandfather; the rest will take place when I return, or without me if I do not survive. You do not need me to visit the hut of a black man in my condition . . ."

"Please, Mr. Niriokiriko Aplika, we will certainly not go to your house in your absence."

"You would have to search it alone if I die. Someone wanted to kill me; my concern, is to know who and why. Do your duty."

He felt weak and leaned on the cupboard.

"It is odd, awful," Dorcas murmured in an irritated tone.

"You are making mistakes, gentlemen," the doctor said, helping Ségué n'Di back to his bed.

"Excuse us, Doctor, but it has been stressed that none of us demanded anything from the victim of attempted murder."

Another agent turned toward Dorcas and asked if she would willingly respond to two questions without importance.

"Why ask them? But if you want to state your names, forenames, and registration numbers, I would tell you how to proceed."

A colleague whispered in the agent's ear, and he pulled himself together.

"My apologies, madam; I forgot your diplomatic immunity. The procedures in this case could indeed prove to be long."

They bowed slightly, shook the victim's hand, and left. Relaxed, eyes twinkling with mischief, Ségué n'Di saw Dorcas off a quarter of an hour later as she took her leave of him. As she walked slowly beside him, he narrated the story of the gold nugget and passed on his n'Ata's message.

"Is such a message really for me?" she inquired in Kinokoroni, quite moved, but without looking at him.

"Absolutely, if I believe my spirit, as well as my body."

She told him that having had to postpone her mission, she would go there shortly before or after his discharge from the hospital.

"I know who wanted to kill me; why did it come to this?"

"Jealousy . . ."

"Really? But you had loved him."

"I had. It is what he does not want to admit."

"Strange."

They looked at each other with affection, and then she took hold of his hand that he squeezed and she left.

CHAPTER 37

THE PROHIBITION OF VISITORS ANNOYED THE PRESS; SOME INSINUATED THAT the attempted murder was in collusion with the authorities. Denouncing the trend of the investigations, *L'Afrique actuelle* suspected "a Western roadblock protecting one of theirs whom the authorities dare not attack." The African-language press unanimously stated, "if the aggressor, identified as Western, were a poor Negro, our anticriminal squad would have removed him from his hut; since it is a white man, alas! Only seen from the back by almost all the witnesses, the guy moves freely around in the dark!"

Three articles signed under the same pseudonym, one in Kinokoroni, the others in English and French, condemned "the duplicity and the unacceptable silence of a government still in a desperate situation despite the improvements made thanks to the strike, the unendurable determination and foolishness of a squad supposedly there to repress criminality, but which, like a rutting bitch with the traces of a male, sniffs after the victim of the crime rather than looking for the criminal among the clan that is increasingly tribal, that is the Westerners. Are we in an Africa that is really decolonized or in the process of recolonization?"

There was itching, real gnashing of teeth, hives, even a kind of hectic fever in Landerneau. A jubilant Greenough sent this complete philippic with extracts of other newspapers to the United Kingdom, Ireland, and the United States. Taking advantage of his old friendship with the still desirable chief supervisor of the central hospital, he contacted his kid and they talked in Kinokoroni; for the first time, Ségué n'Di realized that his "Irish pachyderm daddy" did not have an accent when speaking this language. A leak from the police force, sent from a telephone booth, had informed the journalist that the victim's lines and that of Mrs. Keurléonan-Moricet were "tapped." He was annoyed, complaining while rubbing his hands: "Colonized and under the yoke of others. Ireland was not afraid of the old Dowager! By the late Gordon and the delectable Jew Hannah, it is not in Africa that I would be afraid of finding out the truth!"

Ségué n'Di evoked his remarks at the staff meeting during the international delegation's mission, quoted his "mainly French sources recognized by the representative of the regional office." After the rapid allusions to his success, to the sympathies, because of his work, perhaps also because of his "very modest, not to say unimpressive origins, that Mrs. Keurléonan-Moricet has for me and that some might hardly relate to," he went more into detail and stated: "Born poor, a qualified employee driven back to unemployment by necessity, then newspaper seller before my success in a competition that assures me a certainly enviable status, I owe nothing to anyone. I had never sought assistance from an African, or a Westerner. I never asked for strings to be pulled for me. Why then did someone want to wipe me off the face of the earth? Who had premeditated or financed my assassination? Why does the anticriminal squad that has refused to search my home in my absence insist on running around me and even insinuating incongruous ulterior motives about my employer? If the methods of this squad concerned the professional ethics of its profession, to me, a simple citizen, they are wretched. I will not ask these men to be gentlemen: they have neither the nature for it nor the standing. But up till now, as I am talking to you, what have they tried to find out in the Western fraternity, posh or not? Nothing. It is a Black that a white man had tried to kill off; it is in the Black's house that the anticriminal squad, in the course of its investigations, wants to find the reasons for this attempted assassination. It is due to lack of competence, unless talent consists of bugging the victim and his superiors in Tigony. Why not those from Europe or Japan as well? It would be more complete, wouldn't it? To you who have human experience in life, I say this again because, really, I do not understand why this man who can't be found targeted me. During the shooting exercises in the military service, we were advised to aim well to hit the crack. The assassin who had a pistol missed his prey. Should I express my longsuffering—I am looking for the right word in French—yes, my forbearance? He lacked self-control in wanting to get at my head, also audacity in taking flight; this is hardly courageous. I do not own any arms and can only say from the bottom of my heart that 'the gods of the whole of Africa will be right about this Westerner who accords little importance to the life of a human being, even of a Black of my hackneyed human condition who is still in his hands.' And then, one never knows, since he did not achieve his first goal, he will turn on Mrs. Keurléonan-Moricet herself with whom I was talking when he shot me. Oh no, my God! Not her! Her life is more important than mine.

"Daddy, I want you to find this Westerner sooner or later and publicly reveal the motive for which he wanted to eliminate me. It is necessary because—you know it better than me—there are the Westerners in this country who practice corruption on a large scale; they rule and "remunerate" Africans who help them to create social and cultural poverty through the sapping of the economy. Our peasants also know who carry out ceremonies in order for the gods to rid our country of this bunch. Is it, for example, because I would have refused to cooperate with these illicit traffics that I was attacked?

"At the point where I am and because I am still alive, I want to shout out loud, so that they can also make an attempt on my life: Africans are partners in crime with the Westerners; they are mostly from poor families and had nothing to live on apart from the poor wages that hardly go beyond the end of the month, let alone the trimester. All of a sudden politics have put them at the forefront of the state. The consequences? Misuse of public money, abuse of all kinds that bewilder a youthful generation, eager for independence and freedom, but on whom unemployment lays a kind of granite barrier. Such is the nature of people between twenty and thirty years, which I was part of when I was still selling newspapers."

Greenough banged his fist on the table and shouted bravo, then stated that he had "recorded every word, following the example of the phone-tapping service that is doing its business of collecting the maximum information. In this case, they are like hayseeds. The *Daily Encounter* will publish my entire recording; the foreign news agencies represented in Wanakawa will receive the transcript."

■ ■ ■

Other newspapers reprinted the text the day after its publication. Bubbling with joy, Dorcas did not know how to take it without attracting the employees' attention. At the end of her rope, she retreated into her office as was her habit when she prepared a confidential dossier and uncorked a quarter of a bottle of branded champagne. As she was enjoying a glass, the telephone rang.

"My feelings? Very good: Mr. Niriokiriko Aplika is caustic, but also courageous and of a pugnacity that is difficult to discern in him."

"The people from his tribe are like that. One does not gain anything from attacking them, and when they are sure of being right, they do not shrink back before any authority."

"Those of us who are not from here would have to learn to know and appreciate the differences."

"Oh! You add sensitivity to intelligence in talking like this . . ."

"Did you know that the squad wanted to question me during my visit?"

"Really? I now understand the kid's allusions. I don't ignore the importance of and need for security in a country where millions of Africans, and some Westerners, who, alas! are not legion, struggle for the arrival of democracy. But these gentlemen of the anticriminal squad should not be spared when they operate like partners in crime in their official capacities. I am delighted that my kid has expressed himself with a force, courage, and clarity worthy of his personality. I've known him for fifteen years."

"I very much loved the article signed Nariniki Iya . . ."

"Good heavens! Goody! I will pass on your appreciation; it will please him a lot," he said, then burst out and inquired: "What does your dear and lucky husband think of all this?"

"The duty of confidentiality requires . . . exactly some degree of discretion; but I know that the situation created by this attempted murder within the framework of my professional activities worry him a lot."

▪ ▪ ▪

"Your nigger doesn't lack skill, confidence, or perfidious tricks. And such intelligence woven with arrogance, aggressiveness, and cynicism. Well done!"

"Should I pass on so much praise to him?"

"Come off it! The herring barrel already feels the kipper."

"Ah? So, why not? No woman, even yours, can soak you in her smell."

They walked to and fro in the courtyard of the residence when, starting to get excited, he stated bluntly, "The press that gives so much importance to this issue should be censored; the person who does not have enough guts to lie low behind Nariniki Iya is a scumbag. The courage in pseudonym takes it out on the Whites; what would this country be, what would the whole of Africa be, supposedly independent, without the Whites? Even now that pickaninnies sleep with our women who throw themselves into their sensuality and debaucheries to the point of causing divorces, the white men are still the evildoers, stopping the bloody 'Negritude' from remaining standing, and worthy of what? How we would be happy at home, if these people could take care of their development at all costs!"

She had taken the decision not to stir up the flame any longer and let him taste the distilled venom of his increasingly sleepless nights, just like his home distiller grandfather. But when, after his remark against independent Africa, silence descended on both of them like a blade and, to fill the gaps in the conversation, she said that Greenough seemed to know Nariniki Iya, Gaëtan cursed the journalist as an "idiot, a bastard running after nigger women!"

"Idiot! Is anger or hatred not making you a man of extremes? Bastard? Have you forgotten it? His father was an artist, a great tenor, and I read in an old *Who's Who* unequivocal praises about him; how can a journalist of his caliber lag behind anyone?"

"He is a will-o'-the-wisp! He can only move from one thing to another rapidly, with no character; mixture of a Jewess and an Irishman, he has run away from the problems of either country for those of niggers. Mr. James I-don't-know-what Greenough is more nigger than the niggers; false anticolonialist, uprooted, a nobody anywhere, a contemptible kind."

She heaved a long sigh, said something was going on inside him that completely escaped her. He burst into laughter.

"It is physiologically clear, quite normal: we live together but you have already turned a corner and can understand nothing anymore; you have tasted the nigger!" Despite its force, the blow only rebounded off her and a weak smile hovered at the tip of her lips.

"Are you becoming racist or is it a revelation?"

"Without hesitating, I am confronted by the ambiguity of such a question that's characteristic of your nature; so I say: why not?"

"Strange . . ."

"That is to say? Be plain. I am the reptilian, the tortuous . . ."

"I repeat it in all honesty: no matter what happens, I would like you and me to be human beings capable of seeing each other again, of shaking hands, even kissing each other again; you turn red as a poppy at the slightest word I say to you."

"Shouldn't I have reasons for doing so?"

"We both have everything, and I will be crystal clear: the sediments of racism slip out of your remarks, like a man all eaten up, confronted with an unbearable situation that you never thought would happen. I understand your psychology of someone in a bind, but to talk of Africans with so much contempt, hatred, and racism, whereas you don't spurn sleeping with one or more black women?"

"Where's the problem?"

"Phew! Thanks for confessing."

"Confessing what?"

"Gaëtan, I've been clear; you are sleeping with Myriam Haïlé-Haïkouni and other women, White or Black. It is what you have just admitted."

"You have your . . ."

"I didn't deny it when you had asked me the question without beating about the bush. I'll make you another confession: if I weren't anxious that nothing should leak out which might harm you, nothing but you—because you are terribly vulnerable—I would not make a secret of my relationship with Ségué n'Di. I'll add quite clearly: it is not pity that made me act—you do not need it—but the past, the memories, a companionship, a friendship, and then, love and so on. These are sediments, layers, stratifications that I do not hesitate to qualify as geological, even in human beings."

CHAPTER 38

SHE KISSED HIM ON THE CHEEKS AND WAS WALKING AWAY WHEN HE CAUGHT up with her, grabbing her by the waist.

"I would like us to dine with Myriam."

"Great, good idea!"

She dismissed Malifiki who was about to prepare the meal. She saw that he was sad and explained that they were dining in town, smiled, and went into the bathroom. An hour later, the iron gate opened and the Honda came out at the unhurried speed of their brighter days as a couple. She braked before The Kilimanjaro restaurant when Myriam's Rover stopped. The driver asked when he should come back; she showed him her ringed index finger and he left, hailing a taxi that was passing by.

It was one of the poshest restaurants facing the marina, at about ten kilometers from the center of the city. Wooden paneling, rich oriental carpets on white marble floor, brass chandeliers, and luxuriant green plants: a private open-air alcove had been reserved for them. It was a simple dinner, convivial, sprinkled with subtle jokes, understatements, in which one understood a quarter of the ideas while replying with a burst of laughter, with a vague wave of the hand, or with rapid movements of the fingers.

They left toward 1:30 p.m. When entering her car in which the driver held the door open, Myriam made a mild allusion to Nariniki Iya's article.

"Brilliant! Very courageous! And what a style!" Dorcas said.

"I hope you, too, didn't like these filthy reflections . . . or did you?"

"Friends, do me the favor of continuing the argument at the house," Myriam said, and her car pulled away.

▪ ▪ ▪

Green plants that looked like trees grew behind the wrought iron gate; five hectares of timber wood, fruit trees, of flowered shrubs and rock gardens. The croaking of frogs rose from a distant marshland deep in the heart of the property; softened light danced on the leaves of the trees. Myriam touched the chain bracelet on her right wrist. At the command of the inlaid processor in the bracelet, the high steel gate opened at the same time as the solid carved mahogany door that it protected.

A large hallway with old pink granite floor; on the walls of the living room, paintings from African artists but also authentic ones obtained in Europe, the U.S., and Latin America; rugs from Iran, Turkey, and Morocco covered the floor in a deliberate disorder. Amused and delighted, Dorcas admired what Gaëtan would have called messy; on a wall, separated by paintings, hung photographs, charcoal portraits of Myriam's parents, grandparents, her daughter and son, herself graduating from Oxford, Myriam in a female Dahomean African dress in a photograph signed by Franck Kidjo, Myriam as a student on a tennis court in Los Angeles.

Gaëtan had never been here before, so he looked around everywhere, going from one place to the other. Surprised, Dorcas watched him out of the corner of her eye. In the years since they had met, although they sometimes stayed a whole quarter of a year without seeing each other or calling each other, Myriam preferred to meet him in her second home, in Nirignigy, a villa in the mountains, some fifty kilometers north of Tigony. He was stupefied by the discovery of her home in the city. There was carved Iroko wooden furniture "from the country of the Amazons," she indicated. Dorcas stroked some with emotion. A sculpture of one meter fifty centimeters was like a guard standing in a corner like the guardian in ancient times; a naked man, the serene owner of a powerful penis at rest—one caught sight of his plump equipment at first glance, with the turgescence the artist had wanted to show. Admiring pictures and portraits, Dorcas was covered with goose bumps when she came face to face with this "really beautiful work."

Going to put a vintage champagne bottle in the cooler, Myriam explained that "this superb gentleman, a unique piece, is from Dahomey, now Republic of Benin, the country of my ex, the father of my daughter."

"I instinctively suspected its origin. I was born in Ouidah," Dorcas said.

"Wait!" Myriam exclaimed, hastening to cool the bottle. "I am listening to you . . ."

"I wanted to talk about my African birthplace during the dinner at the residence, but Mr. Greenough spoke of his father. It was really so captivating that I forgot to complete my sentence."

"So, you are Dahomean or Beninois! This is rather marvelous isn't it?"

"No, no! French, of French stock and not Dahomean, Beninois, or whatever!" Gaëtan responded.

Myriam burst into laughter.

"Why this protest? Are you hostile to Dahomey?"

"One cannot be of European, French stock and claim elsewhere!"

"Ethiopian born to Jewish parents, Tigony is my birthplace; my ex-husband is Dahomean. It is a beautiful country in all its diversity. Without exception, those who knew me still regard me as their fellow citizen. Marthe-Esther, my daughter, was born in Kandi. I feel very much at home when I go to the country."

"All the same, Myriam . . ."

"I am happy to hear you talk like this."

"Well, my dear fellow citizen, we can be on familiar terms. From now on, I am Myriam for you as well; for me, you are Dorcas."

They stared at each other, happy, burst into laughter, and fell into each other's arms.

"I was saying that my father was head doctor at Ouidah and my mother, midwife; three of their five children were born at Ouidah, which the natives prefer to call Gléxwé. I am going to tell you an anecdote that I got from my parents: At my birth, one of the nurses said that I was Sika or Adjouavi because it was Monday. The day when the umbilical cord was removed, the African midwife, a good friend of mother, had gotten the authorization from my parents not to throw it away but to bury it in a corner of the hospital. My parents laughed, but were not opposed to such a wish."

"You have never told me a word! What does this mean, that lucky charm?"

"It means that her roots are in this country: we did the same ceremony for my daughter in Port Novo, her father's native city where the elders of his family buried the umbilical cord."

"That is it: although I am French with a Marnais father and a Languedocian mother, I have a very strong attachment to my birthplace. You had not wanted to go there when the children had said: 'Huh! You Beninois, what about spending a part of the holidays in your country?' I took them there; we visited Banamè, the territory of remarkable craftsmen-sculptors who manufacture pieces of furniture; then to Toffo, the village of freshness and charm. Our children did not forget such a visit."

"It is fantastic! What a cultural richness! You learned Fon, Nago, Yoruba, and Mina?"

"Some words here and there in the languages, but Fon is not easy. I was also able to learn quite a number of Yoruba words in the regional school at Ouidah; nothing much was said that I did not understand. Catechism in the religious places, I learned how to pray in Fon. As for my parents, they sometimes spoke Fon with the patients."

"What an experience! You should learn Kinokoroni; it is flexible but easier than Fon, which I understand. It is rather in Yoruba that I can express myself pretty well. Ah, there we are White and Black sisters! Hey! Our friend Gaëtan here who feels isolated—you know, Negritude is not only for the Negro! Anyway, who in Cythera worries about White or Black, when Cypris imposes the rule of the game?"

"Let me go and get the champagne, you are temporarily master of the house!" she said with a burst of laughter.

She came back with the bottle and a crystal bowl full of cashew nuts, almonds, roasted peanuts, and pistachios, brought out flutes, and continued.

"Thus, you were born in a country that I adore! Even if one has had a falling out with a man or a woman and is no longer on good terms, one still should not behave like a wild dog with him or her."

"It is a problem of intelligence and flexibility; all depends on the one side as well as the other," Dorcas remarked, and withdrew at once into her shell.

"Exactly! Donatien is a remarkably intelligent man, but I dropped him because he is afraid of life: sensitive, conniving, with the instincts of a skinflint. Then I, a Jewess, but not a drop religious, I had to soar up; you know, like these sparrow hawks that one sometimes sees far off, very far off in the blue sky of this country."

"Independent and free minded. I felt as though—how do I say it? On our first meeting, on the evening of the gala: your personality had given me a shock like from a water hammer."

"Hey! Hey! You are not going to dump me!" Gaëtan said, half in a jest, half seriously.

"These men! I brought the champagne and tutti quanti and invested you master of the house. Good male chauvinism is still common currency, even in the house of our polygamous ministers, so the women work," she said, taking the bottle.

"No, no, let me serve! I was waiting for you to end your speech!"

"Well done!"

"Well, you have found a friend!" Gaëtan said, uncorking the champagne.

"And what a friend! The Entente Cordiale on board, I am sure."

"Does the dear secretary general of the ICM doubt that two women like us would understand each other?"

"God forbid! By the way, Myriam, I did not know that you are Jewish too."

"Why too?"

"Er—I know there are many in the country, without ever thinking of you."

"Well! It is a fact. With us Blacks, the Semitic features are not as pronounced as those of some of our brothers and sisters in Israel or the Whites; notwithstanding, I will never deny my Negritude, or my Jewishtude," she declared, then turning toward Dorcas, hands semi-stretched as if she was bringing or receiving an offering, she began reciting the verses of a poem in Hebrew:

> "Thy lips . . . drop as the honeycomb;
> and the smell of thy garment is like the smell of Lebanon
> The mandrakes give a smell, and at our gates are all manner of pleasant fruits,
> new and old, which I have laid up for thee."

"Or this:

> "I am my beloved's,
> and his desire is toward me.

Come, my beloved, let us go forth into the field;
let us lodge in the villages.
Let us get up early to the vineyard;
let us see if the vines flourish,
whether the tender grapes appear,
and the pomegranates bud forth:
there will I give thee my love."

Gaëtan applauded keenly. Dorcas devoured her with her eyes as she recited the poems whose sensuality and beauty touched her, without understanding a single word. She was still surprised as she stood up, embraced her, holding her close to her heart.

"Dazzlingly beautiful! It is a gift that I will never forget. And what diction! Who is this from?"

Gaëtan also embraced her and asked for the author of the poem.

"Song of Songs, the most beautiful love song in the world. Jewish or not, whoever wants to broaden or deepen her culture should know certain things about world culture. I began to learn Hebrew at the age of six. I boiled with fascination when I discovered some love texts or religious adoration in my adolescence:

> "If our mouth were filled with song like the sea, our song of praise the number of its waves, our lips of praises like the vastness of the firmament, our eyes lit like the sun and the moon, our hands extended like the eagle of the skies, and our feet lighter than those of the gazelle, we would not suffer.
>
> "Lord our God and God of my Fathers, praise be unto you and the benediction of Your name, for only one of the innumerable kindnesses, miracles, and wonders that you have gratified us with, us and our Fathers in the past."

"I would like to know this book. I will read it; I am going to buy it," Dorcas said, impassioned.

"It is unbelievable! I did not know that you read Hebrew and could speak it."

"But it is also my language! It would be sadly frustrating that I only speak English, French, German, Spanish, Arab, and Russian, my working languages. I live and feel Africa, I am a jubilant Hebrew; I am not Jewish by diet: it is in my blood and my breath."

"Neither Dorcas nor I understood a word of this poem, but what sensitivity! And an emotional burden; there is less sensuality and sensual pleasure in it than in the Song of Songs."

"Good analysis! Haggadah, a religious force, is certainly different from the Song of Songs."

"I know the long passages of the Song of Songs by heart but after having listened to you . . ."

"But no, no!"

"Sensitivity, sensual burden, voluptuousness, all are there; it is exactly what, coming from you, seeps into me. It was as if I was porous at each scansion."

"This great poem is untranslatable; without exaggeration or denigration, none of the translations that I have read—and I have devoured them!—has managed to extract the essence or reproduce the unrelenting beauty of these songs. You must restore the force of its thoughts, when you want to show how they were apprehended and how the events were seen. Cheers!" she said, raising her glass.

"To Friendship!" Gaëtan said, raising his own to toast.

"To Friendship and Fraternity in Africa," Dorcas added.

CHAPTER 39

"I ALMOST FORGOT, GAËTAN—PROBABLY BECAUSE OF THE HEBREW AND MY Franco-Dahomean sister—why don't you like the article of . . ."

"Verbiage and aggressiveness, as well as hatred with the repertoire of the logorrhea of incompetents who pretend to want to raise the standard of living of the African continent. As a matter of fact, they do not build anything! You know it better than me, but listen, Myriam: sincerely, objectively, how many Africans in Europe, after having been bawled out by that bizarre nutcase hiding behind some kind of pseudonym . . ."

"Nariniki Iya," Myriam said, smiling.

"That is it. After their vomiting on the Whites, they only think, in Africa and on the field, of filling their pockets as soon as they arrive on the thresholds of political power, administrative or industrial?" he declared, red and out of breath. Eyes lowered, fingers intertwined, Dorcas seemed to meditate, while Myriam smiled.

"It is funny to be in such a state. I didn't know about your sanguine nature, but what I have just heard radically contrasts with the working sessions where, relatively poised, you metamorphose into a large piece of granite when you want to shatter this or that project. I do not disapprove on the whole of your analysis, but judging from the manner in which you treat Africans, notably the likes of Nariniki Iya, you would send this courageous Ségué n'Di Niriokiriko Aplika, whom a white man wanted to assassinate, to the guillotine."

At these words, Dorcas, who controlled the uneasiness that she felt, paled.

"That one would have been better off not born!" Gaëtan cried.

"How can you think this way, of a young man who came very close to death for motives we still don't know?" Dorcas exclaimed.

"Your reactions are symptomatic and rather telling," Myriam said calmly.

"What of?"

"Of a mindset, a certain conception of independent Africa; also of ethics. I want to go further and say that it is about a syndrome: the poor, citizens of very average means, the well-to-do, or rich ones like me who have all, including this property before taking on my responsibilities, we think with a determination that will surprise in spite of our errors, even our faults that the press and the people denounce more and more, that we will succeed in raising unassailable barriers against neocolonialism and criminal exploitation of Africans by a clique of Westerners. As for the African partners in crime, they will pay dearly."

"Well done, Myriam, for expressing yourself so clearly!" Dorcas was jubilant.

While continuing to develop her ideas as in her quarterly course in political economics at the university, Myriam's middle finger, on which she wore an engraved gold signet ring, touched a button concealed in the wall, and the hidden fastener, difficult to distinguish, opened, and a hi-fi system came out. She took a cassette, slotted it into the deck, hesitated briefly, and started it. The voice of a woman was heard expressing herself in refined English as follows:

> Would this be a lure for the independence of a country with considerable general human resources, with misused technological as well as academic skills, to which the considerable wealth of a subsoil with economic potential like oil, diamond, gold, etc., that attract investors of nearly all the developed supposedly civilized countries? Until when in such a country, will a criminal white man who had shot a young African, without one knowing why, remain a ghost, while the anticriminal squad that one would believe bribed by Western Lobbyists who are much protected by the government, and which I do not hesitate to accuse of assassination complicity, subjects the victim to investigations as unacceptable as they are abjectly absurd?
>
> "It should be said forcefully: the protected Westerners who behave like this

must be hunted down. It is necessary that the law make this bunch dance the dance of Saint Vitus as it possessed their ancestors under Charles VI, but there will be no exorcist priests for them in Wanakawa. Yes, this country . . ."

Head lowered, hands joined in front of her mouth, Dorcas controlled herself in order not to burst into tears. Gaëtan's skin color was like cloth washed, wrung in haste. Since the first words, they had recognized Myriam's voice and diction, and it ruled the room like a silence of mourners. The article signed Nariniki Iya was there with the details of her chosen expressions, style, and violence without concession.

"I beg you to accept my apologies."

"It is funny how you can be mistaken about even those whom you are sure to know. It doesn't matter, but it is important to discover that your acrimonious judgments are held in common with a number of Westerners. They are idiosyncratic to your people who, living in Africa, do not accept that the Africans are masters on their ancestors' land. Some among you harbor an underground racism, which emerges, in spite of themselves? Anyway, circumstances sometimes expose them, while making it possible for them to be unearthed.

"I am going to be quite clear, loyal, and sincere with you; Dorcas is the only witness. Except for some restrictions, also insignificant as far as I am concerned, your views and judgements of Nariniki Iya, alias Myriam Haïlé-Haïkouni, do not affect our friendship. Meanwhile, I am not going to hide from you that your charge against this courageous Ségué n'Di Niriokiriko Aplika, whose view of an African mining company impressed me a lot, even captivated me before his statement appeared in the *Daily Encounter*, it is more than unspeakable and unworthy of a man of your intelligence."

Gaëtan closed his eyes; head bent, highlighted by the collar of his fine blue striped shirt, his neck had reddened; ruddy-faced, mouth half-open in stupor, looking crestfallen, he seemed to hesitate about straightening his head.

"This document is of an extremely rare courage. I have cut out the text in French as well as in English, and it is already filed away. You are not afraid of getting into trouble, if . . ."

Myriam burst into laughter and took hold of her shoulders: "My sister, I will offer you a gift of a copy of the original text; it is on my computer. As for my hypothetical problems in this country . . ."

"You do not think much of the Security Branch of the Police Force?" Gaëtan said, in a very quiet voice.

"The power of the SBPF is all the more strictly limited because it is mainly managed by international civil servants from Europe; listen, the president immediately suspected . . ."

"Really!" Gaëtan exclaimed, alarmed.

"You are a strange chap," Myriam said as she continued: "yes, the president recognized the style, structure, rhythm of phrases and called me into his office, after the meeting with the ministers that I take part in almost regularly."

"You are sure that sooner or later there will not be repercussions?" Dorcas asked her.

"Seated across from each other, he said to me: 'Myri my dear, this article is terrible.'

"'Really, Hali?'

"'What do you think of it?'

"'Sound reactions that seemed right to me not to keep silent.'

"'Why did you do that? You did not even spare your old brother Hali.'

"'Listen Hali: there are more and more dirty Western screwups in our country where you have been in power since independence. I had campaigned and made Jews vote nearly unanimously for you. You offered me a post in the Ministry of Economics, Finance, and Budget; I did not accept it because, irrevocably, I prize my freedom as a free woman, as you know, but I repeat to you. As for the article, the keen onomastics linguist had to realize that the text in Kinokoroni is more frank and direct than those in foreign languages. I could have signed them with my actual name. I gave it up, sincerely, Hali, out of friendship with you, for you alone. It is not because the West takes part in the socioeconomic development of our country that one of its nationals, whoever he is, can think that anything goes, to the point of wanting to assassinate a child of Wanakawa in his own country and remain at large, while gallivanting with his victim's sisters. Have you read the Kai Narikiyingy Report? There are seventeen thousand mulattos—including mine in this country—carrying their mother's name; for 99 percent of the cases, women legally married to these men had been cuckolded.'"

"What was his reaction when you admitted to being the author of the article?"

"You are funny! What would you have liked him to do?"

"Are you untouchable?"

"A sacred cow? No. But as long as I did not commit a punishable crime, attacking me is, deliberately, wanting to provoke not only a simple coup d'état, but spark off a bloody riot. Whoever loves this country and would want to live there should, first of all, get to know our habits, our geological constitution, and our morals. Women like me, there are, without exaggerating, two to three thousand in a population of nineteen million. Listen to me, Dorcas, you also Gaëtan: as a free woman, I prize my freedom and I have given myself solid means to live out this freedom."

"It is an invaluable asset; it is one of your strengths!"

"You see, Dorcas, we are on my property. It had been there well before independence, just as my second home. There is no secret service or squad that will say that I have taken or take kickbacks; from whom then?" She was amazed and burst into laughter before continuing: "I respect the president, my old friend, and I know how to make myself respected. I had said before the general strike, the dismissals that involved the 'suicide-assassination' that had been highly denounced, and whose authors, mercenaries, are now imprisoned, their overall bank accounts frozen, if I were a president, I would never elect a man whose personal wealth was unknown, be he of poor origins or with assets. On the other hand, all ministers, including the president, if there was any, would be subjected to a tight control, certainly discrete, of his way of life, his acquisitions during his term, and the eventual kickbacks, solicited or offered voluntarily by some bribers."

"His response?" Dorcas said.

"He shrugged his shoulders and called me a moneybags' daughter."

CHAPTER 40

THE VIRULENCE OF THE PRESS'S ATTACKS AGAINST THE ANTICRIMINAL SQUAD, its methods, the police as a whole, and the government gave the investigation another direction. Ségué n'Di seemed to be officially neglected, but the security branch of the police force continued to listen in on Dorcas's telephone conversations just as it turned its sights on the "Western community" and those who had criticized the victim's views concerning the creation of an African mining company. Astonished, exasperated, some threatened to "leave the country," others to "take refuge in a sabbatical year to look for a place to crash in Africa."

An article in *L'Afrique actuelle* and another in the *Daily Encounter* stated the existence of a gigantic spider web in the process of reaching the groups that the investigations until now had not been interested in. Going further, one daily newspaper or another explained, word for word, as if they owed their information to a dispatch agency: "Whoever would get trapped in it would not be spared, no matter how powerful the protections of which he is beneficiary. It would not be in the attacker's interest to try to repeat it even by changing target." Slumped in an armchair, Gaëtan was as white as a corpse as he read the article. He sat up and gave Dorcas buried in the same newspaper a worried glance; she came close to him, fitted her fingers between his, and squeezed them without saying a word. When she left for the office where the preparations for her trip sped up, he telephoned her and simply said, "You know, Dor, I love you. I will always love you."

"Hugs, Yvan," she said, and then tackled the dossier for her journey.

The secretaries did not hide from her their pleasure of having been in touch with Ségué n'Di.

"The surveillance is loosening its noose; how is he faring?"

"Pretty good, pretty good, madam."

"He said that his head is bandaged, and that it makes him look like an old Muslim," Runiki said.

"He also said that he sometimes feels like laughing when he sees himself in the mirror, but it hurts him."

"He has not lost his sense of humor, and it is a good sign. He said that if he were a Muslim and did not have enough means to go to Mecca, well, the assassin would have provided it, by giving him at least a turban."

Dorcas laughed heartily with them.

"It is indeed a good sign that he is in such a good mood; I will see him as soon as I can."

"Oh, madam, there is a fax from Harare; it is for him, and it is from Mr. Madjita Minoucodjoyingy. Mr. Niriokiriko Aplika said that he would go and spend two days with him, because of a ceremony for his n'Ata, that means his grandfather," Morika said.

"These things greatly surprise Westerners, but in Africa there are always ceremonies: deceased, mourning, gods, church services, and this and that, even when one does not have money. It kills you, but what can I say? These are our customs and traditions," Anikili, who had had to spend half of her salary the previous month to deal with this type of problem, intervened.

"I know a bit; I heard of it in my adolescence, in Dahomey where I was born."

"What? You, the director of the regional office, you were born in Dahomey?" Samilika exclaimed wide-eyed.

"It is neither obvious nor a novelty, but it is no less true."

"But you are African! Great!"

"Oh!" Dorcas said, patting her face and her arms with her fingers.

"Your skin color? Hey! It is the heart, people's feelings, their reactions to problems and African affairs that count," Anikili said.

"OK, I am going to leave written instructions, but I will call each time I need your help."

"Wow, as sexy as we are, it would be wonderful if someone—why not me?—could be called to take care of your documents," Samilika said, and everyone burst into laughter.

▪ ▪ ▪

He was reading *Géographie humaine* while waiting for his meal when she arrived. He saw her, joy broke out on his face, and he almost stood up, threw himself at her neck, and hugged her. She guessed his feelings, even his repressed impulse. Smiling, she stretched an imploring hand toward him and he put his own in it, and they squeezed each other's hand as they looked at each other without saying a word.

"*La Ragazza di Bube* is beautiful! If I had the means, I would visit the places described and travel round Tuscany."

"I know a bit of the Toscana. I am pleased that you have felt the beauty of things and places seen by Carlo Cassola."

"It is dazzling when a writer makes you feel like knowing the places and the things that he has described, to also meet some of the characters and talk with them, even when they are imaginary, and then, what a delight! What character strength in this novel!"

Strangely in love, Dorcas listened to him, surprised to feel like this with a young man thirteen years her junior. She felt a wave of energy, and she was about to give in, to let herself go to embrace him, but she controlled herself. Happy to be in such a state because of him, a fresh smile quivered on her face with large open eyes.

"I heard that you are going to take part in a ceremony for your grandfather," she said, giving him Madjita's message.

"It is correct," he replied, reading the letter on which he commented: "nice, this Madji; pity that he had to leave Wanakawa for Zimbabwe, but I am sure that he will come back."

"Your colleagues are happy to have talked to you."

"It is quite comforting and feels like family, but because of my face-lift, it is hardly easy to burst into laughter while listening to them."

There was a knock on the door; a nurse gave him a letter in an open envelope. Reverend Father Honokinirifu, "met in the crowd during the courageous strike," had remembered him; he affirmed his "fraternal affection" to him and thought a lot about him in "his prayers to the Almighty Father."

While seeing her off, he asked in the corridors if they were going to see each other again before her departure.

"This evening; at the latest by tomorrow," she murmured, shook his hand, and left

CHAPTER 41

The Gospel According to Saint Matthew was featuring in the Pic Uhuru cinema and she had invited them there.

"A wonderful film, I already watched it three times without tiring of it. Yesterday, my boyfriend took me to see *The Bicycle Thief*; splendid!"

"You should introduce your new boyfriend to us," Gaëtan joked.

"New? I have him permanently; it is Abner-Ron!"

"What a handsome boy! He looks like you; he takes after his father from a certain point of view."

"Your observation is quite relevant, Dorcas!"

"He will break many hearts: such a male beauty does not go unnoticed."

"Oh, my sister, he is mixed-race; some are ugly, but when these types of human beings want to be beautiful, what does our silent Breton think of it?"

"Me, I sometimes find mixtures acceptable. I will not go so far as to look for them willingly."

"This man seems to me to me to be getting weirder. Dorcas, what have you been giving him to eat that does not go well with him?" Myriam asked, intrigued; she then added, "You know, Gaëtan, whose ancestors have crossed Africa, leaving anonymous offspring there, when a white or black man makes love to a woman with a pigmentation different from his, the result, if any, is inevitably mixed-blood. I think I said it, unless you did not listen to me: they are a legion in Wanakawa. My son is one of them, with this precision that it is me, not James, who wanted to give him my family name, since we had mutually decided to have a child. The voluntary cases that carry the parent's patrimonial name are extremely rare in this country. Listen carefully to this which you might not find funny: a man is in an overwhelming minority when a woman whom he makes love to, even his wife, does not want to have a child with him, unless she is of the last vintage; we have women here who desire one or two children from a man who is already married, often a White one; 'the legal wife' is cuckolded, but the couple's honor remains safe. The Westerners who sleep with loads of African women per week, do they know how many mixed-races they breed, only in Tigony? We must pray to God that AIDs does not reach our prostitutes as well; on the contrary, it would be a slaughter at Landerneau," she finished eyeing Gaëtan.

"All the better that officially there are none yet among the prostitutes in the country, but it seems that those from Ghana and Nigeria are infiltrating the corporation. In France, one of my best friends, mother of three children, died of AIDS transmitted to her by her husband; he confessed it to her before her death. He followed her two years later, hated by their children who harped on how he killed mummy."

"That is terrible."

"They sometimes spend their holidays with us," Gaëtan said.

"Ours ought to get to know each other as well, when Dorothy and Yvan junior, more precisely Charles-Yvan, come back to Tigony."

▪ ▪ ▪

Italian films featured in several rooms in the Pic Uhuru; coming out of *The Gospel According to Saint Matthew* Dorcas saw that *La Strada* was showing in Monomotapa and said that she would not mind seeing the original version; Myriam had watched it again last weekend with Ron and James at Nirignigy.

When Dorcas said that she wanted them to go and watch the film, Gaëtan pleaded a working dinner with colleagues, kissed her on the lips, walked away quickly, and started off in his car.

Despite appearances since the strike, Malifíki had the feeling that the couple's gears had lost something of its harmonious movements; but such awareness was not part of his duties, which were more along the lines of suggesting menus while avoiding unnecessary expenses. He was courteous and considerate toward Madam who inquired after his family, the children's education, what they were going to do later, even proposing that he should not hesitate to get back to her if she could intervene to get scholarships for one child or the other in school.

The dinner prepared, the place set, the kitchen and the laundry room where the washing machines had been installed were tidied up. When he saw Keurléonan's car leave, he inquired if he was coming back for dinner.

"No, I will also come back late from the cinema. I will make do with sandwiches, which I will make myself."

She dismissed the butler. The thought of some breast and back strokes in the pool came to her mind, but she dropped it, put on the hi-fi, lowered the volume, put on Miles Davis, and went to change her clothes. Dressed in jeans and a wine-colored blouse, her body swayed to the sound of the music. At the end of the CD, she chose *A German Requiem*; Brahms always moved her. Although infinitely relaxed, she suddenly felt as if a stranger wearing a false toga took her hand, and together they moved slowly as if toward an altar. She sighed, started buttering whole meal slices of bread, garnished them with salmon or smoked barracuda, and wrapped them in aluminum foil with a hand towel, before putting them in her overnight bag.

The requiem made her spirit drift. She entered the garage, opened the car, but changed her mind: the cinema was hardly far. She took three cassettes at random and took a look at the titles; the first was that German requiem playing in the hi-fi system. "My God," she murmured, put the cassette in the Walkman, and left listening to it.

The Monomotapa was a four-story house built with local granite with eight spacious projection rooms. Property of a private African company with many local shareholders, it towered over the left bank of the river, leaning back on the southeastern edge of the eucalyptus forest.

Dorcas walked without haste. Womack and Womack came after Brahms, and she snapped her fingers softly. One of those taxis in which four or six people squeezed together passed by when she got to the paved alley before the entrance of the cinema. It was a VW Beetle in which there was only the driver; she made a sign, the car beeped and stopped, and she got in, telling him where she was going.

"The road is steep and precipitous, sometimes even dangerous to get up there."

"Really? I am not going up there; in fact someone will come to meet me."

She got out of the taxi two hundred meters from the rise, paid, and the taxi, all lights on, reversed down the hill.

She arrived at the foot of the village, circumvented it, and knocked gently on the window, which opened. He saw her, smiled, took her hand, caressed it, came out to greet her, and they crossed the empty courtyard. The door of the hut closed behind them. Dorcas put her arms around him and drew him emotionally to her, her heart beat wildly against his, while he caressed her, rubbing her spine, and she relaxed. The bandage on his head gave her more troubling thoughts than at the hospital. Conscious of her concerns, Ségué n'Di assured her that he was feeling much better.

"There is nothing more for you to be afraid of, promise?"

She nodded in agreement several times. Seated on the bed, arm in arm; they peered at each other, smiling. She brought out the sandwiches and offered them to him; he helped himself, thanked her, and they dined with sorghum beer before making love to each other, happy to be together. She confirmed her departure for Europe the day after tomorrow and told him that a meeting of the international mining committee of Mount Franakiniriyo would be held at the temporary headquarters of the consortium in Geneva; Japan was part of her journey, but exhausted, traumatized, she preferred that the characteristics as well as the facts of the case were clearer, that the company be better structured, better organized, taking into account the wishes of the African partners, natives of Wanakawa.

"You started it like a joke or a provocation that would be of no consequence, but lo and behold, it has followers."

"No kidding!" He was surprised, smiling with his eyes.

"Hold on tight: the most important, even passionate, is Mrs. Haïlé-Haïkouni."

"Beg your pardon?"

"You heard me very well."

"Mrs. Myriam Haïlé-Haïkouni? You have hit the bigger jackpot, if you have her on your side. I assure you that the project is saved; with a personality of her scale, the government and its lobbyists will have no choice but to behave well."

"Your opinion spurs me on."

"I do not know her personally—someone like me, know a landed aristocrat?—it would be rather incongruous. Nevertheless, n'Ata, a renowned sculptor, worked for the members of the extended Haïlé-Haïkouni family and told me about it. This woman is a force, someone of considerable influence."

He seemed happy; he looked cheerful at being informed of Myriam's interest in his ideas. He took her hand, asked what she would do after Geneva, if she did not wish to see her children.

"Certainly, I miss them a lot. I will spend a few days in Stuttgart with my Charles-Yvan. I am his first love and, until the contrary is proven, I come before his girlfriends."

Ségué n'Di put his bandaged head between his hands so as not to laugh.

"Sorry! I forgot that you have such difficulties!"

"Don't worry, I am happy to listen to you talk about your children."

"I will then go to Ireland . . ."

"Oh my! According to the media, things are bad there and Daddy Greenough does not hide it; it is his native country."

"I am going to Dublin. Dorothy, our daughter, is studying there; there is no terrorism. But you will take care of yourself? I would not like you to be sad; you will not be, would you?"

"Do not worry: I will be very careful. I am naturally a loner, but less so since we started seeing each other. As for not being sad, that will hardly be easy; I have been deeply sad since my Old Man, to whom I was very much attached, passed away, even beyond the dead: I have the feeling that he died suddenly because of my action, as if I had pushed him there."

She held him against her, said in a very low voice, "I am not going to bare my thoughts to you; you will not believe me . . ."

"I know it or hear it: you want to keep it so as not to make me sad or annoy me; what do you accuse yourself of?"

"For being a bit responsible for everything."

"Well! I say no; if you love me, do not feel guilty. We know who wanted to take me away from you. You are not him, and he is not you. You had loved him."

▪ ▪ ▪

They came down through the forest plunged in darkness where Ségué n'Di, holding her hand, moved forward like someone having good night vision, guiding her without failing. She talked about "that nugget of an uncommon size," of her regrets of not having met his grandfather, and begged him to be prudent because she had told her husband about their affair when he had asked her categorically. They stopped a short way from the exit of the forest because of the bandage round his head, hugged, giving each other affectionate claps on the back. Dorcas patted him on the cheeks and left. He watched her go out of the forest and behind the Monomotapa building. Hardly was she on the pavement when a taxi passed with three passengers. Ségué n'Di saw her raise her hand and the car stopped; one of the passengers moved close to his neighbor as the door opened.

Dorcas entered, waving goodbye to someone that her neighbors, looking back, couldn't see doing the same on the pavement, while he too, among the tall trees exuding the odor of myrtle in the night, continued to wave goodbye until he could no longer see the back lights of the gangly old Peugeot.

It was almost 2:00 a.m.; Gaëtan had not yet come back from his working dinner. She did not have to give accounts of smelling of a man or the forest, but she ran water for a myrtle bath, got in, happy to cry for the pleasure shared. "How happy I am to have discovered him in Tigony!" she murmured. After the bath, she took the *Roman Elegies* again, got engrossed in it with delight until she fell into a deep sleep.

CHAPTER 42

MYRIAM PHONED HER TO FIND OUT THE DAY OF HER DEPARTURE; AS SOON AS she had made an allusion to the creation of an "African or international mining company of Mount Franakiniriyo," Dorcas turned on the recorder of her cordless phone. Myriam explained her point of view, and wished that she would take account of it in her file and in her discussions in Geneva: "You must avoid at all costs the pretense of 51 percent against 49 percent; the ideal position to fight for would be 60 percent of the shares for Africa, the rest for the West, I mean Europe, the U.S., the Middle East, and Asia. With 60 percent Africa, Wanakawa would have the majority. Mount Franakiniriyo's gold mines will not be exported; we will fight to gain the desired majority. Could you come to the ministry, or alone to the house, if you have time? Sister, the question that, without doubt, you already ask yourself is whether my fellow-countrymen have the means of acquiring so many shares. Don't worry; a drastic review of the bank policies in our country is already on the way. Here, like elsewhere in Africa, billions in Western currencies belonging to Africans are in these banks that are plundering and killing the Black continent; these huge sums of money are used, without the least interest in their owners."

"It is scandalous!"

"Those who have large sums of money there are offered 2.75 percent to 3 percent interest, an insult. The majority of my assets are in Switzerland and Liechtenstein; others prefer France or the United Kingdom. Alas! It will be so as long as we do not create a capital market and a stock market. If you think that I could be of use to you, come to see me; I will give you the numbers of my direct line at the ministry and at home. Ciao! Nice girl!"

On cloud nine, Dorcas laughed, suggested going to see her in the office because she was leaving the next day.

"Come right away. We'll go home; it won't take long; you'll go back to your man and your luggage."

▪ ▪ ▪

She saw her coming down the granite marble front steps of the Ministry for Economy, Finance, and Budget. They embraced; she told her to get into her car, got behind the wheel, and told the driver to follow them in Madam's car. Myriam drove fast, stopped right before the red traffic lights, and left at such a speed that made Dorcas pay attention to her reflexes. Dorcas looked discreetly at her beautiful profile showing her strength and will, a kind of femme fatale; wealth also gave her a power, which she was conscious of. Myriam knew that she was curious about her and she smiled.

"My sister, you are wondering why I work; well, in order not to become idle. When James is in a bad mood, he does not fail to repeat that I have enough means even to provide for my children's needs for fifty years. It is true and my response is always the same: if I had an intelligent guy, creative and hardworking, but frustrated in his office by mediocre bosses, idiots who smother his competences, I would suggest to him that he leave such a company, as compensation, to make life easier for all of us. I am not complicated, but if he proved to be unable to provide for this minimum, I would dump him."

Dorcas laughed till she cried.

"But you are terrible, Myriam!"

"I am going to tell you the depth of my thoughts regarding men. When one has not been lucky to be born rich, it is necessary to struggle in life to acquire the means of being financially secure, so as not to be bound to anyone; to be a woman and be dependent on a gigolo or an idler? Never."

She touched the chain bracelet on her wrist, the iron gate opened, the cars entered; the same gesture for the iron gate also opened the door of the imposing mansion shrouded in a park that Dorcas had not suspected to be extensive in the night.

"Tea or fresh juice?"

"Fruit juice, please."

She touched a button fitted into the wall; a servant clad in African attire came in.

"Haïni, please bring two big glasses of pressed orange or pineapple juice . . . Oh, sorry, I did not ask you for your preference."

"Well, pineapple juice," Dorcas said, looking again at the paintings and the art objects that she had seen the night of their visit.

"Me too."

She took her private business card, gave it to her, and insisted that she should not hesitate to call her, "even late at night." Convinced of having found another dependable partner, but on a scale that could only contribute to the success of the project, Dorcas thought of Ségué n'Di. Myriam inquired after him.

"I paid him a visit; he is much better and will go back home, 'for private reasons.'"

"It is about the funeral ceremonies for his grandfather. It seemed as if you wore a beautiful dress. The young man accompanied you, walking with difficulty."

"It is funny that they take pleasure in following me, portraying me accurately," she said, smiled, and added: "as I was beside him and he showed me notes when he was shot, they would suspect me of being party to this crime that had failed."

"My sister, let it go. The minister of Internal Affairs is not unaware of my views; the head president is in a rabid-dog mood over the fact that the police are unable to find at least the gunman's weapon."

The glasses of juice were brought, and they served themselves. Myriam took her hand and affectionately squeezed it and said that she wanted to "confess" to a woman whom she had found very nice during the gala, before discovering in her a sister to whom she was attached since the evenings spent together. Dorcas squeezed her hand.

"We are friends and sisters, Myriam; whether I remain in Wanakawa or I leave for France or my country of birth that always lures me, I will need you."

"Well! What is wrong? You are not going to leave us? I hope and wish with all my heart that that is not going to happen," she said firmly, her head and eyes lowered as if she begged her.

Dorcas embraced her.

"It is touching to see you sad."

"This is what I want you to know. I have known Gaëtan for the past two years, and he is far, very far from being what one calls a lover for me, but I have slept with him. Although I did not keep records of it, I think it happened five times in two years; it is not a lot."

Dorcas burst into laughter, collapsed on her, hugged her, and kissed her.

"Listen, my sister, others would say: five times in two years, is not that bad. What I only want you to know because I have decided to be deeply sincere is that, even during the evening of the gala, our love was dead before I met you and got to know you. Thus, I was really sad. In conclusion, it is finished: I do not sleep with a friend's husband; that will no longer take place between himself and me."

They got up and went back and forth in the living room, which Dorcas admired again; she moved toward her and gave her her arm.

"I am also going to confess or make some confessions to you, we shall see; Gaëtan and I are going to divorce."

Myriam started, looking directly at her.

"Oh no! What is wrong? You seemed so close, even recently!"

"I suggested an amicable separation; he prefers to divorce and so shall it be."

"It is unbelievable! When I had to divorce Gaëtan, it was for the reasons that I spoke of the other day, but also after five years of more and more unbearable quarrels that were unhealthy for our daughter Akwa Hannah's health."

"The other confession—I did not deny it when he asked me the question without hesitating—is that I love Ségué n'Di; I am very much in love with Ségué n'Di and it is not platonic: we make love when we are together and feel like it. I am going on a trip, and I will be away in Europe for a month or five weeks; could I put his life in your hands?"

Myriam held her in her arms.

"Do not say it to anyone; let no one else know about it, or suspect anything of your relationship with your boyfriend Ségué n'Di. I beg you, my sister, absolute discretion as long as the divorce has not come through; afterwards, absolute freedom."

"Why so much precaution? Would it be shocking to find us together?"

"No! We are above that in Wanakawa! Black-White, Black-Negro have been sleeping together since the colonial era, even before then, as soon as they met and lusted for each other. Why so much precautions? Well, if the rumor of a divorce is added to the attempted murder, which would be interpreted as motivated by your relationship with Ségué n'Di, the anticriminal squad would see an opening that it would hasten to. Gaëtan would be the target of suspicions, open or stifled. The procedure of the suspension of his diplomatic immunity would be stepped-up. Oh, no, not that! He could not have done that! You would not want him to be accused or investigated, right?"

"I believe he is unfamiliar with this problem and does not at all want to be harassed. He does not want to be taken care of, but he is so vulnerable; I would like you to keep an eye on him as well."

"I will do it; I assure you that there will not be sexual relations between us."

"But, that is no longer important, since . . ."

"I analyzed his reaction to my article. Gaëtan is racist; I told him so on the phone the day before yesterday. He confessed as follows: 'Sometimes, something, some deeds make me have racist behaviors and reactions. Am I basically racist? I don't know.' I replied: 'we will remain friends, if you want; but it will no longer be like before.' I added that his reaction was unimaginably negative just because the idea came from Ségué n'Di, of our own African mining company in which the Africans would also be shareholders. This disappointed me, even offended me. My boyfriend of a son develops rashes as soon as he stands beside his mum. These are many reasons that eliminate him. And then, this is what you do not know: James adores your Ségué n'Di; he regards him as his son. At the least leak regarding your divorce, he would rub his hands together; there would be a blistering article. Gaëtan would be torn to pieces, pushed into the abyss. James is very clever and Machiavellian, perhaps cruel when he does not like someone."

"Is it the case?"

"I don't know what Gaëtan did to him, but he detests him. Is it because of our episodic relationship? It is perhaps Ron who put him against him. No, he should not be marginalized. I do not like isolating those whom I could respect."

"Me too, I would frankly not want us to go that far. Myriam, a last favor after my men; find me a house, not too far, at two or three kilometers from the city."

"To rent or to buy?"

"Six rooms, without counting the living room, with a garden, and I will buy it. Later, when I have the means, I will have a house built. If I do not find anything and if life is unbearable, I will go home, I mean to Benin, and settle down there."

"On your return, we will consider all that with equanimity after you have rested; to buy or to have a house built will not be a problem. Dorcas do not forget that I am your sister; I want to help you."

CHAPTER 43

He had driven her to the Wanakawa International Airport and wanted to leave immediately after her suitcases had been checked in. She repeated in a few words the crux of her mission, insisted on the personal interest that she attached to the gold mines, to its mining, even stressed that she would willingly invest in it.

"Invest in Africa? Why not, at the point where you are? You are more mad than in love with a nigger," he flung at her with a low voice charged with anger.

She quickly changed the subject, talked about their children, and asked if he had any specific thought for each of them. He looked at her straight in the eyes, and an ironical smile congealed on his lips. She knew what he was thinking, the scathing message that he would yell: "Dare tell them that you are a whore! That it is a nigger who now screws you!" She heard the words that did not come out of his mouth, nothing for their children; then she came back to the gold mine.

"You know, Yvan, I discovered this mine. To invest there would be a sizeable investment. I am not only thinking of myself; we have two children; it is primary."

"Never, you hear me? I will never invest in any part of Africa; it is not my country."

"I understand you perfectly; nevertheless, had I not been born there . . ."

"That means nothing, nothing at all! Your roots are European, essentially—and I stress—French, whether you like it or not."

"They didn't take roots in France, be consistent," she said, tenderly.

With the announcement of immediate boarding, he hugged her hastily, keen to leave her, but very calm she snuggled up against him, an arm on his shoulders, the other round his waist and looked at him.

"You are unfathomable, unbelievably perverse," he said, disarmed.

"Why? Is it because we are about to go through the divorce that you had wanted? You are mistaken again, Yvan; you will no longer be my husband, but I assure you, I have respect for you, feelings as well, despite everything. We will telephone each other, OK?"

"As you wish."

"I will kiss the children for you," she said when the boarding was announced again.

She turned again and waited a bit to wave him goodbye, but he did not look back as he hurriedly walked away, and then disappeared in the crowd.

▪ ▪ ▪

Malifiki took his weekend time off from Saturday afternoon. Dorcas had made everything available so that her husband could manage alone until the butler's return. Back in the residence, Gaëtan spent most of his time looking for his revolver, rifling through his wife's belongings, going through the nooks and corners of the house, guesthouse, and arbor, cursing. He did not know the house of "that bloody underdeveloped nigger! What humiliation! My wife's lover!"

He refused to think for one moment that "Dorcas could have given herself to that nobody in a hovel or a nigger's dump. All the same, it is not here, in my official residence that they give themselves over to debauchery! That would be the last straw! But when then, goddamn it?"

Red, collapsed on the pink granite table in the dining room, forehead on his forearm, he cried, pounding his fist to the point of bashing his fingers.

"I am going to destroy his face again or kill him for good! I missed him, and he took the liberty of making wisecracks, but I will blot out his shadow from the face of the earth, if I find my pistol!" he decided, getting up.

He pulled up his trousers, went here and there, groaning: "Where in this mess did the slut hide my weapon? In any case, she couldn't have given it to the nigger who screws her! . . . She would be capable of doing so! Whatever she claims, she would be capable of doing it. She is a whore! A whore in Africa!"

He burst into laughter, and then begged: "Lord, help me! It is unbelievable that Dor did this to me, and with whom? A nigger, an underdeveloped man. France, Europe, the United States, almost all the developed and civilized world feeds these people who court our women to the point of taking them; even she whom I loved, adored, succeeded in humiliating me. Africa took my wife. That is their independence. Lord, is that what you want for the Christian world and for its culture that is superior to all others?"

He kicked the chairs, went out like a drunkard, running to jump into the swimming pool, swallowed a mouthful of water, and choked as he came to the point of no return. Then, regaining his strength, in consternation, he swam in a state of total confusion, clutched the aluminum stepladder in panic before he got out. Exhausted, pathetic, he sobbed as he returned to the villa, where he wandered naked from one room to the other, laid down on the divan, and fell asleep.

Exhausted like a falcon whose feathers are all broken, Keurléonan woke around 7:00 p.m., his mouth dry. He was hungry, but suddenly remembered an "undertaking" that made his blood tingle, taking an alternating hot and cold shower. Then he went to Nadikorifu's house, dressed in percale white trousers and matching shirt; tall, beautiful, distinguished, she was the administrative secretary of the ICM. It had been more than a year that he hovered around her without success; she finally gave in. A mother of two mixed-race children, single, she would not mind having a discrete affair with someone high up on the hierarchical ladder who, though not always pleasant or fundamentally equitable, did not displease her too much as a man.

▪ ▪ ▪

They dined in Black Rhapsody, not far from Monomotapa, and then went back to her home, a beautiful villa hidden behind a grass court. They talked about mutual issues. He avoided all allusion to the gold mine "a carnival in very bad taste whose project superintendent would now be a Westerner, as well as the attempted murder," he said and heaved a desolate sigh.

They embraced and caressed each other effusively. Cropped hair, great black almond-shaped eyes, and sensual lips, Nadikorifu was inflamed, and Gaëtan, pressed against her, regretted that such an opportunity had not taken place much earlier. She left him, undressed, went into the bathroom, and came back dressed in a salmon-pink dressing gown. He wanted to see her nude; despite her reluctance, she was hardly against "this male whim." Overexcited, his penis hard, he was in a hurry. Calm, Nadikorifu looked at him with affection, which pacified him a bit and he gave himself time to undress.

Her body was covered with goose bumps, but her desire for him disintegrated when she saw him naked; she felt cold, teeth chattering gently. Tensed, Gaëtan approached her. She took two steps back, eyes wide open, forefinger pointed at his penis.

"What is wrong?" he asked her, surprised.

"You are not circumcised," she said, devastated, afraid.

"Circumcised? You looked at me well, didn't you?"

"I am only stating a fact."

"I am neither Jewish, nor nigger, nor Arab," he declared, scathingly.

"It is obvious that you are not Arab; I don't know whether you are Jew or not; me, I am a Negress woman."

"It is not what I wanted to say! God what conversation when . . ."

"You said it; it is of no importance: I heard it and saw lots of others," she retorted.

"Have you never slept with an uncircumcised white man? Your story of the ablation of the foreskin, that's racism!" he yelled.

She put her dressing gown on again and waited for him to get dressed, which he did in anger and took his leave as if he was fleeing before a fire.

"Mr. Keurléonan, you have raised several problems; I would like to answer in all honesty, if you have the guts and time to listen to me."

"A challenge?"

"A simple request; I would like you to think about it."

"And you address me as 'vous'—

"Just as at the office: the context demands it. I belong to a tribe in which women do not sleep with an uncircumcised man. My twins with the German father were products of a one-night stand; when I found out that Johannes was not circumcised, I threw up. I was sick, hospitalized. We could never again indulge in such pleasure, but the deed had been done, I don't regret it. I don't detect any racism in our customs, traditions, and morals; you have yours that colonization has posted throughout Africa where they perpetuate themselves."

"So, I who very much want to make love to you, I have to get my prepuce cut off! Can you imagine that?"

"I assure you that the wound will heal in ten days. Since I always keep my promises, I would not have valid reasons to refuse to welcome you in my bed."

"Africa really doesn't like me. Everything here is turning against me. I have to make up my mind to go back to France, goodbye for good."

"At this point in time? I do not want to be heartless, but I do not know if many would mourn your departure."

"I will never allow anyone to treat me like that!" he said, getting angry.

"You are in my house. I am not going to hide truths that the whole of the ICM would not bother to tell you, if the situation arrives, except those who were recipients of your injustice and discriminations."

"I am listening to you, madam," he said, his face blood red.

"You would learn about the most stinging judgments concerning you, the most difficult to accept and bear as well, if there was a referendum by the employees. You are not fair, Mr. Keurléonan. Whether the applicants have or don't have the same degrees, the same competency, you extremely rarely accept Africans in such posts; it is a racist exclusion. As the chief administrative secretary, I know all the files. Finally, you like what you like; you give free rein to manipulations among our politicians and those high up in the administration. Your methods go too far; they become alarming and those at the top of the government ask questions. Read the newspapers; is it due to friendship that I am talking to you like this? I need not say more; you know those whom I am alluding to. Professionally as well as humanely, it is unhealthy to prefer an average, otherwise mediocre, person to someone else who is competent, intelligent, and cultured, because the former is White, cousin or nephew of a minister, son of a former mistress, while the other, a Black unknown in the scheme."

He did not turn a hair, was silent for a full minute, and left without saying goodbye.

"No hard feelings, Mr. Keurléonan. I will keep my promise."

"Do not expect me to get myself circumcised; it is not a part of my race."

CHAPTER 44

A DELEGATION OF THE INTERNATIONAL COMMITTEE HAD WELCOMED HER AT the Geneva airport. The mission that she had seen in Tigony had more key figures as well as experts. At the small working meeting that took place the day after her arrival, the regional director of the consortium declared that neither the shadow of suspicion nor any ambiguity should hang over the work, so the presence of Africans among the experts and the technical advisers should be legitimate.

A short private conversation took place between five "Authorities" that she did not know, then she heard say that there were no Africans in Geneva with the competence of the experts that the consortium had been able to bring together. At that assertion, she looked through her address book and immediately suggested two Ghanaians, a Nigerian, and a South African exile in Lausanne; Myriam had given her their names and addresses, had assured her that she would get in touch with them herself, and would give her the details before the preliminary meeting.

"If they accept—impossible that they refuse to assist me—insist on their presence in the capacity of advisers-observers," she had said.

"Don't worry, Myri, I know the delaying tactics; within twenty-four hours, the Ghanaians will have come from the U.S., the Nigerian will drop by from Paris, and Lausanne is within range. Bye! Hug Ron for me."

"He said that he would have gone with you, if you had suggested it to him."

"Oh, the rascal! Next time, I am going to take him from you and we will take off together!"

Her idea did the trick; work was delayed for forty-eight hours. Rubbing his hands, the Swiss declared:

"Switzerland's banking policy would not frown upon the contributions of possible African members; indeed, it is perfectly understandable that the Africans, who apparently have the means, should be the majority shareholders of the gold mines of Mount . . ."

"Franakiniriyo," Dorcas said, who, all smiles, came to his rescue.

"Thank you, dear Director of the regional office, we will quickly get used to pronouncing this name, I assure you. I was saying then that as the mines are in their national territory, there is, as far as Switzerland is concerned, no objection to those who could become the major shareholders."

She did not detect divergences in the opinions of Sweden and Great Britain; the Federal Republic of Germany, France, and Japan, at first only just favorable, explained their reticence. Progressively, with flexibility and an unnerving plasticity, also humor, sometimes cynical thrusts, Madam the director brought out her large artillery that she placed at each crossroad. A number of the delegates said in a private conversation that "that woman, charming and enchanting enough to eat," was "lost to the White world."

"She is a European technocrat in the skin of Blacks that succeed."

"Yet one of the leftist militants produced by May '68."

"Who does she sleep with in Tigony?"

"Her husband is French, Breton, a top international civil servant; we hardly saw him during our trip to Wanakawa."

Two hours after the arrival of the African experts, proud that Myriam had thought of them and suggested that they be invited; Dorcas brought them together for a short briefing and distributed the basic information in the ad hoc file for their lectures, if she or someone else requested it.

"What would you say to a brainstorming session after you've seen the documents?"

They agreed. The international committee meeting held high-level, closed debates without concessions regarding the participation of the Wanakawa natives in particular, and those of Africa in general. Thinking of Myriam, of her wealth, but also of others whom she might suggest, the regional office convinced them that African shareholders, considering their competence in the matter, should be members of the board of the mining company.

The acceptance of her amendment, prepared with her "special advisers," was unanimous. The quibbles and pitfalls of their Western counterparts had been envisaged; the responses or even barricades prepared, they were the first to heave a sigh of relief and applaud when the president of the meeting announced the unanimous adoption of the proposed text.

▪ ▪ ▪

"What a woman! Brainy, but also a hell of a worker!" an African expert said in regard to Myriam, at the cocktail party offered at the end of Dorcas's assignment.

"Getting old like every one of us, is she still as gorgeous as before? It has been more than four years since I last saw her."

"What a question, my old Aïkobinu! How can you get old when you are Myriam Haïlé-Haïkouni?" Seth Adam Atamèkrow asked.

"Myri is a mechanism that breaks its technician when he makes false moves."

"One must be strong, nevertheless flexible, when one deals with her."

"Africa needs women and men of Myriam's quality and strong character, don't you think so?"

"Absolutely, dear madam. We do not lack them; the problem is they stay in the background, play down and smother themselves, but say everywhere that it is the African man who stops them from fulfilling their potential," Aïkobinu intervened again.

"Your question doesn't surprise me, madam. I followed you with a laser during your talks. You are a sort of white version of Myri, a dormant volcano that could erupt at any time. It is unforeseeable," Lalèyè Ladikpé said.

They also heard compliments about the regional director: "Despite some slight differences, her intelligence, competence, command of the documents, and the art of seduction would make her the most important cog in the company."

"I would even say, without restriction, dear colleague, the cornerstone of the Franakiniriyo Mining Company! Ah, I succeeded in pronouncing this name on the first try!"

"She certainly would be a stockholder."

"That wouldn't be unusual, but as part of the Western quota."

"No one knows exactly how much her . . ."

"Probably sizeable, if not considerable. She is a kind of freelance actor, like those very independent people who sell their services at high costs. They are dangerous when they gain access to strategic documents and master them, as she had demonstrated to us."

"No, not at all; nobody will pick a quarrel with her, even if in the business and political world. From now on, you hardly see a woman as a woman, even if she is very beautiful and seductive, but as an individual that you will not hesitate to destroy when necessary."

"Concerning Mrs. Keurléonan-Moricet, there are parameters not to be neglected, her knowledge of the ground and her commitment in the consortium. She was in charge of an investigation into the whole of Wanakawa, but no one knows the result of it."

▪ ▪ ▪

She called Myriam from Stuttgart, gave an account of her mission, and passed on the messages of her "remarkable, efficient and brilliant lobbyists."

"It is crazy that they all like you, what luck!"

"It is Africa itself, more precisely; its governments that often encourage the brain drain."

"I realize it more and more. We will gladly talk about it when I get back. Some could be very useful, and shouldn't be paid at a reduced rate."

Four days of relaxation, walks, jumps from one subject to another, and exchange of ideas with Charles-Yvan, a big redhead with fine features like his mother; in his gait, he rather took after his father. Watching him, Dorcas smiled; the resemblance to Gaëtan when they were students and he was hanging around her at Catho or at Thabor, in Rennes, was striking. She spontaneously kissed him; he gave her his arm and said that like that, they were "like two lovebirds, despite the difference in age."

"Oh you know, age difference or not, me, I am always in love with my big boy!" she reacted.

He kissed her on the neck; they burst out in a merry laughter, which made passersby turn and look at them.

She had sent the file for the divorce proposal prepared with her husband to her lawyer in Paris, and a "juridically acceptable text" had reached him in Geneva. They had been able to agree "clearly on all the points, so that despite everything there is still an understanding, even friendship" between them. Gaëtan had received two copies of the text that he signed with "read and approved" in such a furious hand, unlike his own signature, that Dorcas initially doubted that it was his handwriting.

Quivering with joy, Andréa-Dorothy welcomed her at the Dublin airport as she threw herself into her arms; then she started to hop around her, putting rhythm into steps of an Irish folk dance.

"What a kid! You remained my big kid! I am glad to see you like this my darling," Dorcas happily said in a low voice.

The spitting image of her mother, she had the same face, the sumptuous hair with an auburn sheen, Dorcas's smile with a dimple in the left cheek, the same frank and straight look, and large hands with slim fingers. She gave her mother her arm, squeezed her tightly, and kissed her on the cheek, on the neck as they walked up and down waiting for the luggage. Dorothy stopped and stared at her.

"Why are you looking at me like that, my darling?"

"You look—radiant, and I love you as you are! What a pity there is no photographer here!"

"Radiant, as you say, despite the tiredness? I am rather ex-haust-ed!"

"Tiredness or not, Mum, you are superb!"

"I had rested well with my little darling. He found me 'younger and like a blossoming flower'! I thought it was just to make me happy because I was worn-out. To have worked like a dog, sometimes under stress, confronting a kind of brotherhood that thought of itself, nothing but itself makes me feel that I don't look particularly fresh."

"Your radiance is within you, but it is *oozing*; it is true that it is seeping out despite the tiredness. You are fresh and relaxed. Well, you have a letter from your boyfriend," she said, opening her handbag.

Laughing wholeheartedly, Dorcas felt the semicommercial envelope with the heading of the International Cooperation Mission when she saw her luggage. She slipped the envelope into her bag, and followed by her daughter, she went to pick up her luggage. A taxi took them to a five-star hotel, where the consortium had booked a suite with three rooms, not far from the banks of the Liffey.

"Charles-Yvan spent four days with me; my darling, would you like to spend as much time here in this hotel?"

"Oh! Great, Mum! I am going to quickly inform the Mulligans. Since I am boarding full time, they wouldn't be against my spending the night in my mother's nest."

She patted her on the cheeks and opened the letter. It was from her lawyer, with Gaëtan's visiting card on which his hand was more regular, writing: "Have a good trip; love to the children. You will certainly be missed. Hugs."

"Good news?"

"Yes, especially a file."

"What a life! They do not leave you alone, even when you are with your dearest daughter!"

"I'm afraid not! That's life, big girl." The telephone rang.

"Hello, who is already calling me?" she said, taking her mobile phone. Dorothy went discretely into another room as she closed the door.

"Dorothy gave it to me at the airport—I have read it—I like it like that—You know, Yvan, I am really happy that we agree on all the points; everything is set for a good understanding, as I continue to desire it—Oh really? When then? I left him this morning. He even accompanied me to the airport. You have just done it? His reaction? He laughed and called us *anassortis*: a word that I do not know either in French or any of the other languages that I speak; but—Why so much haste? You are in such a hurry to finish it, even if it means making the child unhappy? Do you want to talk about it with Dorothy as well? She is the older one."

The shock of the phone slammed down to end the communication had the effect of a blow in her ear, but she immediately called him back at home. He was not there. She knew him to be of "incorrigibly bad faith" and did not want him to accuse her: "you left me high and dry when I answered your question," so she telephoned the residence again, then the switchboard of the ICM, stressing that she was in Europe and inquired if her husband was available and did not have a visitor. Having been put through, she was saying, "We were interrupt—," when he retorted: "I understood that you did not want to hear me anymore!"

She controlled herself, kept her calm, and asked again if he wanted to personally inform Dorothy as well. He did not answer; she insisted: "Andréa-Dorothy is in the room next door; would you like to hear our daughter's voice?"

Walled-up in his silence, Gaëtan did not answer, but she waited until he hung up before she put her mobile phone back in the mute mode.

"It was your father," she said, when Dorothy came back into the room.

"You did not tell him that I am . . ."

"How can I forget you, my darling?" she answered, smiling, caressing her face.

"He did not want to say a single word to me, to give me a kiss?"

"There were people in his office, you know, these men are always important in the international civil service."

Suddenly angry, she looked like her father as much as her mother.

"Oh I do not like this, not a drop! I don't give a shit! I don't give a damn about these mister-very-important types, with their wheeling and dealing, from the international civil service! I . . . all those hypocrites! Drips! Visitors? What does that mean? Lords or luxury dogs so that Gaëtan Yvan Keurléonan—I don't like this name!—could not take two seconds to hear his daughter just say: Hello Daddy! And so that his daughter could hear his voice!" she said in tears.

Her mother consoled her: "I assure you, your father, overwhelmed, was sorry; I myself was unable to tell him a third of what I wanted to tell him. I am going to take a bath, relax, and we will go down to dinner in the hotel's restaurant. On our return, you will call him, agreed?"

Sobbing, face distorted, Dorothy shook her head negatively. Surprised, her mother looked at her.

CHAPTER 45

They strolled, going from Dame Street to St. Stephen's Green, which Dorcas liked; they turned back, following Grafton Street, arrived at the former parliament building, stopped in front of Trinity College. Dorcas was excited: she had visited the illustrious institution with her parents, brothers, and sisters, and later with Gaëtan evoking Ireland's Celtic origins, its affinities with Brittany. They strolled along the Liffey which reflected the Custom House; stopping on the Ha'penny, they contemplated the landscape around the Four Courts; the river strewn with the reflections of the buildings not far from its banks ran at its gentle pace. Crossing the Metal Bridge, Dorcas thought again of her parents, especially of her mother exclaiming "Oh! One would think one was in Venice!"

Life in Tigony, in Wanakawa in general, ran as a leitmotif as they changed the subject when Dorothy mentioned her pleasure in recalling places where she had spent her holidays and some of her young friends, although she did "not at all like the clan of these Whites withdrawn into themselves, cautious, arrogant, scornful toward the Africans. I thought of them when I was reading the novel of an African author where a character asked something we should be thinking about: What are you looking for among the Blacks if you cannot stand them? That's fundamental Mum, even at the International Cooperation Mission."

Dorcas alluded to the gold mine, how she had sniffed it out quite by chance in a peat bog valley, on the side of Mount Franakiniriyo. Dorothy gave a whistle of admiration and exclaimed: “Wow! Good Heavens! What a great pronunciation of this name! With the stress, I am sure!”

Her mother blushed, asserting that by dint of hearing her secretaries, the common people on the streets, one gets to pronounce words in foreign languages well, even the most stubborn. Dorothy complimented her for not being indifferent to the social movements and for having taken part in the demonstrations during the strikes. She had read J. F. G. Greenough’s articles.

“Terrific! What courage! What language as well! Who is he? I read the interview that you gave him.”

“A great Irish journalist; some Africans say that he is not a White, that he is one of them!”

“Wonderful! Regarding the interview, how can one not be proud to be the daughter of such a dame? I cut out the article and showed it to some friends as well as my professors; by the way, how is the victim of that damn attempted murder?”

“I visited him at the hospital before I left. The head doctor sent me clinical and administrative information. In his opinion, without last-minute complications, he should be home in a week’s time.”

“Who did that to him and why? They sought the assassin among the Africans, but the witnesses said it was a white man.”

“The anticriminal squad dared, finally, to look into the Westerners, including your mother.”

“You, Mum? The press indicated clearly that Mr. Ségué n’Di was giving you explanations about work in the mine, when a white man shot him, right?”

“It is exact, sweetie, but the police must explore all the possible and imaginable trails.”

“And to sink right into such stupidity up to this point? Africa is not about to decolonize if a white man tries to do in an African and the squad sniffs at the Blacks to unearth the murderer. Kafka is not dead,” she concluded, and they both went to bed.

▪ ▪ ▪

Dorcas visited the places she knew, strolled around the streets, discovering details. She liked the atmosphere of the pubs, the trees, and their shadows on the banks of the Liffey. Dorothy had pointed out a pub to her. They had breakfast there, and she introduced her friends as well as the waitresses she really liked; they found her mum lovely. A big redhead with a face strewn with freckles came in at a leisurely pace; he ogled Dorcas as soon as he saw her and exclaimed in a drawling voice, "Wow! Rather sexy, isn't she," before Dorothy had made the introductions.

"Really?" Dorcas replied, blushing, while Dorothy looked at her, amused.

"Hey, Tony, and you, Arthur, look at her! Who's she?"

"Dorothy's mum; happy, James?"

"Oh sorry!" He murmured, blushing in turn; everyone burst out into laughter.

Back at the hotel, they sat on the settee, talked about this and that, until Dorcas finally told Dorothy everything.

"Great! Things are really happening in Tigony! Like the police squad, you have also finally dared to take the plunge!"

Dorcas staggered, indignant, but keeping her lips buttoned, lowered her head, put her fingers together, and said in a very low voice, heavy with sadness, "Why are you rejoicing like that in such a situation? It is wicked."

"Listen Mum, you are my big Darling and Charles-Yvan's Beloved, OK? There are situations that we do not understand about the two of you. Here is the question which often comes up when we are in Tigony: 'What has kept them together for so many years?'"

"At this point? Why? Are we *anassortis* or rather badly matched?"

"I don't know. You have tastes, opinions, and also lots more that are extremely different. You really look like strangers to each other when someone lives with you for a while and takes note of it: three years ago, in spite of being too young to know better, I had thought that it would not last like that till the end of your days."

"Well! Well!" she murmured, astounded.

Then, looking at her directly in the face, she added, raising her voice a little: "But why, why, my sweet?"

"You are straightforward, loyal, always laying your cards on the table; daddy hedges, doesn't go straight to the point, except when he uses his springboard."

"What springboard?"

"Come now, Mum, you know it quite well! Either he hides in the water afraid of the rain, or uses anger to hide behind, but above all the brutality and violence; yes, violence, aggression, as well as cynicism."

"Please, Dorothy, don't judge him, he is your father. Gaëtan may have all the faults of the world, which is far from being the truth, because I know him better than you do."

"Can I talk to you more openly?"

"What a question! Isn't that what we are doing?"

"Well . . . Do you know that after all . . . Oh, I don't give a damn!"

"I am listening to you; we are talking very openly between mother and daughter."

"Daddy cheats on you. I caught him unawares. He tried to pull the wool over my eyes, but I was not fooled by that. Charles-Yvan also knows it. We did not want to breathe a single word to you about it, so that there might be peace in your flawed marriage, a show of understanding and harmony."

Dorcas heaved a long sigh, explained that there are hardly any couples without that kind of problem, because of one or the other partner, or both; then she added in a conciliatory tone: "Whether your father cheated on me or cheats on me is a matter between us."

"Your private life, of course. Apparently in a couple, hypocrisy sometimes calls the tune and it is better that way."

"You know a lot of things! And if I were to tell you that I have also already cheated and I am still cheating on my husband?"

Dorothy doubled up with giggles, stood up, went to her room, returned, sat down near her, clasped her in her arms, and said, looking her straight in the eyes, that it would surprise her a lot.

"Unless you didn't concretely get wind of his women friends and can't take any more; then, as opportunity makes the thief . . ."

"Opportunity, chance for the discovery of the gold mine, other hazards as well. Your grandfather, juggling with Virgil and Livy, said, '*Audentes fortuna juvat, deis bene juvantibus*.'"

"Translate?"

"Fortune comes to the rescue of the bold, with very willing assistance from the gods."

"Is it true?"

"Yes."

"Does he know it?"

"I did not hide anything when he asked me the question clearly."

"To put the question clearly; all is in the adverb. You have described both your personalities in one single sentence. It is certainly what I said: uprightness and loyalty opposed to blurring and ambiguity. Papa is never straightforward. I said that to him, and he slapped me."

"Gaëtan slapped you? When?"

"Last year; I preferred to keep quiet, for fear that because of me, your beautiful harmony would break up."

CHAPTER 46

SHE HUGGED HER CLOSELY AS IN HER CHILDHOOD WHEN SHE CONSOLED HER after she was upset.

"Is he nice, your guy?"

"He is African, young, not bad. One day he called me a super chick! I love him."

"Great! You have taken the plunge, Mum. Except for chance, opportunity, how did you come up with him?" she inquired, still intrigued.

"My darling, it may seem strange to you that a scientist refers to chance. It doesn't matter; my weakening looked like a suicidal resignation, when chance intervened. It was a trivial movement, like a hand involuntarily touching another that brushed against it in the crowd. It happened when I was taking part in the first march of sympathizers of that strike that the Irish newspapers didn't keep silent about. The thought of a possible intervention of the riot squad and other people with truncheons made the organizers of the strike decide to form a union network. The hand of a young African beside me touched mine; I took his. He looked at me, with the feeling that until then he had not paid attention to his neighbors in this human mass of more than a million people. Why should I ignore him if it went that way? We exchanged a furtive smile of welcome, like everyone, as he was forming a union network with his neighbors. At that instant something moved within me, something I still find it hard to understand, a kind of anguish, which amused me too and which I considered with irony.

"At the same time, there was something within me like a bud that finished growing and that slowly opened: I watched the irreversible blossoming of a flower that absorbed the sun, spreading its perfume. I took flight, felt myself rising up; everything within me was blossoming among the moving crowd that was going back and forth. I held the hand of the unknown man, felt his presence, his internal calm, and his availability. You're going to laugh, my darling, but listen carefully to your mother: I had the feeling that he had taken me, hoisted me on his back, and was carrying me off without knowing where; me even less, except that definitely it was the road of no return and that I could not help but love him, for good, he who carried me like that, even if it I had to suffer because of him. Too bad. I had resolutely taken off. Time does the rest and helps us to build our nest on the tree of the future."

Dreamy, Dorothy collected her wits, moved back a bit to look at her.

"You must have a child with him, Mum."

"Why? I love him deeply; it is the most important, isn't it?"

"Certainly, but I would sincerely like it; I want a colored sister or brother!" she said, her fists clenched, hammering her words as if she were threatening her.

"My sweet, you really want it from the bottom of your heart?"

"It would be unhealthy and cynical if I weren't sincere. Mum, I want a mixed-race sibling!"

"OK, I am pregnant; you are the only person who knows about it."

"Mum! Mum! Phew! You have taken your freedom. You talked about it when you were angry," she said, hugging her with rocking movements, asking her how long she had known it.

"Last week at Geneva, I suspected something and I took it easy, and then I saw a gynecologist. I am two months pregnant with twins, like my grandmother, who had them twice."

"Mum, you mustn't overexert yourself. Do you promise me?"

"I do not want you to feel any animosity toward your father, any disaffection . . ."

"Of course not! Mum, he is my father, fathead, but I love him. He sometimes behaves like an idiot, but you know, he is not bad at all and I adore him. Fiona, the professor of comparative literature, said about a character from Wilde: 'Men of that nature are like certain kinds of drugs: to be shaken before use.' Daddy is like that; any woman would let herself to be taken in, if she hadn't shaken him before giving in to him. I have no experience, but he would not be the kind of bloke who would trap me if I had not been his daughter."

"Fine speech! How many women haven't ever made it and aren't making it!"

Dorothy scrutinized her, murmuring: "You dared, with the great assistance of the gods? It doesn't matter, you dared. Oh! I am now sure, it is the secret of your blooming."

"I have to call my husband."

"Are you going to tell him?"

"The letter you gave me contained the papers for our amicable divorce."

"He's been fair?"

"Anyway, very prudent or inspired."

"Meaning?"

"If he had added the least restrictive clause to my disadvantage in the proposal, I would have informed him of my status, and he would have received the written confirmation."

"How methodical, this woman! I would so much like to cultivate what I take after you."

"My sweet, there is some good, even some excellence in every human being, but also some green fruits, some not yet mature; in all these, we forget the genetic mysteries."

"You are going to tell Charles-Yvan as well about it, won't you?"

"Certainly, but he already knows that we are getting divorced; your father told him about it on the phone. You are sulking!"

"Unbelievable! My father is unbelievable. And your boyfriend, what does he think about it?"

"I told you that you are the only one who knows about it; he is not yet aware of it. Then, he has so many problems, the poor guy! Not being sure of my state, I preferred to keep quiet; he should call me here or in Paris. You did not ask me his name. It is Ségué n'Di Niriokiriko Aplika."

Dorothy startled and exclaimed: "Oh, Mum! Mum!"

"What is wrong with you? Why are you crying?"

"I hope I hope it isn't Daddy who had . . ."

"What a strange association of ideas! Dorothy, my darling, imagine anything you want or are able to, except that my husband, who is not unaware of who my lover is, is the white man who had wanted to kill Ségué n'Di. I want this to be quite clear, so that you don't get eaten up with anxiety in thinking that your—no, anybody, but not Gaëtan," she said convincingly.

"Phew! What a woman! Despite everything, my father still finds in you a supportive and winning lawyer."

"That is normal. I knew and loved him a lot; would I have married him and would I have had with him our two children that you are if that had not been the case? I am talking to you like this because the man I married cheated on me already at the time of our engagement."

"Cut it out, Mum! You are not a dummy and you married such a man?"

"Does Andréa Anna Dorothy Keurléonan regret being my daughter and that of Gaëtan Yvan Keurléonan?"

"You're cornering me; my answer is downright no!"

"I'll only say that I married him because we had chosen ourselves, we loved each other, and he was the one I wanted to get married to. I told him again recently when we could talk to each other without ambiguity."

"He did not know that you knew of it?"

"That's the impression he gave me; in his eyes, I was nothing but a young girl in love whose fiancé cheated on her without her knowledge."

The telephone rang. Dorothy wanted to leave, but she stopped her by taking her wrist. Ségué n'Di telephoned her from a telephone booth on his discharge from the hospital.

"Hodi!" Dorcas answered happily, starting to talk in Kinokoroni. Dorothy, her eyes wide open with astonishment, stood gaping. Ségué n'Di melted with pleasure. Dorcas realized it on hearing him breathe. She mentioned her mission, the development of "your ideas concerning the mining company; they received a unanimous agreement"; she insisted on "Myriam's power as well as efficiency" and finally told him, "the important news, on a strictly personal level."

"That is significant and splendid. What a pleasure to hear you speak to me from so far away in Kinokoroni! In my heart of hearts I had wished for that to happen the last time. I even prayed to my n'Ata's spirit that it would happen, even if it had to cause a scandal in the Western community, but I did not expect it to be so soon. Well, I shout Hurray! I am sure that it will make waves in your family. I proudly take on my responsibilities like a man. Do you remember my Old n'Ata's message? He is also jubilant up there where nobody dies."

She reiterated her advice for prudence, discretion, and caution, and asked if the "confidential items, some of which are exhibits" were in a safe place.

The underpants stippled with pubic hairs emerged in her imagination, held with pegs on a clothesline. She almost laughed, but remembered at once an article in conditional terms signed by André-Denis Arpaillargues sent to the news agencies the day before her departure; then she insisted: "in the event of threats, wherever they would come from, do not hesitate to make it known that the attempted murderer is, from now on, out to get him."

"Is there evidence?"

She answered in a coded language: "The silence welcomes and conceals what speedy action and discretion entrust to it," then added that her children were well, happy in motherly warmth, but impatient to see their father as well as Wanakawa that they missed.

Ségué n'Di inquired about the general reaction.

"The first person informed is in the clouds; her father will be told the truth when, in Paris, I have solved the legal problems with the assistance of experts in the matter. In Geneva, by the way, I had a clip brooch and a beautiful chain made from your gift; it is superb. I will show it to my daughter; she is here, by me."

"Would you tell her that I'd be very happy to meet her? My Old n'Ata, who sees everything, must be happy, even happy that you wear that Funiarikinio gift on its journey to the foot of Mount Kiniyinka. I am really upset in thinking of him."

"I would so much have liked to know him."

There was a long silence; she knew he was quite moved, and she said no more.

"Karinioni," she heard.

There was so much softness, also tenderness in his voice and in that word that she quivered.

"Karinioni icé," she answered and hung up the phone.

▪ ▪ ▪

"Fascinating, you are fascinating, Mum. You learned and speak an African language! You love your boyfriend with tenderness and equilibrium, I felt. You know, you equipped yourself with an undeniable force, a fearful weapon."

"Thank you, my Dorothy. Your appreciation means a lot to me, and what I would like for you as well is that you take the necessary steps to be a free person."

CHAPTER 47

She saw Paris again with a feeling of rejuvenation and that purified blood was circulating through her veins; a thin smile trembled on the face of this woman in full bloom. She was walking in the corridors of the intercontinental hotel where she was staying. Gaëtan had given up resisting, and strolling through the Marais, she looked up toward the building they jointly owned, where a couple of the tenants occupied the four-room flat on the third floor. All she needed was to have a look at it. She had telephoned him before leaving Dublin, to hear his voice, to give him news of their children, to tell him about her desire to go to Brittany.

"It is also France. You can visit all its provinces without going into details with me: it is your private life."

"You are taking everything the wrong way, Yvan. You did not want to talk to our daughter; she was unhappy and cried a lot. You told Charles-Yvan about our plans to get divorced . . ."

"Don't I even have the right anymore to open myself to one of my children to whom I can say what I have in my heart?"

"I don't deprive you of any right and don't discriminate between our children."

He laughed sarcastically and retorted: "Dorcas, the virtuous one, will nevertheless not cover her current private life with a tarp; she will not have the courage to confess to her children that she has a nigger lover."

"How unpleasant and aggressive you are!"

"That is it! Run away when it is a question of lifting the veil so that our children finally have a clear idea of your true nature, who you are."

"Once again, you are mistaken: you told Charles-Yvan of our divorce plans; I made no secret of it to Dorothy; she even knows that I have another man in my life and that he is an African."

The tone of her voice was calm, flexible as if they were next to each other, and she tried to convince him of his mistake in flying off the handle at the slightest word about the objective reality of their lives. It was like before, when she had been talking to him from Dublin and he had brutally cut the communication. Then she had burst out sobbing. Once again, she called him back immediately.

"You will regret your actions for the rest of your life!" he yelled and hung up without her being able to say a word.

Consumed with sorrow, exhausted, her tears still ran when she fell asleep without undressing. Her decision not to go back, even if the point of no return had not yet been reached, was no longer a secret from Dorothy. The crescendo that was characteristic of Gaëtan's behavior no longer had any importance. Even so, she felt an incredible sadness.

▪ ▪ ▪

Coming out of the office of his recent promotion as interim director, coming across Mrs. Nadikorifu Nawewe in the silent corridors of the ICM, Keurléonan took her hand.

"Still a flat refusal, dear friend?" he inquired, bantering.

"You know well that I didn't go that far, my dear Director."

"Your totems don't like me and they are responsible for my marginalization . . ."

"You make me very sad by attaching no importance to our taboos: they are demands that we abide by and have to respect. Take a step, my dear Director; let's see now, it is not the Rubicon!" she said, looking at him with a touch of tenderness in her eyes as well as her voice.

"Ah, Africa! I am more and more unhappy here, alone," he said, heaving a long sigh, and his paleness frightened Nadikorifu.

"No, no," she replied.

"What are you doing this evening, please?"

"Fulfilling a promise; I'm dining with my twins in a restaurant."

"I'm really unlucky."

His low voice, a bit stumbling, was unsteady. Suddenly sad, Nadikorifu became unglued, but held firm. She reiterated her promise if he made the effort to remove his foreskin, which would not cost him his life.

"How do you know, friend?"

His paleness became unbearable. She held out her hand; he shook it, then locked himself in his office, went through some files, signed letters, and left instructions on the "executive sheets" intended for specific sectors.

It was 11:30 p.m. Malifiki, who was to go home with the midnight tram, telephoned to inquire if Mr. Keurléonan was still in his office.

"The interim director left the ICM at 10:30 p.m.; he should have been at home a long time ago, unless he had commitments downtown," the switchboard operator had stated.

The butler closed the door of the villa by slamming it as usual when his employers came home after midnight, left some lights on in the courtyard, and left.

▪ ▪ ▪

Gaëtan Keurléonan cruised the residential area, far from his home as if in search of a sentimental adventure. He went further; the city was now behind him. He left the asphalt lane for one of the crushed granite roads and red earth driving toward the mountain sites. At the foot of Mount Kranataïkani, thirty kilometers from Tigony, he energetically started the high, steep ascent. When he was finally aware of the danger of going up that high, he stopped. His desire to go higher was as great as his dread, and he left the car, continued walking, even using his hands. His nails broke, and his fingers grazed at the touch of the ridges smudged with his blood. About a hundred meters separated him from the peak of Kranataïkani that appeared to him as a challenge. Dripping with sweat, aggressive, red-faced, out of breath, in tears, and teeth chattering, he sat down. The moon was pouring whitish rays over the summit, and they gave the impression that it came down the slopes, blocking off the steep drop to the ravine at the foot of the mountain, before spreading forth into the valley full of locusts.

"No-life forced into a dead end a nigger threw me into it why did she do that to me reduced to such a state in Africa where we were happy because of her out of love for her I refused sensual pleasures that she would never agree to give me so many sacrifices to hear her treat me like a deadwood in our bed what does the nigger give her how does he fuck her obscenities debauchery what feeling can a nigger exude that a white man would be incapable of bringing exotic prejudices should Europe now submit itself to these people's school of fornication as it helps them to live intervening to balance and for the completion of their chronically deficient budget I who by my nature like the intense feelings I have fled from the forest where racked by suicidal impulse I was walking solitary a naked orgiastic fraternal society which I came across men straddling one another who fornicated heterosexuals swapping their dykes with turgid clitorises grown under the yoke of lesbianism on the blankets spread right on the ground of dead leaves and what sordid pleasures put as if into a trance in a hideous world my presence didn't disturb any of them more than one of them invited me to 'fill myself with the nature of things' I declined the offer they called me pathetic deserving to be cuckolded that was already my status here I am hohohoho I need maternal love Mum carry on your dusty knees your tearful little Yvan in a country of savages I gripped Daddy's legs who in the past was discontented because I cheated on my fiancée 'you are shameless you cheat on her and you will also be cheated upon later' was that a curse is my wife now taking her revenge for days gone by and also for present she had seemed to me to be at ease at the hen party of the evening gala I recognized all of them taking part in the orgy in a forest initiatory rite of Whites into fossilized Negritude did she see them frequently with her nigger the slut I will kill that unimportant nigger a shadow in the world of human beings worthy of the name I will sign a confidential report stressing that no nation of our beautiful West should come to the aid of niggers and that the nigger trash left to themselves starve due to extreme poverty despite the wealth so much vaunted of their grounds and subsoils you have sacrificed me to an underdeveloped man you are wrong Dorcas you made an extremely serious mistake I will wipe him off the face of the earth if I know where you have hidden my gun and where your deadbeat hangs out his piccaninny colleagues liars pretended they don't know where he lives 'perhaps on one of the mountains not far from Tigony' I didn't dare go to the police under what pretext perhaps that on your behalf whore they know everything about your orgies and suspect me going by what grounds 'the young man sleeps with your wife Interim Director' hahahaha my wife what a word she is no longer mine it is eight months since we've been living side by side in the same house without sleeping together no longer fucking her I content myself with secretaries in search of promotion or buggering whores eager for such sexual relationships 'oh Interim Director' shut up the cops she has hidden my gun I will buy a Winchester I'll take care of her nigger you will mourn for him widow of a nonentity that you will not marry do you intend to marry him after our divorce I will make the idiotic dream of a bitch crumble the divorce will never come through you hear me never never never I am going to rape you when you come back I will fuck whores I want to contract AIDS I am going to give it to you so that you give it to your ectoplasm of a lover the circle will be closed I want it like that I don't give a bugger about the rest Myriam as well doesn't want me 'you are racist' she told me she the Negress Jewish technocrat set up with so much fortune whose origins no one knows everything in order to be impressive in an underdeveloped country with her old idiot of a second-rate Irish journalist a wreck in Africa oh Dor my love why have you done this to me this terrible blow has knocked me down killed me thrown me on a heap of refuse abandoned to the niggers' stares why yes why look at this I have reached a dead end non-life in life's dead end . . ."

He got up, worn out, drew up his trousers, came staggering back to the car. Suddenly everything appeared absurd to him. Anguished, his heart was beating wildly; violent spasms shook him from the soles of his feet, intensified and stagnated below his belt. His sex began stiffening; the tension was such that he cried like a dog barking at the dead. A mixture of sweat and tears clouded his sight while he said in a low voice: "pathetic wreck my passion for her is killing me in Africa."

He no longer knew how he had been able to get that high and wanted to go down backward. A red indicator on the dashboard started to give successive jerks. The car skidded a little; he got it under control, saw before him a steep path, and took it. Keeping all the lights on, he moved forward with prudence as he murmured: "if I do not kill him I will contract AIDS; I will rape her. They will share it with the person they humiliated . . ."

He had spasms; his hand trembled when he changed to the third gear. Then there was a click, and his eyes opened wide with astonishment.

CHAPTER 48

TIRED OUT, DORCAS WAS SLEEPING LIKE A LOG. SHE HEARD HER MOBILE phone ring as if in a dream; she turned over, changing position, stretched herself, thoughts heavy with sleep, took the mobile phone on the bedside table, and Myriam's voice brought her back to reality.

"Yes Myri, I had a depressing afternoon yesterday; I went to sleep without undressing. . . . What? . . . Oh! Lord, it's not possible!"

A deep loathing for her husband took hold of her, and she trembled, wept, murmuring: "Coward! Coward! That is him absolutely; it is a suicide. He had threatened it to me on the phone, with hidden meaning in his words, talking about the regret that would follow me my entire life—"

"The news dispatch on the Internet is clear: 'according to the official report of the anticriminal squad, it was a suicide. The interim director of the ICM ventured onto the slope of Mount Kranataïkani; peasants who perceived something strange alerted the police force in the district. Mr. Keurléonan's car was found in the ravine, at more than a hundred meters from the foot of the mountain. The ballistics showed that it was a car accident; according to the squad, the deceased did not want to fail in killing himself.'"

"The soul of a coward. I defended him when Dorothy revolted. Our daughter wept because her father had not wanted to talk to her and hug her on the phone; to end it all, he revealed his nature and his identity. My God, why did you do that, Yvan?" she said in tears, her teeth chattering as if she were under the yoke of a fever.

"He had visited me in the office the day before yesterday; Ron was with me because of his laptop and was not particularly pleasant, grumbling, 'You can't separate me from mum like that,' as Gaëtan wanted to talk to me alone. The motive for his visit was not disclosed, and my answer must have disappointed him. We went into the garden of the ministry, and he stated without preamble: 'Your sister and friend Dorcas cheats on her husband!'"

"'Really? You, you have never done that.'

"'That's not kind; is that your answer, or did you know about it?'

"'I am not a pink notebook agency, but these things are rarely a scoop in a marriage. The alternative is no longer going to be simple: either you break up the harmonious union, or it is a cordial agreement with its hypocrisies.'

"'That is a pragmatic analysis, although disappointing.'

"'Do you know your wife's lover, if she has one?'

"He hesitated before saying no; then I asked an existential question: 'What is tormenting you, my dear Gaëtan?'

"'I don't personally know the man she has taken as . . . a lover, oh! I find it difficult to tie this word to Dorcas, but he is an African.'

"'Lord! What is the problem? She was born in Africa; you deny her these ties and this part of her roots. You cheat on her; is she aware of it? You are funny.'

"He suddenly went fiery red; I remembered having seen him like that in a negotiation where the Russian ambassador had ensnared, taken aback, and put him in a difficult situation. He wanted to leave angry. I took his hand as I accompanied him to his car before hugging him. My sister, you have to come back quickly . . ."

"Myri, I want to hold you in my arms—"

"Me too. I would love to be with you, but listen: 'Your home was secure, / Qayîm, and your nest perched on the rock. / But the nest belongs to Béor; / until when will you be Assur's captive?'"

"Do you find answer and solution to everything in the Bible?"

"Not to everything, but it helps me to understand some problems of life, to face them, avoiding the politics known as those of the ostrich. When I was a young girl and had my first disappointment in love, my grandfather—who introduced me to Hebrew—made me sit on his knees and recited this which I repeat to you in English: 'He asked for water, / she gave him milk, / in the nobilities' / beaker she offered some cream / —those who love you, let them be like the sun / when it rises in its strength.'"

"Thank you, Myri, you can't imagine how much you have calmed me down; what does the morning press say . . . ?"

"James produced a dreadful article, suspecting Gaëtan of having a heavy as well as obscure load on his conscience that he preferred to take to his grave. One of these days, the future will shed a glaring light on the nature of such a man. You will see to it more on your return. I will try to convince him to do away with his suspicions, which I consider serious but baseless."

▪ ▪ ▪

Deeply traumatized, sometimes on the verge of a nervous breakdown, her unwavering will not to harm her condition, however, made her climb the hillsides. Being in command of the situation, she put her life in order, thought of the method to adopt to inform her children, confirmed her departure, and returned to Tigony the day after with the first Swissair flight to Nairobi; an Air Afrique flight brought her back to France with her husband's mortal remains, where their children joined her.

Tense, overwhelmed with sadness, but elegant in her mourning suit, with her determined appearance that she never forced; she strangely resembled the young girl with whom her father or brothers and later Gaëtan Yvan Keurléonan danced at the socialite parties.

The funeral took place in Brittany. They devoted four days to visits, receptions, and property problems before the departure to Dublin where "it would be good to draw strength from each other." Weakened, Charles-Yvan gave his mother his arm from time to time, or put his arm around her waist; she had to accompany him to Stuttgart and spend a week with him.

"Life must get the upper hand and go on, Mum; you have to reorganize your life," he told her as he hugged her at the airport before they separated.

Dorcas gave him her arm, walked a few steps at his side on getting out of the hall, held him in her arms, rocking him, and left him as if fleeing. Then she took hold of herself again, looked back, burst into tears as she saw him departing, head lowered, back stooped as if he had aged twenty years in the space of a week. The mobile phone rang in her handbag. She thought of Myriam as she took the call, but heard her son's voice say before he got into the taxi: "Don't worry, Mum, I love you."

The mobile phone rang again. Dorothy, wishing her "a very pleasant return to Tigony," added: "Mum, you know it better than me, but, I repeat: 'Many waters cannot quench love, neither can the floods drown it.'"

"Many thanks, my darling; I am relieved, very happy to hear you tell me this broad truth again."